Re-disc kind of novel

THE UNCERTAIN FUTURE OF THE SILVERMANS

Victor Canning

This edition published in 2019 by Farrago,
an imprint of Duckworth Books Ltd
13 Carrington Road, Richmond, TW10 5AA, United Kingdom

www.farragobooks.com

By arrangement with the Beneficiaries of the
Literary Estate of Victor Canning

First published by Hodder and Stoughton in 1937

Ebook ISBN: 9781788421744
Print ISBN: 9781788421782

With grateful acknowledgment to John Higgins

Have you read them all?

Treat yourself again to the first Victor Canning novels –

Mr Finchley Discovers His England
A middle-aged solicitor's clerk takes a holiday for the first time and meets unexpected adventure.

Polycarp's Progress
Just turned 21, an office worker spreads his wings – an exuberant, life-affirming novel of taking your chances.

Fly Away Paul
How far could you go living in another's shoes? – an action-packed comic caper and love story.

Turn to the end of this book for a full list of Victor Canning's early works, plus – on the last page – the chance to receive **further background material**.

Contents

I

It should be the duty of every clear-thinking citizen to resolutely, and without stint, assert the right of individualism against the might of public monopolistic companies, for in many ways the old-established family concern is the basis of our country's prosperity …

Swanbridge Messenger (From a report of a speech by Captain H. C. Lowthern, M.P.)

Swanbridge was asleep. The shops showed blind faces, the newspaper placards were full with their proclamations of news already twelve hours old, and about the pavements and gutters lay burnt matchsticks, crumpled cigarette cartons, and bent omnibus tickets. In the daytime this litter went unnoticed, but now, with a cold January wind to lift the scraps of paper into dance, there was a fantastic suggestion about the moonlit, humanless streets, as though each piece of waste was the night-time presence of one of the mortals who walked the streets by day, and in the shrill whine of the wind and the dry flutter of paper it was easy to imagine a thin echo of the voices that filled the air during the day.

Over Swanbridge the four-faced clock tower of the Town Hall was poised, each of its fatherly moons watching a different district of the town and throwing a robust challenge to the true planet which, sailing high against the racing clouds, was dying quickly into its last quarter.

One face looked towards the east, where the steeple of St. Dunstan's Church glimmered like steel in the moonlight against the dark yew-trees that moved uneasily in the wind. Beyond the parish church, mis-shapen in the light and shadow of the night, the town gave way to long meadows and orchards, and the land rose slowly to the downs that ran in a curving north-to-south sweep which formed part of the rim of the natural basin in which the town lay. In the south the main street, with its ribbing of smaller streets and lanes, dropped sharply towards the River Troon. Directly about the town side of the river there were no houses, and the meadows, whose winterly flooding had stopped any building upon them, were given over to allotments that suffered little by the floods and gained each year a layer of alluvial deposit that made vegetables and flowers flourish with the coming of spring and summer. On the other side of the river, which had a higher bank, were one or two villas, a stretch of open land used as a recreation ground and a favourite pitching-place for travelling circuses, and the playing-fields of the Grammar School and the various athletic clubs in the town. To the west the town stretched away past the hospital, the railway station, and the locomotive yards, in row after row of houses, some new, some old, and most ugly, until it thinned and trickled into orchards, wheat-fields, and twisting country lanes. The northern clock face shone on a jumble of gables and red roofs that marked the oldest part of the town. Even the broad main road which came sweeping southwards from London to the outskirts of the town had to crib itself within the narrow walls of overhanging houses as it passed through this quarter, and the straightness which it loved was sacrificed to a succession of twists and bends that were cursed by lorry-drivers and traffic policemen a hundred times a day.

It was in this part of the town, as the clock began to strike midnight, that a light still showed, impudent and assured. It came from an uncurtained window on the first floor of a building which stood on the east side of the road. It was an old building. The first floor overhung the ground floor by some feet, like a frowning forehead, and in the centre, below the forehead, was a wide doorway supported by two carved posts. On each side of the door were windows of diamond-paned glass—long, shallow windows that were never intended for commercial display purposes. The roof of the building was covered with warm red tiles, most of them discoloured by growths and twisted with age, and was cut into three dormer projections that seemed on the point of toppling into the roadway in their anxiety to lean over and see what was happening on the pavement below.

Looking at the building, you might have said that it was an inn, and you would not have been far wrong, for at one time a sign had swung over the low doorway showing a chained bear. Now there was no sign, but along the face of the building, just below the lighted window, in black lettering ran the words The *Swanbridge and District Messenger*, and, in the show-windows of the ground floor, photographs of local events were pinned to steep ramps, and placards announced the headlines of news items to be found in the latest issue of the paper. On the right-hand side of the doorway was a small black board, no bigger than a quarto sheet of paper, which stated that these were the offices of the Swanbridge *Messenger* Company, and beneath this pronouncement, in small white letters that almost escaped notice, were the words: *Editor Matthew Silverman.*

* * *

Sitting in his room at the front of the *Messenger* building, Matthew Silverman frowned as he heard the town clock strike midnight. From the heart of the building came the continuous low rumble and tremble of machinery. In the street, even at night, it would have been scarcely audible, but in Matthew Silverman's room it enlivened the whole atmosphere, and sent a faint tremor through each piece of furniture. The rotary press was still printing off the weekly edition of the *Messenger*, and the vitality in its whirling rollers and rods was too much for the machine to hold. The energy escaped in a roaring madness of noise about the printing room and vibrated with quickly lessening force through the offices and works. While the paper spun through the maze of machinery, the whole building hummed the song the press bellowed, and to Matthew in his room the faint noise and the persistent pulse were as much part of him as the beating of his own heart. But even his pleasure in the sounds of the press did not stop his frown. They were late tonight. Usually at this time the press was still and the packers were racing with their last bundles. There had been nights, memorable because of their rarity, when the works had been still and dark long before the town clock began to toll the midnight. For the press to be still going after midnight was unusual.

He got up from his chair and left the room, making his way down a narrow stairway to the main corridor that ran back from the front of the building to the printing room. The corridor ended, and he was crossing a tiny unroofed square of cobbles—all that remained of the once famous inn yard of the Chained Bear. The rest of the yard had disappeared to make way for the printing room, the foundry, and above them the composing and linotype rooms. Matthew opened a door at the far side of the little yard and was immediately engulfed in a flood of light and sound.

The press was roaring away, spewing out its papers in neat quires that were snatched up by the packers and hurried away to the packing-shed. At each end of the terraced rotary press stood a mechanic, eyes and mind concentrated on the elaborate machinery and hands ready to regulators. Aloft, another mechanic worked his way from point to point, a monkey figure sporting with an oilcan in a mechanical jungle through which, travelling so quickly that it seemed still, streamed a river of white paper, its bosom gathering a flood drift of type and pictures until it poured finally from the machine in a breaking spate of printed pages.

"How much longer?" Matthew asked the printer.

"Fifteen minutes—if nothing happens," answered Mr. Phipps. He was an oldish, little man with a large, balloon-like stomach that seemed to be kept in place by the belt-band of his trousers. All the week, except on Thursdays, Phipps's stomach existed happily with the belt about its middle, but on Thursdays, as though the excitement of press day had filled it with elation, it lifted above his belt, and he moved about his machine like a pouter pigeon strutting in a dovecote. His assistants he forced to wear blue overalls; for himself, he wore a shirt and a greasy pair of dark trousers, kept in place by the belt which had been with him through the war and which was studded with regimental badges that he would polish in those intervals when there was nothing he could find to do to his machine and when Matthew was not about.

"If nothing happens." Matthew knew what that meant. Something generally did happen; the paper broke and lost them twenty minutes, or something went wrong with the inking, or the stop press slipped and began to strike wildly, high in the column, until Phipps could clamber aloft to adjust the fudge box.

"One day, I suppose," he shouted to Phipps, "we shall get everything run off to schedule!" As he spoke he knew that such a thing could seldom ever happen in a newspaper office, only his irritation with the present delay prompted him to make the remark.

"Maybe," said the printer. He was not anxious to enter a discussion about efficiency with the old man tonight. It would not have been wise.

"Maybe!" Matthew caught him up. "What?" he shouted above the stamp of the press. "What the devil do you mean by that? Maybe!" Some people were too vague. They fogged their minds with a load of silly expressions that could never bear examination.

Phipps smiled, and, shaking his head hurriedly as though he had not heard, darted away towards the top deck to see to some bearing that needed no attention. "Maybe!" he said, quite loudly and safely, as he went. "What the devil do I mean by that? The old bear's looking for a fight tonight; but he won't get it from me. The paper's an hour late—and the world has come to pieces …"

Matthew picked up one of the copies and left the room. There was no real need for him to remain so late. Phipps was capable of dealing with any emergency which could arise now, and the packers and vanmen knew their jobs better than he did. It was a tradition, however, that the editor of the *Messenger* should stay until the final copy was printed, and Matthew was the last person to disregard a tradition.

He went back to his room and sat down with the paper on his desk before him. He had sat in that room hundreds of nights before this, with the *Messenger* before him, the sound of the press in his ears; and always the fresh folds of the sheets, the smell of still damp print, and the paper's limp virginity brought to him an intense feeling of satisfaction, satisfaction not with himself and the part he played in its production, but a satisfaction that was more diffused. He was glad that life was so arranged that a paper could be printed and that he could sit at night, when the town slept, feeling its freshness and looking at the tidy columns and crossheads.

A horse-breeder watching a group of foals trying their legs in a paddock is glad, not alone from the importance he plays in their well-being, but glad simply because there are horses; and Matthew was glad that there were papers. This love of type and presses was part of the Silverman heritage. His father, James, had known it, and when he had died in 1910, after a cold caught by standing bare-headed at an open-air memorial service to King Edward VII, his eyes had been fixed, not on his family about the bed, but on the latest edition of the *Messenger* in his hands. Matthew's grandfather, Jacob, who had still been editor at seventy-three, and despite his doctor's warnings persisted in climbing the narrow stairs to the editor's room, had been found unconscious at the bottom of them one evening with a *Messenger* in his hand. He had died without regaining his understanding. And before him there had been the founder of the paper, Matthew's great-grandfather, John Silverman, a man who had welcomed difficulties. He had founded the paper in 1834 and had died at sixty from overwork.

They were before Matthew as he sat in his chair. A dark oil-painting of John, done a few years before his death by a local artist, took the centre place on the wall, and flanking the painting were two large photographs of Jacob and James, and in all of them showed the same features; a firm, small mouth to give incision to commands, and large eyes set deeply and saved from fierceness by an open, humorous expression. They were men of strength; nothing stopped them from their purpose when they had determined it; and yet, although they were given to bigotry when they believed fiercely in an opinion, they never let their stubbornness overcome their natural kindness and humour. What the *Courier*, a rival paper, had said of James Silverman in his obituary notice was true of all the men who had held the editorial seat: "When he growled it was impossible to say whether he was angry or only pretending to anger, but when he laughed there was no doubt of his feelings; and he often laughed …"

In Matthew Silverman there was a great deal of the spirit which had possessed his three forerunners. His staff called him a bear—not inappropriately, since he sat in what had been the best bedroom of the old Chained Bear. His growls were not those of a chained bear. He was a genial bear, fond of company and appreciative of the sweet things in life. If he differed from his predecessors, it was that often when he wanted to laugh he decided that it would be unwise. He was very much aware of his position as editor.

To look at him it was difficult to guess his age. He was of middle height, with a slight stoop that had come from life in an office, and his gold-rimmed spectacles, which he wore for reading, gave him a slightly curious, probing air. His dark hair was thin and grey, with streaks which, coming early, had given him a dignity that befitted his position. Although he read very little in books, he gave the impression of quiet, smiling scholarship suited more to a university don than a country editor. As the editor of the *Messenger* he was liked. His tender affection for Swanbridge, his ready championship of it in any dispute, and his welcome in every Swanbridge circle, marked not the busybody but a man who had identified himself so firmly with the welfare of the town that without him the town itself would have seemed incomplete. At home that respect was tempered by a gentle ridicule of the importance which belonged to him outside as an editor. In his own house he dropped from his public pedestal and yet managed to retain against the joyful blasphemies of his children and the mild criticisms of his wife a position of affection and respect. No one ever mentioned family love in the house, yet love dwelt there, and it proved itself simply by the firm declaration that only a Silverman might criticise a Silverman. He was fifty-five years old and had been editor of the *Messenger* since his father's death. He maintained that tolerance was one of the greatest virtues, and that it was an editor's duty to see all sides of a question. To these two principles he added a fierce defence of any attack on the *Messenger* and family traditions, no matter how logical those attacks might be, and he had a happy knack of getting his own way with a minimum of discomfort to all parties, and his way was generally, though not always at once admitted, the best way.

* * *

Matthew was about to open the paper when there came a knock on the door. He dropped his paper, looked at the door, and frowned.

"Come in," he said.

Being editor of a country newspaper gave every Tom, Dick, and Harry the right to invade his room with requests, supplications, and grievances; but he had supposed that he might be allowed a little solitude at midnight. What did they imagine he was?

The door opened and a slight, fair-haired young man edged into the room and stood at the side of the large open fireplace.

"Oh, it's you," said Matthew. Although his tone was cold, he was glad. Here was the lamb coming willingly to the slaughter at a moment when he felt the need of blood-letting. "What are you doing in the office still? I thought you'd gone. You've caused enough trouble for one night." Then he held up his hand in a severe gesture, and above the roll of the press they heard the clock striking the half-hour. "Do you hear that?"

The young man nodded, and then, because he was reckless from fatigue and knew Matthew would be roused by the obvious misinterpretation, he said "Some of the townspeople are talking about getting up a petition to have the chimes stopped at night. Keeps them awake, they say."

"That's not what I mean, and you know it, Mr. Barnes." Matthew rose to the bait, and Barnes smiled to himself as the float went under. "I mean that if my father were sitting where I am now and heard that clock, and also heard the press still going, somebody would be shot for it. We're late; later than I've known for years. In fact, I can't remember being so late in the whole of my—no, that's a lie. There was an occasion. But that doesn't affect matters tonight. We're late, Mr. Barnes; and why? Would you like me to tell you?"

"I know, Mr. Silverman. I'm sorry, but it wasn't really—"

"It wasn't really your fault." Fault! He knew it wasn't strictly Barnes's fault, but, then, no error was solely the fault of one individual; a man did wrong by virtue of a thousand uncontrollable and foreign circumstances, yet that was no shield to offer against a hearty trouncing—and Matthew felt himself entitled to trounce the young man. "A worn-out excuse. I suppose you'll have the teleological impudence to ascribe the origin of your plight to Adam and Eve? In my young days, when we started to do a thing we did it, and if we couldn't do it we didn't moan that it wasn't our fault. It wouldn't have been any good—at least, not to any one of those three gentlemen looking down at you from the wall there."

Barnes shuffled before the fireplace and decided not to answer. He knew that, once the Silverman ancestors were mentioned, Matthew was good for fifteen minutes. The old man, he felt, was being unjust, but he could see that he meant to rant on and would not welcome interruptions.

As he finished speaking, Matthew was surprised to find that his mind was less concerned with Barnes and his three ancestors than with the impression that perhaps he had used "teleological," taken from a sententious *Times* leader that morning, incorrectly. He pulled himself together and glared at Barnes. Barnes had been sent out to cover the speech of a local M.P. at a small town twenty miles away. The text of the speech had been sent to the office by the speaker days before the meeting. Locally it was an important speech, and to print the *Messenger* without it would have been to disappoint many of the readers and annoy the M.P. Barnes had gone to make sure that the speech delivered was the same as the one already set up in the office, a normal precaution—and the speech had been different. At the last moment the M.P. had spoken impromptu, scrapping his arranged speech. Barnes took the new speech down, and telephoned the office to hold the page until he got there with the new speech. Matthew had congratulated himself on a smart reporter when the message had come into the office; but when Barnes had not returned and time moved on past the usual hour of printing, he had begun to alter his opinion of the reporter.

"It was your fault, my boy. Don't deny it. I don't say it was your fault that your motor-cycle had to skid and put you in the ditch. I don't think it was stupid of you to borrow a bicycle and begin a leisurely journey on that to the office; but it was crass, glaring imbecility to let the van I sent out to see where you were pass you twice without so much as giving it a hail. I know what you're going to say." Matthew raised a hand to stop Barnes from speaking, though the reporter had no intention of talking. "You'll tell me that it was going so fast that you didn't get a chance. Well, if you, as a reporter, can't stop a news van, then there's not much hope for you."

Barnes knew it was useless to tell him what the rest of the office already knew—that the first time the van had simply ignored his shouts, and the second time it had been going so fast that he had tumbled into the ditch with the bicycle on top of himself to get out of its way. Matthew, he thought, would never know that.

"Well, what have you got to say for yourself?"

"I suppose on that showing I'm not a very good reporter, sir."

Not a good reporter! Matthew sat forward in his chair and began to roll up the fresh *Messenger* as though he intended to use it as a cudgel. What was the matter with these young men? They were too complaisant, too ready to make a false admission for the sake of peace. Peace was all right, but there was no need to make yourself a doormat to get it! He liked to see spirit—in its proper place—and, because Barnes had not shown spirit now, he considered he should have done so.

"Don't stand there and lie to me!" he roared, shaking the paper angrily. "You know perfectly well that you think you're a fine reporter." His eyes travelled up and down the tall, slim figure. There was nothing in some of these young men, but they had a surprising vitality. This Barnes had been busy all day reporting, had spent his evening taking difficult verbatim at a political meeting, and on top of that had skidded from his motor-cycle, and then cycled fifteen miles against a vicious east wind. He was standing before him now with his suit a little rumpled, his hair tidy, his eyes beginning to fill with sleep, and not complaining. The sight of his tiredness suddenly touched Matthew, and he was ashamed that he had settled his anger against circumstances upon Barnes, who was only partly to blame. He went on in a gentle tone: "Well, we'll say no more about it. You go on home and get some sleep. I'll have a word with that vanman in the morning."

The young man hesitated.

"I haven't asked you what I really came in about, sir."

"What's that?"

"I wondered if you'd be good enough to let me have the day off next Tuesday."

"The day off!" Matthew sat up stiffly and eyed Barnes fiercely. "Whatever for? As a reward for your services?"

Barnes laughed timidly. "No, not that, sir. You see, there was a letter waiting for me when I got back tonight. There's a chance for me to get a better job on a London paper, and they want me for an interview on Tuesday."

"So the *Messenger* isn't good enough for you, eh? What do you want to go on a London daily for? They're not newspapers; they're daily suppurations!"

"The pay is better and there's more excitement," said Barnes quietly.

"Money and excitement!" burst out Matthew. "What does a young man like you want with either of them? Trash, both of them. Cultivate the firmer, more decent virtues, boy, and let those who will run with the Gadarene swine, itching with devilish excitement and full of beech-nuts."

Matthew flopped back into his chair and looked at Barnes, expecting to see some sign of appreciation for this last phrase. It was good. He must remember it. Barnes's expression of patience was unaltered, but he said very firmly

"I'm afraid I don't altogether agree with you, sir." Matthew looked up at this change of tone. For a moment he was about to take up the argument. The tired lines of Barnes's face stopped him. He tapped his teeth with a pencil for a moment, and then said quietly:

"Well, different generations have different opinions. Perhaps I overstated my views. Still, overstatement is necessary at times. However, I won't stand in your way, if that's what you really want to do. You can have the day, my boy, and I hope you don't regret it. There's a future here for you if you care to stop."

"Thank you, Mr. Silverman." Barnes smiled and then went towards the door. As he reached it the vibration of the press through the building ceased. He stopped and looked across at Matthew, and the older man returned his look. He gave a little nod of approval, and then, as the reporter opened the door, he called across the sudden silence: "And I wish you all the luck in the world, Barnes. You deserve it."

II

Those married people who do not want
children no doubt have good reasons
for their attitude, but I am old-fashioned
enough to believe that there is no
happiness comparable to that which
inhabits a happy family.

Swanbridge Messenger (From an editorial)

The Silvermans lived in a large villa quite near St. Dunstan's Church
and on the main road. It stood in its own grounds, and was almost
completely masked from the roadway by a shrubbery of thick
rhododendrons and laurels. Behind the shrubberies were laburnum,
birch, and a few fir-trees. In the front of the house, formal flower-
beds dispersed the gloom of the trees, while at the back a tennis-lawn,
sunk below the level of the house, gave the garden a terraced look,
an impression of openness, which was furthered by a wide stretch of
orchard that ran for nearly a hundred yards until it ended in a high
redbrick wall. On the other side of the wall was a public footpath
leading from the lower High Street to the fields which pressed closely
around the outskirts of the town. A gardener, Fuller by name, who
was deaf, looked after the garden, helped by a boy of fifteen.

The house had been built by Matthew's father in 1898, three
years after he had become editor of the *Messenger*. From the outside
it was an overwhelming aggregation of sharp gables, green barge-
boards, wide, sash-framed windows, unexpected points of roof,
sudden sproutings of chimneys, and occasional wastes of red brick

and plaster facing. Looking at it, you would have said that the man who designed it must have been obsessed by the desire to incorporate in one building something of all architectural styles and a great deal of his own originality; and you would have been right, for the house was designed by James Silverman himself. It was true that he had employed an architect to assist him with the technicalities, but the architect had soon found that his sole duty was to oppose sensible arguments to James's fantastic ideas and then to capitulate with good grace against James's equally fantastic insistence. By the time the house was built both the architect and the local contractor who was building it under James's persistent and hindering supervision were men of fretted nerves and worried faces who would dive quickly into side-streets to avoid the editor when they saw him coming.

"A house," James had been fond of saying, "is as important to a man as his clothes, though he is allowed to add more decoration to his house than he can countenance on his clothes." Yet, curiously enough, although the house was such an odd mixture on the outside, within it achieved a unique atmosphere of comfort and convenience. The rooms were pleasant; there was light where there should be light; and if the fireplaces were now old-fashioned they still warmed the rooms in winter with gratifying efficiency. A week before the house was ready for occupation General Kitchener had overthrown the dervishes at Omdurman, and, when the news came through of the entry of Gordon's avenger into Khartum, James, who had been worrying with the problem of what name to give his house, was filled with inspiration, and across the white gate had been painted in black letters the name Khartum.

At half past seven on the morning after Matthew's talk with Barnes the sound of a gong vigorously beaten went echoing and jangling through the house. The noise woke each member of the family and produced different responses.

Matthew heard it in his sleep and then was awake, sitting up in bed and rubbing his eyes. His thin hair was ruffled, and the crumpled folds of his pink and blue pyjamas gave him an odd concert-party air, as though he were an ageing pierrot who had come home and tumbled, too tired to undress, into bed. The last notes of the gong vibrated through the house and he was out of bed. He put on his dressing-gown and, with his mind already thinking of the duties which lay ahead of him that day, he began to perform the inflexible ritual which marked his rising in the morning. He went to the window and looked out, noticing that it was time Fuller swept the dead leaves from the lawn. He took three deep breaths and then, because the air was cold with frost, shut the window hurriedly and went along to the bathroom. While his bath-water was running he shaved himself. Later he would return to his room and dress himself with the leisure that made dressing in the mornings a pleasure to him. He would spend some time deciding which tie he would wear, and then go downstairs to read his letters and the paper in his study before breakfast. In the summer he took them into the garden.

In her room next to his Mabel Silverman, his wife, heard Matthew go along to the bathroom and, as the water began to run, she murmured a faint, "Oh dear, time to get up." Then she got out of bed, pulled her wrap about herself, and slipped her feet into comfortable mules. With a feeling of guilt she lit the gas-fire, and spread her underclothes on a chair before the heat and went out to the other bathroom. She turned the water on in the hand-bowl and tried it with her finger until it was running hot. She began to wash. She had never been able to abandon herself to the recklessness of bathing first thing in the morning. Indeed, brought up in a country rectory where baths had been a weekly and exacting ceremonial of heating water in a copper and carrying it pail by pail to the discretion of a hip-bath in a bedroom, she had never entirely rid herself of the notion that a daily bath was somehow a wicked waste of time and water. She would have her wash now, and then later in the day, when everything had got used to the daylight, she would come up and bath in comfort, taking her time.

Five years younger than her husband, she was a woman of no great distinction. She was big, comfortable, and kind. She believed in being kind to everyone, and imagined that the greatest part of kindness was to see that everyone she came into contact with ate well. And perhaps she was not wrong. If any of her children were unhappy, she prepared them tempting foods, if they were unwell, she prepared them less solid but still tempting foods; and, if she were faced with any problem that seemed beyond her solution, she would retire to the kitchen and start to make meringues for tea, and in her annoyance at their failure she would forget her worry.

She stood now before the gas-fire, dressing, and wishing that the mornings would not be so cold; her mind beginning to go over the domestic arrangements for the day, for, although she would never have dreamed of opposing any interference of Matthew's, she had somehow managed to maintain a vigorous control of the household arrangements, even though he had remarked sometimes that there was no need for her to worry with things so much when she had a perfectly good housekeeper and servants. The daughter of a country clergyman, she cherished a kindly distrust of all servants, except Gibby, who had come to Khartum with her from the rectory at the death of her father.

Loraine Silverman heard the gong, rolled over in bed, and lay half awake between the sheets, wondering if there would be any letters for her. She heard her father go along to the bathroom and, a little later, her mother padding to the other. There was silence for a while, and then came the sound of someone coming slowly along the landing. Something bumped on the mat outside her room, and she knew it was Gibby with her shoes. She sat up in bed, keeping the sheet around her shoulders, and cried: "Gibby! Oh, Gibby, dear!"

The door opened, and a woman wearing a black dress, her white-grey hair drawn tightly back to a bun, came into the room. Her face was wrinkled, and her hands had that brittle appearance which comes with age.

"Well?" she said, and drew her mouth into a firm line as though she were getting ready to say "No."

"Oh, Gibby, be an angel and light the gas-fire. It's so cold in here. I couldn't possibly get out of bed until it's warmer. There are some matches in that bowl on the table."

"You coddle yourself up too much, young lady. That's why you're always catching colds. I'll do no such thing. Your father wouldn't approve."

"Oh, Gibby, please ..." Loraine smiled pleadingly at her, and the old woman gave in.

"I'm a fool to let you wheedle me so," she said, and moved towards the fireplace. Loraine had always been her favourite, and she did for her things which no amount of persuasion or flattery from the others could have made her do.

Gibby was only one among many from whom Loraine evoked willing service. There was an appealing, innocent quality in Loraine that demanded protection. Her physical appearance emphasised this quality. Her eyes were large and bright with a perpetual curiosity, like those of deer; and her lips were full, conspiring to a half-pout that only disappeared when she smiled, which was often. Her hair in disarray still maintained, as if by design, that careless beauty which is given only to the young, and as she sat up in bed its vagrant fairness over her clear skin stirred even the unromantic Gibby. She was nineteen, more fond of games and dancing than of books, and her look of fragile charm, as her friends who played hockey with her knew, covered a sturdy contempt for hard knocks and an ability to look after herself.

"You're an untidy minx!" grumbled Gibby, picking up some of her clothes from the floor at the foot of the bed and spreading them over a chair by the fire.

Loraine smiled, and then stretched her arms and yawned luxuriously. "If I weren't untidy, Gibby, you know you wouldn't have the pleasure of going round putting things tidy for me—and think what a loss that would be to you."

"If you're going to sit up in bed like that, you'd better put this round your shoulders, otherwise you'll have a cold." Gibby handed her a dressing-gown.

"Thank you, Gibby." Loraine took the gown, and, as the old woman went to the door, she was wondering whether Gibby had ever had fun in her young days, gone to dances and had men around her … "Oh, Gibby," she called before the other could leave the room.

"What is it now? I've got a lot of things to see to. Miss Alison will be sleeping, and—"

"Never mind Alison. Gibby, are there any letters for me downstairs? Bring them up, there's a dear."

Gibby's mouth went firm and she shook her head.

"You know what your father says—those who want their letters must get up to read them. I wouldn't go against his orders."

"But you have done before."

24

"Maybe, Miss Loraine, but not today." She opened the door and then paused, half in the room and half out, and added: "There's nothing for you, anyway, 'cepting a bill."

No letters! Loraine fell back on the pillows and frowned. What an awful start to a day! If she were dictator, she thought, she would make a rule that everyone wrote one letter a day to someone, then no one would need to start the day without a letter. It was exciting to have letters—strange letters and familiar letters. She spread her hands towards the glow of the fire and wondered, without much hope, if Gibby were only teasing.

She lay, inconsolable and crushed by the gloomy opening to her day, until someone knocked gently on her door and her mother's voice said:

"Time's getting on, Loraine dear. Don't be long."

"All right, Mummy," she called, and with a sigh slipped expertly from the bed on to the rug before the fire and began to do exercises with a fierce vigour.

Alexander Silverman heard the gong that morning. Some mornings he did not hear it, for his bedroom was situated at the top of a stunted little tower which graced one end of the house. The tower had been James's greatest inspiration. It had expansive windows along two of its sides and a tiny balcony around the outside, and it was here that James had determined to make his study and begin an astronomical career. Astronomy, he had long felt, was his métier. Unfortunately, the strain of having a study right at the top of the house, and the inconvenience of being able to watch the stars only at night when he was tired, had soon sapped his enthusiasm for the room, and he had given it up. It had been left empty, a storage for the detritus of a large household which was reluctant to jettison all its waste, until Alexander had become old enough to make a claim for it. Despite opposition, he had made it his bedroom, and had found unexpected support from his father, who pointed out at great length that by using the room they were making another and more convenient room available for guests.

The sound of the gong came thinly up the narrow stairs that led to the room, and Alexander, sleeping lightly, woke and sat up. Gibby, he thought, took a fiendish delight in hammering the gong.

"What the hell does she think she is?" he muttered to himself. "A Zulu with a tom-tom? Damn' noise!" And he turned over and determined to go to sleep again. A few moments later there came the thump of his shoes being laid down outside the door, and Gibby's voice said loudly:

"Did you hear the gong, Master Alexander?"

"Did I hear it!" Alexander poked his head from under the sheets. "Of course I heard you kicking it around. What do you think your name is—Minnie the Moocher?"

"What's that?" came Gibby's voice.

"It's all right, Gibby. It's a joke. I didn't expect you to laugh."

"Your father's almost finished, if you do want to bath," came the unconcerned reply, and Alexander beat the pillows in mock frenzy as he heard her going away. " 'Peace, you mumbling fool! Utter your gravity o'er a gossip's bowl; for here we need it not,' " he cried. He liked Gibby; she was a good soul; but it was too much to expect anyone to be even-tempered these cold mornings. Not on any day, he supposed, was any man really normal until he had got a good lunch inside him. That was why—he followed the theory out, taking a delight in it—those men who could rise and eat a breakfast equivalent to a lunch, hogging meat and swilling cups of tea, were so jovial and smooth-tempered. Bad temper throve on cereals. Eating cereals was an American habit, and the American national characteristic was dyspepsia. One had only to look at their films; constipated orgies ... Their architecture was not so bad, though. But, then, they had wisely developed it from a European tradition. Wait until he was qualified and started to practise! Christopher! He'd show them ... He began to build dream buildings, and for ten minutes he lay upon his back staring at the ceiling. He saw the sun shining on tall white façades, buildings that reached to the clouds, pure and clean in line; towns studded with green squares, running water cooling the main thoroughfares, and a happy people living in houses and flats which were open to the sunshine and air of life ...

He had a thin, virile face, and his skin was darkly pigmented. He was unlike any other of the Silvermans; no one would have said that he and his elder brother George came from the same stock. Alexander's features had a clean, vivid freshness, as though they had been newly released by the chisel of a master from some rough core of stone. He had a long, almost Jewish nose, with wide nostrils, and thin, sensitive lips, and his eyes were as dark as his ruffled hair that spread against the white pillow.

Suddenly he smiled to himself, and his face was that of a schoolboy delighted with a piquant obscenity. Into the midst of his dreams had come sailing a lovely phrase: "If American films are constipated orgies, the English are constipated economies." He must use that; not at home though; they would be shocked.

A breath of cold air came across his face from one of the windows which was open at the top, and the coldness reminded him of the river. If only there would be a few heavy showers and they had the sense to keep the lock shut at Chaffley, then the river meadows might flood, and with this kind of weather there would be some skating ... Men envied the birds their powers of flight and clumsily imitated them, but the birds could never hope to have the joy of skating. Was the emotion a physical or a mental one, he wondered; like the downward swoop on a swing which sent a tingle through your stomach, was that physical? The sound of Fuller's barrow squeaking along the drive stopped his reverie.

He reached out a hand and looked at his watch. It was late. He lay for half a minute more, wondering whether he would bath and shave. He could put on the gas-fire and warm his clothes while he was doing it. What an awful nuisance this washing and shaving business was. How many years of his life did a man waste doing it? Ten? Probably more than that. Well, this was one morning he wouldn't waste.

Steeling himself to the divorce, he jumped quickly from the warm bed and grabbed at his clothes, pulling them on hurriedly in the hope that he might be into them before he felt the cold. Then, with a dressing-gown covering his trousers and loose shirt, he ambled down to the bathroom. He would wash, and he would clean his teeth. The bath and shave could go. Christopher! There were some people who didn't clean their teeth regularly. The dirty swine!

As Alexander went down the stairs he beat a tattoo on the door of the room in which Alison, his ten-year-old sister, slept.

Alison made no reply. She was awake. She had been awake long before the gong had sounded, staring at the window with her round eyes and wondering. She was not wondering anything, but just wondering. That was the way she amused herself in the early mornings when she was awake and the rest of the house slept. The game was to stare out of the window until you forgot the window and the edge of the bare birch-tree, and then some thought came into your mind and you went on thinking, and in the end you never knew what it was you had been thinking about or what the first thought had been. Time went very quickly when she did that.

The gong had interrupted her wondering, and she had lain for a while, waiting. She had not waited long. A faint scratching came from the outside of her bedroom door, and she jumped, regardless of the cold, from her warm sheets and ran to the door, which she opened cautiously. A young Skye terrier wriggled through the crack of the door, and stood on the mat wagging its tail and looking up at her.

"Ssssh! Micky," Alison whispered. "Go on—sikum!" Micky understood the signal, and with a jump he was on the bed and burrowing into the depths of the sheets, and Alison followed him into the bed. She pulled the clothes tidily about her and lay with her feet stretched down into the foot of the bed, her toes resting on the warmth and comfort of Micky's body. When Alexander knocked on the door she was telling Micky a story. She was a plain-faced little girl, with straight brown hair and very serious eyes.

When Gibby came in, Alison was still telling the story. She stopped as the door opened, but Gibby had heard her speaking.

"Who were you talking to?" she asked suspiciously.

"I was telling a story aloud," answered Alison. "About a dragon that kept a petrol pump. It was on the wireless the other afternoon."

Gibby's only comment on the modern trend of fairy-stories was a loud sniff. Alison was too young to use the bathroom, the hand-basin being too high for her, so she washed in her bedroom. Gibby came in each morning to put out her clean clothes, pour hot water into the wash-hand bowl, and to stand by while she washed to see that it was done properly. Alison resented this supervision. She watched Gibby putting out her dress and said:

"Have I got to wear that blue thing today? I want to wear my pink dress. It's Hilda's party today, and I shall have to wear the pink party dress."

"You'll wear the blue dress until it's time to change for the party, young lady, and don't let me have any nonsense from you. Now come along, dear, you must begin to get dressed, otherwise—" Gibby stopped suddenly and, lifting her chin into the air, began to sniff. Her eyes narrowed, and her mouth—it may have been in order to conceal a smile—set very tightly. "Alison!" she exclaimed indignantly, "I can smell dog! You've got Micky in here again!"

"Micky?" questioned Alison with very wide eyes, her face limpid with innocence.

"Yes, Micky, that nasty, smelly dog!" And Gibby leaned over the bottom of the bed and shot her arm under the sheets. There was a muffled squeal, an upheaval of the clothes, and she brought her arm out, holding Micky in a firm grip.

"How could you, Alison?" she said as she pushed Micky into the passage and shut the door on him. "Don't you know it's not healthy to have a dog in the bed, with its fleas? Ugh!" The horror of the thought stopped her speech, but Alison was not horrified.

"Micky hasn't got fleas, and, besides, I like him in bed with me."

"All dogs have fleas!" snapped Gibby. "Now come along and wash or I'll let your mother know about Micky. Come along!"

"Oh dear," Alison sighed, and for a moment Gibby was reminded of Mrs. Silverman; "you make me feel very sad." She got out of bed and approached the washing-bowl.

* * *

The breakfast-room at Khartum was at the back of the house. It was a long, pleasant room with french windows that opened to the terrace overlooking the tennis-lawn. Round the lower part of the walls ran a cream-painted wainscoting, and above this a pale blue wallpaper set with water-colours. The blue-and-white colouring gave an impression of the sea, and the southerly aspect of the room made it warm whenever there was any sun. At the one end of the room a fire burned brightly in one of James's old-fashioned tiled grates, and at the other end stood a long Welsh dresser full of china that had been with the Silverman family for years.

At twenty minutes to nine the gong sounded again, and by a quarter to nine the family were at breakfast. Alison was the last to come down. She saw her father's eye upon her, and as she slid into her place she said apologetically, "I'm sorry I'm late, Daddy."

"You'd better not be late down to breakfast when you go to Aunt Adelaide's," said Alexander, pouring milk on to his shredded wheat. "If you're late she says you can't want any breakfast, and takes it all away."

"That wouldn't worry me," said Loraine. "Breakfast is the most fattening meal of the day."

"I wish you would eat something at breakfast, instead of just sipping at hot water," complained Mrs. Silverman. "It worries me. Can't you make her eat something, Matt? It isn't healthy, I'm sure."

Matthew laughed. "I don't suppose she'll keep it up for long. Meanwhile, it's probably quite healthy for her to do a little fasting."

"It's reversing a natural instinct," said Alexander sharply.

"What is?" questioned Loraine. She never let any remark from Alexander slip by her if she considered he was being clever at her expense.

"Your slimming to be attractive. It's the part of the male to attract the female, not the other way round. In nature it's the cock-bird which has the colours."

"I don't slim to be attractive, but because it's nice and pleasant to be slim."

"Stop quarrelling and get on with your breakfast, both of you," commanded Matthew indulgently. Loraine and Alexander seemed to take a delight in annoying one another. He added, "I notice you haven't shaved this morning, Alexander? Don't you think it is rather disrespectful to the rest of us to come to table looking like a hairy savage?"

"Perhaps he's going to grow a beard to make himself attractive to women," suggested Loraine, delighted at the change of conversation.

"Hairy savage!" Alexander was indignant. "Why, father, I'm only seventeen. I don't have to shave every day yet. If I did shave every day it would only make it grow quicker and stronger. Why"— he ran his hand quickly over his chin— "I can hardly feel it."

"You may be only seventeen, but if you're going to shave you should shave every day. You're dark, remember. But"—Matthew smiled—"I'm not forcing you to shave. If you want to grow a beard, do so by all means. You would look quite distinguished, and cause a lot of amusement in the town."

"Why do men have to shave and women don't?" asked Alison in the pause while Alexander sought to find a reply to his father.

"It just happens like that, dear," said Mrs. Silverman, quickly opposing the awkward problem and banishing it altogether by putting a piece of toast on Alison's plate. "Eat some toast, dear, there's a good girl."

Loraine caught Alexander's eye across the table, and he scowled at her.

"I think Alex would look charming with a goatee," she said sweetly.

"Is there anything interesting in the paper this morning?" asked Mrs. Silverman, fearing a fresh outbreak.

Matthew wiped his mouth with his napkin and nodded. "There is, my dear. That is the function of a daily newspaper, to bring you something fresh each day." The family were used to these humorously intended pomposities.

"And a country newspaper to confirm what everybody already knows!" put in Alexander. That was a good dig at the old man.

"A neat point, my boy," Matthew admitted with dignity; "but quite erroneous, of course." Alexander was inclined to adopt a little too flippant an attitude towards the *Messenger*.

"I see there was something about this new liner the Cunarder people are building," said Loraine. "They're all set to win back the Blue Riband for Britain."

"And we'll do it," said Matthew proudly. "We're a great seafaring nation, and it is only proper that the honour of the fastest crossing should come to us."

"Why is it only proper?" questioned Alexander.

"Because the world expects it of us. British means the best."

"I don't see what difference it can make to the world which ship crosses the Atlantic in the fastest time. As long as there is one fastest ship, it can't make any difference if it's a French, English, or American boat."

Matthew shook his head. This was a tendency among the young people of today that he most deprecated, this slightly irreverent disregard of their own nationality.

"But it does, very much so. If it's a French boat, then the world regards its speed as uncomfortable; if it is American, its speed is unreliable; but when it's English, then it is speed with comfort, assurance, and correctness."

"You're too chauvinistic for me."

Matthew chuckled gently. He was used to being accused of many things.

"When you're a little older, my boy, you'll appreciate that the world is not full of socialistic hot-heads like yourself. Why, it doesn't seem so very long ago that it was George who was kicking against everything like you're doing. Now look at him, as reasonable a person as you could find in the whole of this county."

"George is too reasonable at times," said Alexander.

"He's coming home today," put in Mrs. Silverman. "There was a letter from him this morning. He's only stopping for the night and then going on to Oxford tomorrow."

"I wish I could go to the University right away, without having to stop at school another year," said Alexander wistfully. As he finished speaking the telephone bell began to ring in the hall.

"I'll go," said Loraine, jumping up before anyone could stop her.

"She's thinking that it may be from her darling Philip," Alexander said, smiling and shaking his head at the folly of young love.

"It's probably the butcher," said Mrs. Silverman.

Loraine came back into the room and, standing behind her chair, looked towards her father. "It's for you," she said delightedly, and winked at Alexander.

"For me?"

"Yes, you're for it. It's Uncle Abner. He says he's just finished looking at last night's *Messenger*—"

"Well?" They were all looking at Matthew, waiting; for this was no new situation to them. When Uncle Abner telephoned on a Friday morning it had only one significance. "Well, what did he have to say?"

"He said he knows that M.P.s frequently use split infinitives in their speeches, but it is the duty of a good newspaperman to correct them when reporting. There were two in the report of Captain Lowthern's speech."

Matthew pushed his chair back and stood up, his face wrinkling into a frown. That interfering, critical old monkey of an Abner! Had he nothing else to do?

"He makes me tired, that man. I believe he waits up all night for the *Messenger* and then goes through it with a magnifying-glass looking for faults. Doesn't he appreciate that the English language must be elastic? Elastic! If we want to use split infinitives we will— and that's that!" He left the room, pulling at his nose in irritation.

"Oh, dear," Mrs. Silverman murmured, "I do wish Abner wouldn't do this each week. It puts your father out for the rest of the day."

III

... this unusual behaviour of the nuthatch. There are other signs that this mild weather is not likely to last, and those who know how to interpret Nature's storm signals will not be surprised by unexpected inclemencies.

Swanbridge Messenger (From "This Week in the Country")

George Silverman was the eldest of Matthew's children. He was twenty-three, and in his last year at Oxford, and Matthew was looking forward to the time when he would come back to take up his duties in the *Messenger* office. Since the time of John Silverman, the founder of the paper, the eldest son had always served the *Messenger* ... Jacob, James, and Matthew, they had all been the eldest sons, and now George was soon to come into the office.

He had already spent a year at the office, between his leaving school and going to the University, and had shown, Matthew considered, a genuine enthusiasm for the work. He was steady and reliable, could write good English, and had an air of worthiness which inspired respect and confidence in others. He would make an ideal editor when his time came. If anything, Matthew thought, he was perhaps a little too conscientious. He was sitting in his office, gazing at his large fireplace and thinking happily about George. It was nearly his lunch-time. That morning he had spoken to the vanman who had missed Barnes, and he had called in Mr. Selway, who acted, among other things, as sub-editor of the *Messenger*, and reprimanded him for allowing two split infinitives to get into print.

"It's the duty of a good newspaperman to see that M.P.s speak decent English!" Matthew had pointed out. "Some of you young fellows want to make the English language too elastic!" Mr. Selway, who knew his Matthew, offered an apology and took the first opportunity to withdraw. On reaching his room he showed the copy of the *Messenger* to Barnes, and, pointing to the marked errors, said significantly

"Uncle Abner's caught us out again!"

* * *

While his father was thinking about him in his room, George was driving back to Swanbridge from Hampshire. Since the New Year he had been staying with a college friend, and now, before going up for the Hilary Term, he was returning home for a night. George was very conscious of the duties of an elder son, and he considered it right that he should go home before going on to Oxford. And, even if he had not considered it dutiful to go home, instead of driving straight to Oxford, he had a very good reason for calling at Swanbridge.

He drove a small car to which his great bulk gave an exaggerated appearance of tininess. He had the hood down and the windscreen partly open, so that the cold air came rushing back into his face, sweeping over his short, crisp hair. A heavy coat and scarf protected his body from the cold. The car bounced and swayed and rattled, but George sat solidly within it, his face as grave as a judge's, his body offering itself to all the vibrations and bumps and conquering them by its sturdiness. His face was much the same as Matthew's had been at his age—the face of a Silverman; but instead of Matthew's stooping, academic slightness George had a burly, robust frame.

George was thinking that he liked the winter. A man knew what to do with cold weather; the sharp wind was a direct challenge and could be fought by exercise. In the summer the heat sapped all the vitality from one's body and left one listless and defeated. He looked around at the winter scene almost with affection. The grasses in the ditches were brown and dead, and patches of hoar frost showed in the deeper shadows of the hedges. Away to his left a line of hills showed blue against the pale grey of the sky, from which the cold had long drained all other colour. The cottage gardens were wildernesses of dead plants, the brittle, brown scaffolding of clumped hollyhock stems standing naked against white walls, and the hedges, stripped of their leaves, disclosed the secrets of summer in the mouldering nests of thrush and blackbird. There was little life to be seen on the land. The rooks wheeled and cawed over the dead fields, and clouds of gulls settled on the hard furrows, facing into the cold wind. The cattle stood in the lee of the hedges, each with a small cloud of vapour rising from its nostrils. There was little movement in them, not even the spasmodic flirting of tails, for the flies of summer no longer attacked them. No buds, no bursting leaves, no thin points of seed shoot … The earth had locked everything tightly in its grip.

George liked the wintry barrenness. It was hard; it was physical. No leafed hedges and tall sways of luxuriant grass hid the clean sweep of fields and downs, and the air which poured into his lungs was sweet and icy with health, not warm and laden with dust and pollen.

The journey to Swanbridge was mostly across country, missing the wide main roads, and it was well into the afternoon before George turned on to the splendid trunk road that linked Swanbridge with the coast. At three o'clock he swung his car through the drive gates and drew up with a thin squeak of brakes and a protest of gravel before the doorway.

"Have you had your lunch?" his mother asked, after he had made his greetings.

"Yes—stopped on the way up." He had taken a glass of beer at a small and dirty public-house.

"You're sure you won't have just something now?" Her eyes regarded him affectionately. If she had a favourite among the children, it was George. He had been her first, and now, looking at his healthy body, his square, honest face, she found herself suffused with a strong pride.

"No—really, mother."

"Can I borrow your fruit barrow for an hour, George?" asked Loraine.

George was on the point of telling her that she certainly could not borrow the car when he stopped, and then said very deliberately: "Of course. Be careful with the top gear, though. The lever jumps out of place sometimes."

"I will," cried Loraine, and she was gone before he could alter his mind.

"You ought not to let her drive it, George. She's not safe in a car yet by herself. And you know how nervous Matthew is about cars."

"Don't worry, mother. Loraine can look after herself. Still, I hope she doesn't muck it up. Where is Dad?"

"He's at the office."

"And Alexander?"

"He's working in his room."

"Working! That's a good one," laughed George. "I must go up and talk to him. I hope Dad comes in to tea; I want to see him." His tone as he said this was serious; but his mother did not notice it. George often was serious. It was a good thing, she thought, to have one serious child in the family.

* * *

Alexander was working. He was seated at a table before the long window on the south side of his room. As he looked out he had a view of the orchard and the serried dips of roofs in the river part of the town, and beyond them a dark barrage of elms which marked the far side of the river fields. Before him was a drawing-board and about the table were scattered a compass, protractors, set-squares, and pieces of paper with hurried sketches on them.

It was a comfortable room. In front of the gas-fire was a deep cane armchair, and the mantelshelf was laden with books, amongst which the works of Aldous Huxley and Sinclair Lewis predominated. A large fitted cupboard held all his clothes and an assortment of sports wear, tennis rackets, and hockey sticks. About the walls, in no apparent order, were pictures, some framed and some just fastened with drawing-pins. There were groups of school theatricals, in which it would have been difficult to recognise Alexander unless he were pointed out to you, two etchings of Canterbury Cathedral, some drawings taken from a motoring magazine of racing cars, a black-and-white caricature of George Bernard Shaw, honoured by a passe-partout frame, and one or two water-colours.

When George entered the room, Alexander was sucking the end of his pencil and staring out of the window. He turned quickly at George's sudden entry and said:

"Hullo, scavenger! Don't they teach you to knock before entering a room at Oxford?"

"Scavenger yourself," retorted George politely. "I did knock, only you were so busy day-dreaming you didn't hear me."

"Perhaps I was deep in thought," admitted Alexander.

"Day-dreaming, I said." George looked over his shoulder at the drawing-board. "What's that supposed to be?', he asked, indicating the sheet of cartridge paper which was pinned to the board.

"What does it look like?"

George did not answer. He sat down in the armchair before the fire and began to fill a pipe.

"I can understand your silence," Alexander said sympathetically. "You're overcome by the sheer beauty of the design."

"Beauty my eye! It looks like a barracks."

"Barracks! Alexander stood up in his indignation. "Barracks! You unenlightened oaf! There never was any barracks that had the line and grace of this building, and look at the almost perfect balance. I rejected a lot of ideas before I decided upon this one."

"What is it?" George was amused by Alexander's anger. He liked his younger brother, and, although he never let him know it, he had a sincere respect for his ability. George knew his own limitations, and he realised that if Alexander lacked the more phlegmatic virtues of steadiness and thoroughness, he had a quick brain which might one day prove him to be a genius. That Alexander was to become a genius was only George's idea. Alexander had a modern dislike of the word, and, as he had never yet had to do any, believed fervently in the power of unremitting hard work.

"It's a girls' school, such a school as this country has never seen before. And I doubt whether anyone will ever have the enterprise to put up such a place; at least, not for another fifty years. You see"—Alexander picked up the board and brought it to George—"this is only the front elevation, and doesn't give much idea of the inner economy of the place. You see, films are going to be the greatest teaching medium in a few years, and I'm designing each classroom on the basis of a cinema, but not the cheap, flashy cinema. I want to get an atmosphere of intimacy. There'll be a projector in each class—"

"Are you going to have pretty girls selling chocolates and cigarettes while the films are showing?"

Alexander replaced the board with dignity on the table and said gently and sadly, "You're a Philistine."

George did not answer. He sat staring into the fire and puffing his pipe. Alexander was suddenly aware that George was not in a jocular mood at all.

"What's the matter, George?" he asked.

George lifted his feet to the fire-rail and said, "Just how much do you think it means to the old man to have his elder son take over the editorship of the *Messenger* when he's too old for the job?"

"What a question! Why, I guess it means everything in the world to the old boy. And why shouldn't it? Ever since the days of old John Silverman the eldest son has taken over the paper. It's a family tradition, and you know how the old folk bow down to tradition. Anyway, I think it's a good tradition. I'll bet when you're editor you'll be as snotty about the *Messenger* as the old man can be; no irrevelant criticism, no jokes; and you'll want your eldest son to take on the job when you're through with it."

"I shall never be through with it."

"What do you mean?" Alexander did not at once read any serious intent in George's words. George usually did his analysing in a conversational way, with Alexander putting forward arguments for him to attack.

"I mean I shall never be through with it because I'm not going into it!" George made the pronouncement deliberately and with satisfaction. Alexander was the first member of the family he had told; he had begun to break the ice, and, feeling himself in action, he was more at ease in his mind than he had been for the last few weeks.

It was some time before Alexander could reply. Then he said quietly: "Not going to work on the *Messenger*! Do you mean that?"

"I shouldn't joke about it." George's reply let down Alexander's flood-gates.

"Wow!" He sat down suddenly and then began to chuckle. "Christopher! Won't there be a rumpus when you tell the old man! He'll go mad. But why don't you want to work on the *Messenger*?" Alexander was amazed at George's declaration. Solid, honest George, destined to inherit the mantle of editorship, the true successor to the great traditions of the Silvermans, suddenly renouncing his intention of following in the steps of his forebears! It was almost biblical, Alexander thought; and then he was overpowered by a curiosity to know why George had changed his mind.

"I shall have to see the old man today some time," George said. "I've been thinking this thing over for a long time, and I can tell you it hasn't been an easy decision to make. I considered how much it might hurt the old man, and then I had to consider my true feelings. No, it wasn't easy …"

Alexander knew it had not been easy. George, conscientious and fair, would have gone over the arguments one by one and then made up his mind like some machine spewing out a product after tortuous hours of subsidiary processes.

"What are you going to do, instead of newspaper work?"

George hesitated a moment before replying, and then, with a frank look at Alexander, he said seriously "I'm going to enter the Church."

The simplicity of the utterance destroyed Alexander's first reaction, which was to roll upon the floor and howl with laughter. All he could do was to stand before George and murmur, "You're going to enter the Church?"

"That's it," said George. "And I'm glad you didn't laugh, Alexander. It's a very serious decision for me." No one, hearing him, could have doubted his sincerity.

"It sounds a bit like the Oxford Group Movement to me," said Alexander, recovering himself.

"No, it isn't that. I sympathise with the movement, of course, but this is more than that. I want to enter the legitimate Church. I feel I can do more good there than in a newspaper office. There are plenty of people willing to take that kind of job, but not so many who want to go into the Church. She needs young blood, and I'm going. I've made up my mind, and nothing can stop me."

"I can see that. But there'll be hell's own row when the rest of the family find out. Still, you've got your own life to live. I wouldn't give up architecture for a paper, so why should you renounce the Church for it? You know I'll stand by you."

"Thanks, old man."

Alexander sat down by the table and began to scribble meaningless designs on his board. Life was the funniest puzzle going. Here was dear old George coming calmly into the house and, without warning, dropping a bomb before them all. Perturbed as he had to be by the knowledge of what was to happen when his father knew about it, Alexander could not help feeling a certain eagerness of anticipation. Golly, was there going to be some fun!

* * *

When the gong sounded, Alexander and George went down to tea. Loraine was back from her drive, but Matthew had not come in. Alison had gone to a friend's party.

"I suppose Dad is coming home to have a cup of tea?" asked George.

"I think so, dear," replied his mother. "He generally comes in about now for a cup, and then goes back to the office until dinner. Why? Did you want to see him about something?"

"I just wanted to see him. It's nothing very important."

"Don't you believe that, mother," said Alexander quickly. What was George hedging for? They had to know sooner or later, and surely it was as well to begin right away?

"Alex—don't." George began to make a protest, but Alexander would not allow it.

"Go on, tell them now and get it off your chest."

"What is this all about?" Loraine came from the window towards the fireplace, holding a cup of tea carefully, like a competitor in an egg-and-spoon race.

"It sounds very mysterious. Surely our Georgie hasn't gone and got himself into some trouble?"

"That's it," Alexander said. "One of the town girls at Oxford has made a fool out of him and he's got to get married right away."

"George!" Mrs. Silverman started up in a flutter of alarm. "What will your father say?"

George put his hand on her shoulder and scowled at Alexander.

"He's only fooling, mother. Of course not."

"Thank goodness! Of course, George, I should have known. Alexander"— she turned towards him—"you ought not to make such jokes. They are in bad taste."

"I was only fooling. Can't we have a little fun in this family at times?"

"I know you and mother would like to discuss the ethics of family jokes. But I'm more interested to know what it is that George wants to get off his chest," said Loraine.

Well, Alexander had as good as let the cat out of the bag; he might as well tell them, thought George. He moved to the fireplace and got his back to it, so that he could dominate the whole room. His position comforted and assured him, and he said:

"I'm not going into the *Messenger* office when I leave the University. I'm going to enter the Church!"

The effect of this announcement on Loraine and Mrs. Silverman was to be expected. Mrs. Silverman, caught in the act of pouring a cup of tea, sat with the teapot raised elegantly in the air, directing a thin stream of brown tea into a cup. She sat perfectly still, her face turned towards George in a look of pathetic horror and despair. For a second or two she made no sound, until the noise of tea running over from cup into saucer drew her attention to the mess she was making on the tray. She put the teapot down and succumbed into the depths of her chair, making small moaning noises which might have come from the sight of the spoiled tea-tray or from George's calm declaration of apostasy.

Loraine's reaction was more direct. She dropped her cup of tea to a convenient table, placed her hands tragically to her forehead, and collapsed into a chair, where she lay shaking her head ominously, murmuring, "What will father say?"

Alexander stood by the window enjoying the scene.

"Well," said George anxiously as the two women continued to look at him as though he had suddenly materialised by the fireplace, "can't you say something?"

"Oh, dear, George …" Mrs. Silverman felt it was her duty to pull herself together and be calm. All she could do was to look helplessly at George and wonder why he had done it. "What will Matthew say? What will he say?" The thought was too potent for her, and she lapsed into silence.

"What will father say?" Loraine savoured the thought slowly, then she sat up, tugged her blouse into neat lines, patted her hair, and added: "Whatever he says, I don't want to miss it."

"Yes, what will father say?" Alexander took up the question and grinned at George.

"Well, you're a helpful lot," said George, a little irritably.

"Oh, George, dear … you know we'll do what we can …" Mrs. Silverman began, but the thought of their ineffectualness stilled her.

"I knew you never had much sense, Georgie," said Loraine sympathetically, "but you've certainly got courage."

"Yes, the courage of a terrier, ready to tackle something too powerful for its strength. Well, George, here comes the protagonist. I hear the footsteps of the respected paterfamilias in the hall. We shan't be long now, folks"; and Alexander subsided gently into a chair by the window and prepared to enjoy himself.

George shut his eyes, and, though none of the others knew it, he was praying for strength.

* * *

Matthew was in a good mood. By the afternoon post there had come to him a letter which had made him forget Uncle Abner and filled him with good humour. He had not troubled to disguise it even to his staff, though he privately considered that for the good of their souls it might have been wiser to have done so. It was one of his dicta that an employer should always be enough of a tyrant to exact implicit obedience, yet not so much of a tyrant as to have obedience marred by nervousness. That another of his favourite sayings was, "I like to be regarded as the father of a large, happy family, rather than an employer of men," caused him no qualms. If any of his staff had confronted him with his contradictions he would have wriggled from the embarrassment by pointing out that even the father of a happy family must sometimes be a tyrant.

There was to be in Swanbridge a great rally meeting in aid of the League of Nations, and to this meeting a well-known duchess, whose seat was in the neighbourhood, had persuaded Austin Swing, the novelist, to give an address. The duchess would be out of the country at the time of the rally, which was billed for the middle of February, and Matthew had written to the famous author offering him the hospitality of Khartum for the night of the meeting, and the letter had been from Austin Swing sweetly accepting his invitation in those verbose and glittering phrases which had endeared Mr. Swing to a large and susceptible feminine public.

Matthew laid his hat and coat carefully across the hall table, glanced into his study to see whether any letters had been delivered for him at the house, noticed through the window that Fuller had swept the lawn of leaves, thus saving himself from the reprimand which Matthew had intended to give, and then he made for the sitting-room in which he knew the family would be at tea. George was home, he knew from the car outside.

He stopped for a second outside the door and then, opening it with a wide sweep, he entered, beaming at his assembled family. Alexander was the only one who noticed at once his good humour; the rest were too occupied with the thought of what was to come.

The scene pleased Matthew. The cheerfulness of a room brightened by firelight on familiar things, the sense of intimacy that comes from association with a room for years, and the presence of his wife and children, happy and glad to see him—Matthew respected and was glad of family life. He stood by the door for a moment, his scholarly face beaming, his spectacles catching the light.

"Ha, just in time, am I, to save something for myself from you hungry people?" He advanced smiling.

"Here's a cup of tea for you, dear. I've just poured it out." Mrs. Silverman had the sound instinct of getting something to be balanced into Matthew's hands. It might deter him from violence.

"Thank you, my dear." Matthew took the cup. "And I'll have a piece of that chocolate cake. Nice to see you home, George. Quite a pleasant surprise. Talking of surprises—Mr. Austin Swing, the celebrated novelist, who is to address the forthcoming League of Nations meeting in this town, has done us the honour of promising to be our guest on that occasion!"

Matthew looked around for the gratification which was due from this statement. Mrs. Silverman, George, and Loraine said nothing. Alexander said very loudly:

"What, that awful pimp?"

But Matthew's good humour was not tried by Alexander's irreverence.

"I did not expect a disciple of Aldous Huxley to be enthusiastic about Mr. Swing. Nevertheless, there are some million lovers of literature in this country who share the opinion with me that Mr. Swing is a great force, and an ornament to letters."

"He's an ornament all right, and, anyway, who cares what a million morons think?"

"I'm sure we shall be glad to have Mr. Swing," said Mrs. Silverman hurriedly. "I read one of his books—*The Golden Fortress*—and I must say I enjoyed it, and I'm sure I'm not a moron—whatever they are. Do sit down, Matthew. It makes me nervous to see you standing up with that cup of tea."

It was then that Matthew became aware of the strangeness which hung over them all. George had done no more than nod to him. That was not unusual; George never said a lot; but why was he watching him so anxiously, as though he were a young boy playing near the edge of a precipice? And Loraine, who was, he knew, a Swing fan— why had she let Alexander's remarks go unchallenged?

"I expect you're hungry, dear. Shall I cut you a large slice of cake?"

Matthew recognised his wife's nervousness. He looked at Alexander, and was met by a pair of dark eyes that gave him no hint of trouble. Loraine was tapping her saucer with her spoon, and avoided his look; but George met his eyes, and he knew that whatever was wrong was to do with George. He was vaguely annoyed at his temporary exclusion from them. A father should have the confidence of his wife and children.

Very deliberately Matthew sat down, putting his cup on the floor by his feet, and then he said:

"What's the matter? You all seem very quiet."

"Why, whatever makes you say that?" Mrs. Silverman felt that she had to do something heroic to stave off the disaster. Perhaps, if she did, George would suddenly think better of his decision, and it would never be known to Matthew. No one took any notice of her.

"We've got reason to be quiet," said Alexander slowly. He knew George would not resent his interference. Unless someone spoke up and started the ball rolling, anything might happen. "We've got news as well as you." A look flashed between Alexander and George.

"Yes, we've got news, Dad." George took him up, and went on: "But I'm afraid you may not find it so pleasant."

"Hullo, this sounds serious. This sounds gloomy … What's all the trouble?" Even as Matthew spoke jocularly, he had a feeling that his humour was out of place. Anyway, why didn't they tell him instead of keeping it back?

"It is serious," George went on steadily. He was in it now, and there was no turning back. "You see, father, during this vacation I've been doing a lot of thinking, and I've come to a decision. I want you to release me from my promise to go into the *Messenger* with you when I come down, and let me go into the Church instead!" It was done; the tension about the room slackened, and then tautened as Matthew sat forward in his chair.

"What on earth are you talking about, my boy?"

"About my future … I want to go into the Church, not be a newspaperman."

Matthew felt all their eyes upon him. George—he repeated the words to himself—wanted to go into the Church. The desire had the immature quality of a child's longing for impossible playthings. George was asking for the moon. It was so absurd that Matthew refused to consider it seriously.

"Nonsense, George. This must be a whim. It'll pass. You can't do a thing like that." The boy was obviously not serious about it, though it was time he began to cease having wild enthusiasms that passed and were soon forgotten. Matthew overlooked, in his eagerness to convince himself that it was only a whim, that George never had been given to wild enthusiasms.

"It won't pass, father. My mind's made up. I want to go into the Church," George said steadily, and Matthew knew that he had made up his mind. Then, like a reservoir bursting its dam, he felt an immense resentment surge within him, uncontrollable, straining for liberty. It was almost as though he were a detached observer of the calamity, safe on the sunlit slope of the hillside watching the waters rise into a crested head and rage, towering, along the valley, their lusting roar fainter in his ears than the song of larks above the hill heather. The vision passed, leaving him angry and rebellious.

"But you can't!" He sprang to his feet and, doing so, kicked his cup over. The jingle of crockery annoyed him, and he glanced downwards. He resented this sudden intrusion upon his good humour. It was an insult.

"Mind your cup, dear—" began Mrs. Silverman.

"Damn the cup!" bellowed Matthew suddenly. Why were they all concerned about cups when there was this monstrous thing to be faced?"I won't allow it! I won't allow it! Don't you realise what you're doing? Four generations of Silvermans have seen an eldest son in the *Messenger*, and now, because of some silly undergraduate fancy, you want to upset all that."

"It's not a silly undergraduate fancy."

"It is! Don't contradict me! I'm older than you are. Do you think I don't know that you'll have forgotten all about the Church in a week? You're a Silverman, and your place is in the newspaper, and that's where you're going. The whole of my life I've looked forward to having you with me, and you're not going to alter my plans now—just for a whim. Don't answer me back!" Matthew roared, as George started to speak. He stamped across the room, kicking a footstool from his path. "The Church! What good would you be in the Church? You're a newspaperman and your place is in the *Messenger*. Never in the whole of my days have I heard such damn' tomfoolery, and never did I expect to hear it from you. I thought you were sensible, but you're not; you're soft; you're fuzzy-headed and as volatile as a schoolgirl. Well"—he swung round on the rest of the family, his eyes blazing and his face wrinkled with rage—"what about the rest of you? I suppose you're content to sit around and let him go on with his foolishness? Isn't there any sense amongst you? Am I the only sane person in the room?"

"I don't see why you should be annoyed because George decides he'd rather spread Christianity than news. It's just as worthy—"

"Silence! No one's speaking to you!" bellowed Matthew, quelling Alexander in a moment.

"Matthew, Matthew, dear." Mrs. Silverman was alarmed at his anger. She was sure it wasn't healthy for him to carry on so. "Don't be so violent."

"Violent!" Matthew shouted the word. "Violent! What else can I be when I'm greeted at my home-coming, after a hard day's work, with such news?"

"You might be sensible and give me a chance to speak," said George. He was not frightened by his father's outburst. He had expected it, but it was not going to shake him from his intentions.

For a moment Matthew felt himself insulted by George's request that he should be sensible. That he should be sensible! The impertinence of these modern children—had they no respect for age, for traditions, for the hand that fed them?"I am being sensible! If I had not been sensible all my life it would have been hard for all of you—and I had hoped that you"—this at George—"at least were level-headed."

"Do you mean that I am not level-headed?" asked Alexander indignantly.

"You're as scatter-brained as a lunatic!" Matthew said tensely. "And, what is more, if George thinks—"

"Please, Daddy, I do think you might give George a chance to speak." It was Loraine who spoke, and the quiet tone of her voice affected Matthew. He hesitated. She was right. George had every claim to make his defence. No one should accuse him of being hot-headed and unjust.

"All right; but it can't make any difference!" he said, dropping into a chair and blowing his cheeks out as though the air were full of poison gas.

There was a pause before George spoke, and in that pause Matthew suddenly realised that he had gained very little by storming, and he was half ashamed of himself.

"I'm sorry about this," said George, "but I can assure you, Dad, that it is no sudden whim. I've been thinking about it for months, and I've gone very carefully into my responsibilities. I know I promised to go into the paper, not only because you wanted me to, but because I

48

wanted to. I'm unhappy, too, because the tradition must be broken. But since I've been at Oxford I've come to see that I can do more good by entering the Church than I can by going into a newspaper. There are plenty of men ready to take that kind of job, plenty of worthy men, but there aren't so many these days who are ready to devote their lives to the Church, and the Church needs men. It needs young blood, and I feel that I have been called to work for Christianity. That's all there is to it. I know it sounds bald, but I mean every word of it. If I didn't, do you think I would stand here and say what I have said, knowing the pain it must give you?"

As George was speaking, Matthew saw that his son did mean everything he said, and he saw, too, what a struggle George had had with his loyalties to the *Messenger* before he had come to a decision. Suddenly his anger went from him and he was curiously proud of the boy. It took courage to do what he had done. George was solid, sincere, and he knew that if he suffered because of his son's decision that suffering was no less than George, too, had borne. Matthew was ashamed of his outbreak. He had let his emotions take control of his senses, and that was not wise. He got up and went to the window, staring out without speaking. The garden was dead, and the sky through the branches of the orchard was deepening into the darkness of night. Behind him in the room the firelight was throwing warm shadows, and out there was a friendless darkness. John, Jacob, and James ... What would they have done? They had never faced such a problem. To them the *Messenger* had been all. And to him the *Messenger* meant everything; it was his life; but that was no real reason why it had to become George's life; no reason why, because he loved it so, he had to offer his son to it as a sacrifice ... George was no longer a boy; he was a man, and entitled to make his own life, to make his own mistakes and forge his own triumphs... One day, perhaps, George would find that he had made a mistake—or he might not. It would have been easy—Matthew knew George well enough for that—to have pleaded with him, reminded him of his age, his life's desire to see George in the *Messenger*, shown him the wreck he was making of a life's ambition—yet Matthew could not do that. Even in his despair he had to be honourable.

He turned and looked across at George.

"I hope you're not making a mistake," he said; "but if that is how you really feel I don't see why I should try to stop you. We must all make our own lives these days, so far as we can. We must get along without you at the office, that's all. If ever you change your mind, son, you know there's a place waiting for you there."

Before any of them could speak, he walked to the door and left the room.

IV

Sir, I hope that you will allow me
space to reply to "A Mother of Five."
A woman's place is not necessarily in
the home. I also am the mother of five,
but this has never prevented me from
following my profession. What about
Florence Nightingale?

CONSTANT READER.

Swanbridge Messenger (From "Our Mail-bag")

Later that evening George and his father had a long talk in the study. Matthew held to his decision and did not try to dissuade George from his purpose. Their conversation concerned itself chiefly with ways and means of helping George to enter the Church. And even here Matthew found he was of little assistance beyond agreeing to George's proposals. George, characteristically, had worked everything out.

When George went, Matthew remained alone in the study. Outside, the evening had turned suddenly milder, the frost had gone, and great gusts of blustery wind were hurling rain before them—rain which was already swelling into gutter torrents and dispelling the litter which had been whipped there by the wind during the last few frosty days. The drops beat a steady tattoo on the study window, and the wind, as though aiding them in their efforts to get in, shook the panes of glass with rising violence. Matthew did not hear the storm.

He sat in his chair, his chin held between his cupped hands, staring into the fire. The light from a green-shaded reading-lamp picked out his profile, while the fire put life into the shadows which underlined his features.

He could not pretend, he was telling himself, that George's decision had not hurt him. Any other man would have been hurt. It had meant so much to him to know that, when he passed on, George would have remained, a Silverman, to look after the *Messenger*. People could say what they liked about family traditions, but really the traditions which persisted only did so by their own virtues, because at the bottom they were sensible. Yet it was necessary these days to be open-minded. Young people were more frank, more honest with themselves, and less in awe of their parents. Jacob Silverman, the son of John, the founder, had been completely under the domination of his father; and James, too, had in turn never questioned Jacob. And to Matthew himself it had never occurred to do any other than his father commanded. But, then, he had always wanted to join the *Messenger*, had looked forward to doing so, and he knew that, although Jacob and James would never have dared to question their fathers, they had never wanted to; they had all wanted to join the *Messenger*. George did not want to—and Matthew knew that he had no prescriptive right to make him. In fact, he knew he could not make him. Nowadays no father had that much power over his family, and perhaps it was a good thing that it was so.

He began to pack his pipe. Funny. He smiled to himself. Here he was, fifty-three years old, and for the last twenty-four years he had lived and worked, thinking all the time that when he died there would be a Silverman carrying on with the *Messenger*. Now all that was to be changed. He was to be the last, although he had two sons. George was to become a preacher, and Alexander an architect ... Alexander could never be persuaded to join the *Messenger*. You couldn't drive these young people; the moment you began to hamper their freedom they fought fiercely. They resented older people interfering with their lives, though they lacked the experience of age which was necessary to direct their lives into the right channels. The only way they could be influenced was by making them think their decisions were born of themselves, and that was not easy ...

Matthew looked up as there came a knock on the study door.

"Come in," he called quietly. The door opened and Alexander came in.

"Am I interrupting you?"

"No, son. What do you want?"

"I heard you say some publisher had sent you a review copy of a book about pygmies. I wondered if I could borrow it. It might be interesting to know something about the happiest race under the sun—that's what they call 'em."

Matthew smiled. Alexander seldom made a simple statement. If he wanted a book he said why he wanted it. If he went for a walk he had to observe that it was healthy to do so, and if he spent an afternoon reading in his room he would point out that it was pleasanter to sit indoors in comfort than to tire the body by strenuous exercise.

"It's on my table, somewhere beneath the papers and stuff there."

Alexander tilted the shade of the reading-lamp and began to rummage for the book. His father's table was the one thing in the house which Gibby dared not tidy.

"Well, and what do you think of George's desire to go into religion?" Matthew put the question casually, as though he were making conversation until Alexander had found the book and left the room.

Alexander stopped turning over papers for a moment and looked round at his father. All he could see was the top of his head over the chair, each hair picked out in a gold film against the fire. "Do you want my views on George or on orthodox religion?"

"On George. I've heard you on religion too many times."

"I think he's doing the sensible thing. There are not enough men and women doing what they want to do these days."

"Do most men and women know what they want to do—when they're young, I mean?"

"That depends. George knows what he wants, and I know what I want, and there are hundreds of others who know. Some people, of course, never do discover what they want to do. Anyway, unless you stick out for what you consider is your vocation when you're young, you're lost. You can't change horses when you're old and settled in a job." Alexander wondered whether his father was sounding him. When George had broken his news, he had been too occupied with the stir it had made to examine it in relation to himself. During dinner, however, he had begun to see that it was possible that his father might make a request to him to give up architecture and join the *Messenger*. In fact, he was sure that Matthew would ask him at some time, and he would have to refuse. Although he knew that his father would not attempt to force him, he rather looked forward to the moment. If he could have done, he would have agreed to give up architecture, but that was impossible. It meant altering his whole life, his future, his dreams and aspirations.

Matthew's distress hurt Alexander. He knew the agony of mind which possessed his father, yet he had, he told himself, to be sensible, not sentimental.

"Yes, I suppose it is. Still, it's difficult when you've made up your mind to a thing for years suddenly to find that it isn't going to happen after all. Family tradition is a fine thing as long as it isn't allowed to produce discord ... though I often wonder whether some traditions aren't worthy of sacrifices ..."

Here it comes, thought Alexander. This was the point where his father made his appeal to him. He picked up the book on pygmies and turned away from the desk. The feel of the cold, firm covers beneath his fingers gave him steadiness. It was going to be hard to disappoint him; but he had to do it. The old boy was already broken up about George. It seemed cruel to make it harder for him, but one had to be hard these days ... parents were too emotional.

The wind rattled the windows. Matthew said nothing for a while. Alexander found himself trembling with a nervous excitement. Then his father spoke.

"Have you found the book?" he asked quietly.

"Yes, I—"

"I hope you enjoy it. You must tell me about it when you've finished it."

Alexander was outside the room before he had recovered from his surprise. He could have sworn that his father would have asked him then. He glanced down at the book in his hands and he was aware that it was not surprise which had confused him. He was disappointed. He was the only other son; he had the right at least to be asked whether he wished to take George's place.

* * *

Alexander went into the sitting-room with his book. Only Loraine was there, turning over the leaves of an illustrated magazine and sitting close to the wireless, from whence came the raucous dialogue of two comedians.

"Hullo," grunted Alexander, dropping into a chair and opening his book. "Why aren't you out with the dashing young Philip?"

"Because," said Loraine, without looking up, "I prefer to stop in and listen to the wireless. These two are very good—Alexander and Mose."

"They sound too laryngeal for words."

"We're very superior tonight, aren't we?" said Loraine, without any animosity. "I seem to remember you once saying that Clapham and Dwyer deserved a Nobel Prize for their work."

"Your mind is too literal. A little exaggeration at times gives colour to a statement, and generally does no harm. And now, if you will be silent, I will endeavour to read my book, though the booming inanities of Messieurs Alexander and Mose are going to make it difficult. I have not yet acquired your happy facility of reading and listening to the wireless at the same time." That would touch her on a sore spot, thought Alexander.

Loraine was not annoyed. Her mind was only half occupied with the conversation. She dropped her magazine and looked across at Alexander. Her hair was bright against the dark stuff of the armchair. She crossed one leg over the other and, holding her foot high, worked her ankle in and out of the heel of her loose shoe with a faint clipping noise, taking a pleasure in the friction of the leather over the silk of her stocking. Although she was two years older than Alexander, she was conscious, without any feeling of resentment, that he was in many ways older than she. She liked him, but outside the house they had few common contacts; she had her friends and he had his. At times his seeming lack of conventional emotions worried her. He made such outrageous, unorthodox statements, and nothing seemed sacred to him. He spoke openly about religion, sex, and society in a very disturbing way; and where Matthew and others smiled at Alexander, and discounted his remarks by his youth, Loraine found herself unable to persuade herself that Alexander did not honestly think as he spoke.

"You've been talking to father in the library, haven't you?" she asked suddenly.

Alexander looked up quickly. What was she driving at?

"Yes," he said simply.

"And I suppose he asked you if you would give up your plans about architecture and take George's place?"

"What if he did?"

Loraine flipped the leaves of her magazine through her fingers. "Nothing, only I can't help thinking what a shame it is for him to have all this happen. It would mean an awful lot to him to know that one of you would be carrying on with the *Messenger*. Do you feel that you did the right thing by refusing to go into the office with him?"

"How do you know that I refused?"

"I can guess what you would do. Don't think I'm blaming you, Alex. I'm not. You've got a right to refuse, I suppose. But it does seem an awful shame for the old dear. All these years thinking about it … and then this happens."

"It's not such a tragedy as you make out. I'll admit it does seem a pity that the tradition is to be broken, but you surely don't think a tradition like that is worthy of human sacrifice, do you? Why … it would almost be a blood rite!"

"I don't see that it would be such a sacrifice for you. After all, you haven't properly started your studies for architecture as yet, and you can hardly know whether you're going to like it. Everyone says it's interesting to work for a paper; reporting and all that. You might find that you liked it an awful lot, Alex. Please, why don't you give it a chance? I'm sure father would let you try it on the understanding that if you didn't like it after a year you could leave and take up architecture. It would make him so happy."

"Not me!" said Alex definitely. "I'm not going to give up architecture merely to spend my life messing around with garden fêtes and county council meetings. I should hate working on a newspaper."

"I don't see how you can possibly tell whether you would like it or not."

"No, you may not; but I do, and I'm not going to do it. If you're so keen about the tradition why don't you offer to take George's place? No profession is barred to a woman these days! Poor old Philip, I wonder what he'd say about having an editor for a wife ..." Alexander returned to his book with a snigger which infuriated Loraine.

"You funny little beast!" she snapped. Then, very deliberately, she turned the wireless on as loudly as it would go and walked out of the room without a glance at him.

A few moments later George came into the room to be met by a blast of oscillating chamber music.

"Must you have it as loud as that?" he enquired piteously.

"Have what? Oh, the wireless," said Alexander, with an artless smile. " I suppose Loraine must have been listening to it. She's just gone out. I was so immersed in my book about pygmies that I hadn't noticed it was so loud."

"Pygmies?" said George, switching the wireless off.

"Yes. If you're thinking of taking up missionary work, I should go to one of those tribes. The women are a most handsome lot. Would you care to see some of these pictures of them? Elles sont toutes nues ..."

"Don't be a dirty-minded little beast," replied George with heavy dignity.

"I'm sorry. I forgot your change of life." Alexander returned to his pygmies.

* * *

James Silverman had been the second of the four children of Jacob Silverman; the eldest had been Isobel, who was born in 1853, two years after the marriage of Jacob to Anne Granger, the daughter of an army officer. Three years after Isobel's birth had come James, and six years after his birth Anne had considerably surprised herself and her husband by being brought to bed of twins, Samuel and Adelaide. They were the only twins recorded in the family history of the Silvermans, and Jacob and his wife were proud of their meritorious achievement, but the twins, as though they resented their alliance by birth, had never cherished that sweet concord which is supposed to be the sign of their close relationship. From the moment they had been able to speak and express their thoughts they had disliked one another. Samuel had died at the age of thirty-seven in circumstances which were seldom referred to by the Silvermans. Great-aunt Adelaide was still alive, but had long outlived the triumph she had felt at surviving Samuel. Both James and Isobel were dead, and Adelaide was consequently the eldest living Silverman. She and her sister, Isobel, had been very close to one another. As young ladies they had decided, after much discussion, never to marry, and to pass their lives undisturbed by the repugnant presence of males. But when Adelaide was twenty-one, and easily repulsing the few attempts upon her affections, and Isobel was thirty, and considering herself safe at last from the unwelcomed attentions of men, Abner Cartwright had come into the Silverman household. He was a friend of Samuel's, and older than him by three years. Within three weeks he was engaged to Isobel, and at the end of six months they were married. Adelaide had forgiven Isobel her apostasy, but she had never forgiven Abner.

No one had known a great deal about Abner. He had settled in Swanbridge at his marriage, and he had a great deal of money. By his marriage there had been one child, Peter Cartwright, who married Mary Haydale, the daughter of a local doctor, in 1911 and he had been killed in action in 1914, when his only child, Reginald Cartwright, was ten months old.

Abner now lived in a quiet house on the northern outskirts of Swanbridge, and with him lived his widowed daughter-in-law, Mary Cartwright, and her son Reginald.

At breakfast, the morning after George had made his disturbing announcement, Matthew stated his intention of going to call upon Uncle Abner. It was not usual for him to make public his daily movements. The family read nothing strange into this innocent remark. Only Alexander wondered why his father should be seeking Uncle Abner's company. Uncle Abner was a great critic of the *Messenger*, and the two men, although they were friendly, never went out of their way to seek one another's company.

Matthew found Abner sitting before his fire reading *The Times*.

"Well, what do you want at this hour of the morning?" he asked before Matthew had taken a seat. "You should be in your office attending to business."

"Business takes one outside the office sometimes," Matthew replied. He did not mind Abner's tone. Abner was seventy-five, and accustomed to speaking his thoughts. He was a thin, brittle-looking man, his face white and folded with loose flesh that hid the lines of his lips. His hair was white, and he wore it *en brosse*. His legs were wrapped in a plaid, and by the side of his chair lay an enormous Alsatian hound whose hackles started to rise as Matthew entered, and then as quickly dropped.

Seeing that Matthew evidently wanted to talk to him, Abner folded *The Times* carefully and, with a movement which suddenly made his age seem ridiculous, he threw the paper adroitly on to a near-by table as a man throws a quoit. As it landed neatly and safely, he turned to Matthew with a grin of self-approval in his old grey eyes.

"Well, what do you want?" he said, and one hand dropped over the side of the chair and began to play with the loose fur at the back of the dog's head. A large signet-ring encircled one of the fingers.

"George came home yesterday."

"Then he ought not to have done. He should be in Oxford by now."

"He's going back this afternoon. He gave us all rather a surprise."

"That's unlike George. He is not a man of surprises. He's one of those who can write an autobiography at twenty and then proceed to live the life as it is written. And a good job, too. The trouble with this world is that there aren't enough sure men in it like George. I like George; I've always liked him; but I don't see why you should make him an excuse to come up here interfering with my reading of *The Times*. I'll give you two minutes to go before I set Pelang on you."

"This is serious, Abner," said Matthew quietly. He leaned forward in his chair and told him about George. Abner listened without interruption until he was done.

"So you're going to let him leave the *Messenger*?"

"Yes, I am," answered Matthew. He knew what Abner was thinking. For all his criticism of the *Messenger*, the paper and the Silverman tradition meant as much to him as it did to Matthew. The eagerness with which he conned each week's issue for mistakes came only from a desire to have the paper perfect, and the greatest period of Abner's life had been during the few years of the war when Matthew had gone to the Front and he had taken over the editorship temporarily. Although he belonged to the Silverman family only through his marriage with Isobel, he was more Silverman now than he was Cartwright.

"Then I think you're a damned fool! If he were my boy I should lock him up in his room without food until he came to his senses. You can't let this thing happen. Do you know what you're doing?"

"Perfectly," said Matthew, enjoying, without showing it, the rage in Abner which he too had felt when George had first told him his intentions. "But fathers can't do that kind of thing these days. It isn't rational. George has every right to change his mind, and I have no right to force him into a life which he feels is not congenial to his gifts!"

"Balderdash! You talk like a lecturer. You can't apply principles like that to human beings. You have every right to force him to do what you wish. It's the sensible thing to do. You have your authority as a father, and the last resort of authority is force. You must use it."

"I shall not. If he wants to go into the Church, he shall. It's hard for me, but I've no right to expect too much of the boy."

Abner was suddenly complaisant. He could see that Matthew had made up his mind, and it was not Abner's practice to hammer against stone walls. "And what do you propose to do about the *Messenger*? There's always been a Silverman on it?"

"I know, and so I hope there always will be."

"But there's only Alexander. He's got nothing in his head but architecture. He was up here the other week criticising this house until I felt like boxing his ears. He actually told me that it was a crime to make servants carry coals up two flights of stairs, and that I was as good as a slave-master for making them live in the basement! And then he had the audacity to say that I had plenty of money, and, if I liked, he would design a new house for me, full, I suppose, of electric fires and rooms that looked like miniature Wembley Exhibitions."

"He's at that stage, but it'll pass and he'll quieten down."

"I hope not," said Abner fiercely. "I like the boy to be like that. He's got spirit. Often he reminds me of Samuel in many ways. Poor

60

old Sam—if he hadn't been so fond of the bottle he might have done great things. Alexander has his spirit all right. Let's hope he doesn't get his bad habit. But if you're thinking of taking him into the *Messenger* you're mistaken. If he went he'd never stay there—and I don't think he'd go. Not unless you force him to."

"I can't and shan't do that."

"Then what are you going to do if he won't come?"

"I haven't thought about that."

"Then my advice to you is to go home and think about it, because you'll have to face it whether you like to or not."

"I wonder," said Matthew, almost to himself.

"What's that?" snapped Abner, who hated people to mumble.

"Nothing ..."

* * *

Alexander was worried by his father's silence. He had expected to be asked long ago if he would care to join the *Messenger*. Matthew had had plenty of opportunities. It wasn't, he told himself, as he went up to his room after breakfast, that he wanted to join the paper; but at least he had the right to be asked. He was the second son, and, if it really came to it, he supposed he could make as much a success of being an editor as he could of being an architect ... Not that he wanted to, of course.

He tried to work, but his thoughts kept reverting to his father. Why had he gone up to Uncle Abner's? Saturday morning was a fairly busy one at the office, and he usually made a point of being there early and staying late. He stuck at his board for an hour, and then, defeated by his thoughts, he threw down his pencil and left the room.

As he passed Loraine's room she was sitting on her bed, idly polishing her nails and staring sideways out of the window. She was humming slowly to herself and thinking. She had been doing a lot of thinking since awakening that morning, for with the morning had come a great thought. Loraine often had great thoughts on awakening, but they usually lost their brilliance by the time she had read her letters and eaten her breakfast. This one had persisted.

If you're so keen about the tradition, why don't you offer to take George's place? No profession is barred to a woman these days. That was what Alex had said. She had been too angry with him at the time to take any notice of the remark. When she had awakened this morning, the words had slipped first into her mind from some depths of her memory, and there they had stayed. Why didn't she take George's place? The more she thought about it, the less absurd it seemed. Women—Alex was right—were going into all professions these days, and doing their jobs as well as any man ... Doctors, lawyers, aviators, preachers ... Why shouldn't she join the *Messenger*, and in time become the editor of a provincial paper? It was such an easy solution, too, of Matthew's worries. She was a Silverman, and the elder daughter. If only her father would take her, she was sure she could make a success of the job. She would work hard, not rely upon her sex to help her out of difficulties, and force them to take her as an equal, to forget that she was a woman. Learning shorthand would be a bore, but she was willing to do that. It was the first thing.

She rummaged in her cupboard amongst her old school-books and found a Pitman's *Elementary Primer of Shorthand*. She sat with it on the bed for a while memorising the simple grammalogues. Then she put down the book and forgot the grammalogues in the much more exciting occupation of dreaming about herself as an editor. The editor's room at Bear Yard could be made to look quite attractive ... chintz curtains instead of the bare windows, and some antique Jacobean furniture instead of the odd jumble of stuff there was now; and she could get a pair of wrought-iron dogs and a basket for the open fireplace, and burn real logs instead of a gas-fire. Writing the editorials and reports would be difficult, but that would come in time.

How would her father take her offer? She knew how much this meant to him, and she didn't want to hurt his feelings. Anyway, it was the only solution for him if he wanted a Silverman in the office ... He was sure to take her. Suddenly she was glad that George and Alexander did not want to join him. It was giving her a great chance. There might even be little notices about her, when she became editor, in the papers and magazines. Perhaps a photograph, as she was good-looking ... Through the window she was aware of Alex on the tennis lawn. He was knocking a golf-ball about with a putter and frowning every time Micky made a pounce at it. Then she saw her father. He had come into the garden from the orchard. His stooping figure came up the pathway, and she saw him stop and say something to Alex.

She slipped towards her dressing-table and began to powder her face. Now was the time to catch him, before lunch. If she told him now she would lose that nervous excitement which was possessing her body and be able to enjoy her lunch, and it would make him happier and he would enjoy his. He had taken very little breakfast. She took one last glance at herself and ran from the room.

V

HURLDEN. The Church Organ Fund
benefited by a whist drive; winners
of which were Miss A. Silverman,
Mrs. G. Tobart … A pleasing
musical interlude was provided
by Miss Hildegarde Peters.

Swanbridge Messenger (From
"News of the Neighbourhood")

Alexander did not at first notice his father standing on the edge of
the court. When he did, he stopped knocking the ball about and,
shouldering his club like a rifle, walked across to him.

"Hullo, father. I didn't see you come in through the orchard. You're
back early, aren't you?"

"Yes. What are you doing? Improving your putting?."

"Oh, just knocking a ball about."

"I must have a round with you when I can find the time. From
what I hear, you're pretty good."

"Not really. If you want a good game you should get Reginald to
play. He's very good—much better than I am."

"Oh, yes, Reginald …" Matthew mouthed the name with a
certain sad reluctance that made Alexander look up, as Matthew had
intended he should.

"Good Lord, why do you say it like that? What's the matter with
Reg? He hasn't got leprosy, has he?"

"No—at least," said Matthew, smiling, "Abner hasn't said anything about it, if he has. But I was thinking that Reginald may soon be partnering me in something far more serious than a game of golf." The black branches of the fruit-trees above them cut the pale sky into a thousand odd pieces, and a cold wind shivered among the dead leaves on the path.

Alexander was aware of a sad desolation in everything—the cold earth clasping the withered weeds of summer, the melancholy croak of a pair of daws about the chimneys, the leaf-clogged stagnation of the pond in the orchard ... Suddenly they were all symbolic of sadness which came from this drawn-shouldered man who was his father. It would have been fanciful to imagine that Matthew had aged in the last two days. He had not done that, only there was about him a suggestion of complacent weariness; he was no longer a quiet, smiling don, happy in his scholarly abstractions, but a man unable to lose himself in his natural meditations because of the insistence of some malignant anxiety.

"What do you mean?" asked Alexander, guessing in his heart what his father meant, but not daring to believe it until he heard it uttered in words.

But Matthew was not eager to satisfy Alexander; eagerness now he knew would be fatal. Matthew knew Alexander, and he knew men, and he realised that the birth of some emotions cannot be hurried.

"I've been having a talk this morning with Abner," he said.

"About George?" Alexander asked the question, doubting his wisdom.

Matthew nodded. The boy was fresh, innocent, and so guileless. "In the morn and liquid dew of youth ..." For a moment he wondered whether he was doing wrong. Ethics, he decided, only made a man too nervous to distinguish between his duty and his desires; the greatest judge, the supreme arbiter, must be instinct, and his instincts were sound.

"Yes, about George," he went on. "Abner, you know, is more Silverman than most of us, and I felt that he should know right away. He was upset, of course."

"I'll bet he was."

"But he recognised the common sense of not forcing George to do anything against his will. For an old man Abner has some remarkably modern views."

"I've never noticed that. He's one of the old brigade."

"He doesn't like the idea of the Silverman tradition being broken. He had a suggestion to make, though, which may save me."

And that suggestion, thought Alexander, is obvious. First of all they will ask me to go into the *Messenger*, and, when I refuse, they will invite Reginald to take over the job, and he, although he might kick against it, will have to do as Abner tells him.

"Yes, he had a suggestion," said Matthew, guessing what Alexander was thinking. "Reginald, you know, is in a way a Silverman, and if he joins the *Messenger*, and becomes editor in time, then Abner and I will both be happy. Don't you think it's a good idea?" He looked up slowly at Alexander.

The boy was staring straight before him, his eyes lost in contemplation of the fruit-branches. Through his mind was singing the thought that they had asked Reginald. They had asked Reginald before coming to him, the second son. It was an insult, an injustice. How could they have been sure that he would have refused?

Matthew turned away for a moment. There was a discomfiting beauty in the disappointment on Alexander's face, the trembling, poignant disappointment of youth.

"Why," said Alexander with effort, "why didn't you ask me if I wanted to join the *Messenger*? I come next after George, don't I? I have the right?" The last question was posed fiercely.

"Why—Alexander!" Matthew swung round in surprise, his grey eyes wide.

"Well! Hadn't I the right to be asked?"

"Of course, my boy. But I never thought you would want to join. You're so taken up with architecture that I thought—"

"Damn architecture!" said Alexander suddenly. "Damn architecture! Who wants to build houses for mankind when he can take a hand in forming their opinions and informing their minds? What does Reginald know about the *Messenger*? He's interested only in motor engines and playing golf! He's a mechanic!"

"But I never knew you felt like this."

"You never even tried to find out! How could I know myself until the chance came? A man doesn't make up his mind like working out a train journey weeks ahead. Things come to him as he turns some corner in the road. I want to join the *Messenger*."

The power of his son's cry invaded the disquiet of Matthew's soul, conquering his doubts and killing all his fears. This was the Alexander he saw so seldom and loved so much. The sweet bitterness of the moment hung about him, saddening him yet satisfying. Only those who have known the fear of losing the love and respect of their children, he felt, were entitled to such revelations. He answered quietly:

"I'm glad you want to—and you shall. Abner will be as glad as I am, and I know that he hasn't spoken to Reginald yet, so there won't be any unpleasantness."

Matthew took the boy's hand for a moment and squeezed it. Then he hurried towards the house, but, though there was a little smile about his lips, his eyes were wet with tears.

Alexander watched him go into the house. Then, feeling the golf-club in his hands and seeing the white ball at his feet, he gave it a mighty swipe that sent it flighting into the orchard, where it rebounded from a tree-trunk, a vicious white bullet, and clanged resonantly against the corrugated roofing of Fuller's garden shed.

"And I'll wake that sleepy little rag up and make a paper out of it!" he confided to Micky fiercely.

* * *

Loraine met her father in the hallway.

"Hullo, Daddy! Why," she cried, noticing his flushed and happy face, "you look as though you're pleased about something."

"I am, Loraine, my dear. I am happy." He put his arm around her and held her affectionately. "Alexander has just made me very happy. He's offered to give up his architecture and join the *Messenger*."

"Oh!" Loraine bit her lip in quick annoyance; but Matthew did not notice her reaction. Swiftly she recovered herself and smiled at him. "Daddy, what good news! I am so glad for you! And," she added, without any reluctance, "it's rather splendid of Alex to do that."

"Yes, he's a good boy. Now I must find your mother and George."

He was gone, leaving her alone in the hall. For a moment she was terribly unhappy. It was just like Alexander to spoil everything for her. Then she realised that he could not have known …

"Oh, Loraine, you're crying! There's tears in your eyes." Alison had come quietly up to her and was staring at her.

"Don't be stupid. They're not tears. I've got a cold coming on, and it's making my eyes run."

"Your nose isn't red as though you had a cold—"

But Loraine had gone up to her bedroom. She stood at her dressing-table, tidying her hair and powdering her face. The redness about her eyes was soon gone. Then, as she turned from the glass, she saw the shorthand primer on her bed. Thank goodness, she thought, she wouldn't have to learn all that stuff. Alexander was welcome to it …. She lit a cigarette and went calmly downstairs.

* * *

That afternoon George set out for Oxford. Alison was with him when he started, for he was taking her to Aunt Adelaide's house, which was on his way. Alison was subdued at the thought of her stay with Aunt Adelaide. Hitherto she had met her aunt only infrequently, and her impression was not favourable, but she could not escape the invitation. When Aunt Adelaide suggested that one of the family came to stay with her, that suggestion was a command. Her invitations were not, however, common, for she preferred to live a quiet life, her only companion being her secretary. She was constantly changing her secretaries. They came and went with a frequency that left her undeterred in her search for the perfect secretary. She busied herself in all the affairs of the village and a great number of charities and, while she admitted that a secretary was indispensable to her, she would not admit the indispensability of any particular secretary.

"I don't see why she wouldn't let me bring Micky," said Alison peevishly.

George laughed. "She doesn't like dogs. But you don't want to worry. She's really very nice. I enjoyed myself when I first went to stay with her. It's only her manner."

"Alex says—" began Alison.

"Whatever Alex said about her you should take with a grain of salt. You know what Alex is like."

"Yes," said Alison, leaning back and pursing her lips, "he is rather prone to misstatement."

George glanced at her in astonishment for a second, and then his eyes were back on the road. She startled him sometimes by her odd, grown-up ways. She had an uncanny, precocious habit of stating opinions in words which came strangely from her infant mouth; opinions that were shrewdly true, as though her young eyes saw through all shams to the real person.

Presently the car swung to the left from the main road and began to follow a twisting lane leading to the village of Hurlden, which was ten miles from Swanbridge.

The house was a tall, two-storeyed Georgian construction, covered in summer with red Virginia creeper. On either side of a finely proportioned but somewhat paint-blistered doorway were two rounded bay windows of the period, and the house was flanked on one side by a long line of poplars, from which it took its name.

"Here we are," said George, as he stopped the car before the house. " I'll come in with you, but I mustn't stay long. I've a good way to go." He flung the end of his gay scarf back over his shoulder and took Alison's bag from the seat.

"Miss Silverman is out at the moment, sir," said the maid as she let them in. "Will you go into the drawing-room? Miss Peters is waiting for you there."

"Miss Peters?" George looked at the maid quizzically as he dropped Alison's case.

"Miss Peters is the new secretary, Mr. Silverman."

"What, another of 'em? I suppose she's like the rest—glasses, protruding teeth, and wispy hair, eh?"

The maid, who was a plump, good-looking creature, smiled tolerantly and made no comment. She opened the door for them and announced meekly, "Mr. and Miss Silverman have arrived, Miss Peters."

They were in a tall, well-lit room that was crowded with elegant cabriole-legged china cupboards, tapestried chairs, and highly polished occasional tables. Over the floor was a thick carpet of a uniform brown shade. A large mirror above the mantel gave the room an impression of spaciousness that was helped by a pier-glass hanging near the window. On every ledge, shelf, and projection was poised some china ornament or vase; the cupboards were full of delicate tea-sets and dishes and the mantelshelf groaned under the press of china figures.

Alison felt herself contract as she entered the room. She knew at once that she would always be nervous there, and afraid to move with ease.

"Good afternoon. I'm Miss Peters."

From a chair near the fireplace arose a woman, a young woman. She moved across the room towards them with a tall, statuesque grace which gave her a firmness and assurance that the porcelain figures lacked. In the room, so full of dead things, of fragile imitations that strove to catch the semblance of nature, her body breathed a warm flush of realness, and proclaimed her to be apart from the spirit which was sequestered among these memorials of an older generation. Seeing her move easily and bearing herself well, George found himself thinking of Galatea and Pygmalion. Some artist had made this creature, and, when he was done, a higher agency had breathed life into it.

"I'm George Silverman, and this is Alison ... I brought her. I'm on my way back to Oxford ..."

"Yes, I know. You were expected. Miss Silverman was so sorry, but she was obliged to go out. Won't you sit down? I'll ring for tea."

She turned to the bell-push, and George took the opportunity, while her eyes were from him, to observe her more closely. She couldn't be any older than he was, he told himself. Yet she had a maturity and poise that many women never attained. The skin at the nape of her neck as she leaned towards the bell-push was brown. She turned quickly and found his eyes upon her. She did not blush. Instead, she smiled easily and waved gently to a chair, and George realised that her face was not pretty, not so distinguished as her figure. It was a frank, slightly masculine face, intelligent, yet wearing a pleasant frown when she was not smiling. Her hair was thick and dark brown, and it came back in a smooth wave from her temples to lie snugly on the nape of her neck.

Alison liked her right away. With some people, she knew, you had to wait for a while until you discovered whether they were nice. She felt at once that Miss Peters was nice, and she knew that the formality of polite questions that gradually slipped into intimacy and confidence was unnecessary with her.

"Do you like living here?" she asked Miss Peters, after the maid had brought in the tea and she sat eating her cake.

"I do."

"I'm a bit afraid of Aunt Adelaide. I don't know whether I shall enjoy it here," Alison confided.

"You mustn't be like that. She's very nice. Only she doesn't like people who are afraid of her, and so many are."

"And with good reason," said George. "She can be a Tartar when she likes."

Miss Peters made no direct reply to this. Her eyes flashed George an agreement, and he was left with the curious conviction that Aunt Adelaide had found a secretary who knew how to deal with her idiosyncrasies.

Alison, seeing that they were likely to begin a conversation in which she would have no part, said quickly:

"I think it's wrong to guess what things are going to be like. It's easier for them to happen."

"What do you mean?" Miss Peters looked at Alison.

"I mean"—Alison struggled to swallow her cake—"I mean that I shouldn't worry about whether I'm going to like it here, but just come and see whether I do. Then I can't be mistaken. We were mistaken about you, Miss Peters. Weren't we, George?" Alison turned her round eyes on him.

"What do you mean?" George stared at her.

"About Miss Peters," said Alison resolutely. "You said she would have glasses, protruding teeth, and wispy hair, didn't you?"

Miss Peters laughed and shook her head; George blushed and almost upset his tea into his lap.

"Alison! Miss Peters, please. I said nothing of the kind. When the maid told us Miss Peters was waiting, I naturally enquired who you were, and ... well, Aunt Adelaide's secretaries usually are rather peculiar, and I said that I supposed the new one was ... well—"

"That the new one had glasses, protruding teeth, and wispy hair?" finished Miss Peters, smiling at him. "I'm sorry I've disappointed you."

"But you haven't. I mean … well …" George escaped by raising his cup and taking an enormous draught, letting the subject die. Damn Alison! A small sister was a curse. This Miss Peters would think he was just an oaf.

"You're on your way back to Oxford?" She came nobly to his relief. "It's a lovely town, isn't it? I lived there for some years."

"Did you?" George seized this new topic eagerly. "Yes, it's a grand place. I shall be sorry to leave. This is my last year. You get attached, you know …"

"You're in a hurry, aren't you, George?" put in Alison calmly. "You said you could only stop a few minutes."

"Then we mustn't detain you," said Miss Peters, making to rise. "Alison will be all right now."

"Really," George protested, "really, I'm not in all that hurry. I was only speaking comparatively."

"Well, you mustn't let us detain you."

"Oh, I wouldn't do that. I've got plenty of time." He had the impression that secretly she was laughing at him, and he felt himself growing angry with himself.

"George is going to be a clergyman, Miss Peters. I think he'll look nice in a black suit and a white collar, don't you?"

"They are certainly very becoming to some people," she confessed, and George wondered whether there was a shade of deeper meaning as she said *some people*. "Your father told Miss Silverman about it over the telephone this morning. She was speaking to me … Please forgive me; of course it's not my business."

"Oh, that's quite all right, Miss Peters. I don't mind your knowing. Everyone will know very soon. You see, I've decided that newspaper work isn't my line. I'm going to read for the Church."

"Why, that's magnificent, Mr. Silverman. The Church needs all the men it can get. There are many fine men in the Church."

"You think so?" George questioned her eagerly. It heartened him to find that she approved his step, though he did not ask himself why it should.

"Could I have another of those cakes, please, Miss Peters?"

They were both suddenly aware of Alison.

* * *

That evening—it was Saturday—Matthew sat in one of the Swanbridge Constitutional Club's armchairs, smoking his pipe and reading the evening paper. There was a happy confusion of sound and warmth around him. From the billiard-room came the soft mutter of men's voices, the click of ivory balls, and occasional bursts of laughter.

Sam Hardwick, the owner of the town's largest shop, a provincial Gamage's, whose advertising the *Messenger* valued, wandered over to him, a cigar in one hand and a whisky and soda in the other.

"Hullo, Matt."

"Good evening, Sam."

"Had a busy week?"

"So, so. And you?"

"Bit quiet for us now the winter sales are over. Still, can't grumble. I met that new editor of the *Farley Courier* yesterday. Smart fellow."

"So they tell me. The *Courier* needs somebody with brains to do it good."

Sam laughed. "That's almost what he said about the *Messenger*."

"Impudence!"

"He seemed to think," Sam went on affably, "that as soon as he gets going his paper will drive yours out of business. Says he's already getting some of your sales in the outlying districts. I hope it's not true?"

"If it is, then I haven't heard of it, and I should be the first to know," Matthew said easily, and added "You never want to believe what one editor says of another, Sam."

"Perhaps not. By the way, I met George this morning. He tells me he's going to be a minister. That isn't so, is it?"

"Yes; he wants to do it, so I didn't stand in his way. He's a good boy."

"Dunno that I should give up my eldest so easily to the Church. Not that he's likely to want to go, though." Sam's fat paunch shook with his own joke.

Matthew dropped the paper. "You probably would if it came to it, Sam. Young life is precious stuff, and it doesn't do to warp it to your own ways. Tolerance is a great virtue these days, and we older ones mustn't lag too far in the past. I've no patience with the bigot or the man who thinks so much of himself that he never thinks of others. Alexander is coming into the *Messenger* in George's place."

"That firebrand!"

Matthew laughed. "Weren't you a firebrand when you were seventeen?"

"God knows," said Sam, sighing and surveying the curve of his waistcoat. "It's so long ago."

" 'The thought of our past years in me doth breed perpetual benediction …' " quoted Matthew gently, and then, because Sam was an advertiser and a shop-man and not a man of letters, he said affably, "Finish that whisky and I'll buy you another."

VI

Exciting Incident. Tragedy Narrowly Averted.

Swanbridge Messenger (Headline)

It was raining. The hills to the north and east of Swanbridge were hidden by dark tangles of cloud, and the whole countryside was noisy with the steady voices of rainwater. The gutters of the houses ran full, flowing over, to fall with splattering cascades to the pavements and yards. Rain fell steadily and heavily, regiment after regiment of drops, upon the town and country. It battered the dead copper of the beech-leaves that still clung to the thick hedges and, carrying a load of waste, it swept into drains and runnels, choking them and stemming into muddy pools that parted, like the Red Sea before the hand of Moses, as the wheels of motor-cars sped through them. In the steep lanes of the hills it washed the soil from the stones and made a hundred rugged little gullies, destroying ants' nests, uncovering pupae, and forming tiny drifts of mud. In the streets it coated the tarmacadam with a treacherous sheen that gave little hold for braked wheels, and it sent people hurrying under the shelter of umbrellas and mackintoshes.

Down by the river, the carcass of a dog, long stranded on a dry spit, was taken off by the rising flood and borne, gyrating slowly in the current, towards the distant sea. Water voles sought the upper chambers of their holes, and the freshet at the side of the Grammar School ground, unable to empty its load into the river fast enough, began to overlap its banks, and a spread of dark water moved across the turf. In a wretched cottage between the railway works and the corset factory, water began to drip through the ceiling of a bedroom into a bath on the floor and, at the sound of the tinny bastinado, a man upon the bed raised himself and shouted angrily to someone below-stairs … By midday all the locks along the river would be open and the water-meadows would be in flood, cattle would be drowned, cars would get stuck in flooded patches of road, and cottages would be isolated on willow-fringed islands of meadow.

The rain seemed conscious of its strength. It needed the help of no wind. It poured down in a slanting onslaught, determined to wash everything before it, cleaning the slates, clearing the gutters, burnishing the roads, flooding the fields, damping ceilings, and soaking into timbers.

* * *

Matthew Silverman stood at the window of his room and looked out into the street. The water streaming over the glass distorted his vision. People lost the probity of their normal figures and became dwarfed, bent, and obese. He was smiling at the oddness when there was a knock on his door. He turned to find Alexander standing on the mat.

"You sent for me, sir?"

"Yes." Matthew left the window and sat down at his desk. He motioned Alexander to a chair. "I want to talk to you."

This was Alexander's first day at the office. Apart from making arrangements about his not returning to school and settling the date of his starting at the office, he and the boy had not discussed in any detail what was to happen when he came into the business.

Alexander said nothing. He knew his father very well. He was not so sure of the man who was editor of the *Messenger*.

"I suppose you know why I sent for you?"

"To give me a general idea of what I am supposed to do."

"In a way, my boy. I purposely have said nothing to you until today because I felt that it was not appropriate. Now, Alexander, I'm not going to give you a lecture, or to repeat a lot of moralities to you. I don't think that's necessary. But there are one or two things."

"What things?" It was natural, Alexander supposed, that a man taking his son into his business should be a little pompous.

Matthew paused, rubbed his chin, and glanced around the room before replying. The faces of his ancestors in the office looked down upon him, approving but grave, he thought. This was an important day in his life.

"First of all, I want you to get one thing very clear. At home I am your father, but in this office I am the editor and you are one of the staff. So you will understand that you cannot expect privileges."

"Of course, sir."

"Another thing you must remember is that now you are a member of the staff you must do nothing in your official or private life to bring the *Messenger* into disrepute. Not that I think you are likely to. You know what you're expected to do here—learn as much about everything as you can. Reporting is far from the whole job. At the moment I don't suppose you know minion from nonpareil, and, although I must confess I know little about its mechanism, there's no reason why you shouldn't know as much about the printing machine as Mr. Phipps. You've come into this of your own free will, and I don't doubt your keenness; now it's up to you to prove it. In a district like this a newspaper is an invaluable part of the community; we've got a trust for our readers, and nothing must ever interfere with that. What's your shorthand speed?"

"About eighty words a minute, sir."

"You'll have to improve a lot on that before you can take on anything important."

"I'm already attending some classes run at night in the Grammar School."

"Good. I've asked Mr. Selway to keep an eye on you. If Mr. Barnes were not leaving us soon, I should have handed you over to him. But Selway will do. He knows his job ... Well, that's all, except that I'm more happy than I can say to have you here."

"I'll try not to disappoint you, sir." Alexander rose. He had forgotten all about architecture. He was on a newspaper.

Matthew watched him go, and in his heart he knew that Alexander would never disappoint him. He was already improving his shorthand ... there was keenness. He turned towards the window and stared into the street, and this time it was not the rain on the glass which was blurring his vision.

* * *

Roger Selway took Alexander in hand. Jolly Roger, as he was known, was a plump, jovial-faced, warm-hearted bachelor of thirty-five. He had a smile for everybody, a joke to suit any and every company, and he knew that it was his destiny to be no more than a senior reporter on a provincial newspaper. He lived with his widowed mother, and was the secretary of innumerable clubs and committees. He was always busy, and yet always had time to stop and talk interminably on any subject. His hair was thinning and brushed back to make the most of it, and if ever he was wanted in the office and could not be found it was pretty certain that he would be leaning up against the bar of the Three Feathers Hotel drinking beer, of which liquid he seemed able to take enormous quantities without impairing his equilibrium or speech.

He greeted Alexander effusively, which was not unusual, for his greetings were always effusive.

"Well, well, the fall of primogeniture. Second son acquires brother's birthright. Local boy makes good. But what, my sea-green incorruptible, are you doing in this haunt of the bourgeoisie? Your place is in Hyde Park selling copies of the Daily Worker."

"My place is here," said Alexander, unperturbed. He knew Selway. "For some inscrutable reason I have been assigned to your care. You are to be my instructor, and guide me through the intricacies of a provincial newspaper."

"A Daniel come to judgment. The pure white flower of an unspotted life come to cast its fragrance over this fetid air. And let me tell you, young man, that your father is wise—oh, wise beyond Solomon—in putting you in my care, for if there is anything to be learned about provincial newspapers, then I am the one to teach it. Some day you will thank me. Barnes here"—he nodded to where Barnes sat at the other end of the reporters' room—"would be a good mentor—if I may use the word, though it has an ugly Latin ring which does not please my essentially Anglo-Saxon ears—but he would show you the *Messenger* as an efficient machine, an organ that fulfils a want. But I, I shall give you not only that. You shall have the romance and the pathos, the joy and the sorrow, the mistakes and the heart-wrenches, and all the mad abracadabra that goes to make a provincial newspaper. The penny-a-line local correspondents who write screeds about local fêtes, the simpering brides and ungainly bridegrooms who seem to get married only to have their photographs in the paper—and then complain because we spell their names wrong—and a hundred others—you will meet them all in good time. Meanwhile—"

"Meanwhile, what?" interrupted Alexander, tiring of the speech.

Selway folded his hands together in a benediction.

"Meanwhile, you will begin work," he said.

"Work?" Alexander looked at him.

There was an indulgent smile on the man's face. "Yes, work. The word, no doubt, still has a fantastic ring for you, but we take it in our stride. Some day, if you're very good, you may be able to do that. Meantime, as I said, you will work. On this piece of paper is the name and address of a gentleman who, we were informed by telephone this morning, saved a young girl from being gored by a pig; to be exact—a boar. You will get his story. Like most heroes, he will, no doubt, be incoherent and reticent. You must supply his deficiencies."

"But—" began Alexander.

Selway interrupted him. "I know, my lad. You are about to say that such an important assignment should be given to someone else. This is a sign of our belief in your ability. Go, boy; the office bicycle awaits below-stairs!"

Alexander did not argue. He went. The address was of a small cottage on a farm, which he knew well, on the outskirts of Swanbridge.

* * *

The woman who came to the cottage door at his knock regarded Alexander with distrust. He was very wet; his felt-hat brim drooped dejectedly towards his shoulders, and small rivulets of rain poured from him. "Does Mr. Hobbs live here?"

"He does. What might you be wantin' with him?"

Alexander forgot that he was wet and uncomfortable, and said with some pride, "I'm from the *Swanbridge Messenger*. I'd like to talk to him, if I may."

"I'll see," she said, and disappeared into the cottage. She reappeared almost at once and ushered Alexander into the kitchen. It was a large, slate-floored room backed by a long horsehair sofa and heated by an enormous kitchen range. Before the open bars of the fire sat Mr. Hobbs, himself on one chair and his feet on another.

"Good mornin', sir." The man nodded civilly and then was silent.

"Good morning," replied Alexander. "I'm from the *Messenger*."

"So the wife said," answered the man.

"Did she?" Alexander found himself saying.

"Yes, she said you were from the paper." The man relapsed into silence, and Alexander remembered Selway's remark that heroes were generally reticent and incoherent.

"Do you mind if I sit down?" asked Alexander.

Mr. Hobbs said he had no objection, and Alexander sat down on the sofa and was greeted with a low growl from a cocker spaniel that had been curled at one end of it. He took out his notebook, opened it nervously to its first page, a page white and eager for notes, and then licked the tip of his finely sharpened pencil.

"Do you mind, Mr. Hobbs," he said, "telling me a few things about your adventure this morning?"

"My adventure?" Mr. Hobbs turned towards him curiously.

"Yes, you know ... the boar and the young woman you saved."

"Good Lord!" Mr. Hobbs started into a sudden vivaciousness. "Do 'ee mean to say you've come about that? I couldn't for the life of me put a reason to your coming at first."

"That's what I'm here for. We want to know about it so that we can put it into the paper."

"Put about me into the paper?"

"That's it, if you'll give me a few details."

"Of course, sir. Why didn't 'ee say at first what it was you wanted? Why, it's all very interestin' too, though I must say I didn't think it was anything the papers would bother about. You see, I've had tussles with Father William afore this."

"Father William?"

"Yes, sir. That's what us calls the old boar. He's a bad-tempered beast. Well, it was like this—" Mr. Hobbs settled his legs more comfortably on the chair and began his story. Father William was usually kept locked up in the big barn, though there were times when he had to be allowed in the meadow with the gilts and sows, and this was one of the times. Mr. Hobbs described how he had had a feeling that morning that Father William might cause trouble; his reasons for this were many and obscure, but Alexander put them down. He had been mending a gap in the fence at one end of the meadow when he had heard a scream, and, turning, had seen a young girl being chased towards the stile by Father William. He had picked up a length of wood and dashed towards the boar. Seeing him coming, the boar had abandoned the chase after the girl and charged towards him. Mr. Hobbs, knowing Father William of old, had stopped the charge with a well-directed clout on the boar's snout. Father William had snorted, shaken his head in sad anger at such unfairness, and turned obediently back towards the sows. Meanwhile Mr. Hobbs, full of pride at a duty well done, had seen the young girl well over the style and then returned to his fence. On the way he was suddenly caught in the small of the back by something that felt like an express train. He fell upon his face in the mud, and had to lie there while Father William, a master tactician, methodically trampled on his legs. Before Mr. Hobbs could recover his wind and arise, Father William had tired of his sport and had wandered back to the other end of the field, leaving Mr. Hobbs free to take his bruised but not badly cut legs back to his cottage, where a doctor soon had them bandaged.

Mr. Hobbs enjoyed telling his story. It took him exactly one hour and a half to recount it, and the only interruption was from Alexander when he broke the point of his pencil and had to borrow the labourer's pocket-knife to make a fresh point.

Heroes, thought Alexander, as he cycled back to the office, are generally reticent. He not only knew Mr. Hobbs's life-story, but Father William's, and the main facts in the careers of a few of the more celebrated of Father William's progeny. Nevertheless, he felt he had a good story. He realised that he would have to cut it a good deal for the paper.

"This," said Selway, as he read Alexander's account later, "is a most interesting saga."

"I'm glad you like it." Alexander flushed with pleasure.

"I do. It reminds me so much of my lost youth. It has—if you understand me—a bloom upon it." As he spoke he took out a red pencil and began to mark through it. "I shall look forward to the other three volumes. Meantime, this advance note of its forthcoming

81

publication will do very well for next week's *Messenger*." He handed the account back to Alexander, and the boy saw that of his two hundred lines only twenty survived.

"But you've cut practically all of it out!"

"That is so—all the trimmings; the facts remain, and as a newspaper we are most interested in the facts."

"But, damn it!" Alexander was indignant. "I could have written what you've left in from what we were told on the telephone by the doctor."

"That is so," agreed Selway blandly. "But it was such a lovely morning, and you looked so pale from your incarceration in the office, that I thought the fresh air would do you good." Selway saluted him with a low bow and left the room.

"I shouldn't let that upset you," said Barnes kindly when he had gone. "Most of us start off like that."

"Oh, that's all right. I suppose I was a bit long-winded."

"I know. The thing to remember, however, is to say what there is to say as simply and as directly as possible. You aren't writing fiction, but retailing facts. The people who read the report will put in all the fancy trimmings from their own imagination. Here you are; here's an example of the necessity of cutting reports down. Take this pile of local correspondents' reports and go through them, cutting them down to the bare minimum. You'll see what I mean then. These people get a penny a line for all that's printed, and naturally most of 'em write as much as they can. The thing to remember with a local paper is that we don't ever have to bother about finding enough stuff to make up our pages; we have to worry about finding space for the stuff which should go in."

He handed a sheaf of reports to Alexander. They kept him busy for the rest of the day, and he soon began to forget his own hurt, taking a delight in condensing two hundred words to thirty.

* * *

Alexander was quick in learning. Selway kept a watchful eye upon him, and was always ready with pleasant ridicule when he made a mistake, for he saw, with an acuteness which most people might not have accredited him with, that Alexander, like most people, resented ridicule, and, unlike some, never forgot the blunder which had caused it.

Slowly Alexander watched the muddle and confusion, which had been his impression of the *Messenger* office, smoothing itself out into an intricate but efficient process. Although the gathering of news interested him most, he was not blind to the importance of the means which brought that news into the homes of thousands of people each week. Within a month he knew his way about and was accepted by the rest of the staff. He could use, though but slowly, a linotype machine, and, although he lacked the manipulative skill of the men in the composing room, he could handle a stick and make up advertisements from the type cases, and at proof-reading he grew as critical as Uncle Abner. He became a great friend of Mr. Phipps, and his favourite lurking-places, when he was not to be found in the reporters' room, were in the covered yard where the great rotary machine stood, and in the little foundry next to it where the semi-circular plates for the printing machine were cast.

He still made mistakes. He was sent to get the details of a fire which had broken out in a small house near the gasworks. A slatternly woman, the wife of a railway worker who lived in the house, described to him what had happened.

"The oil lamp was knocked over and it caught the whole of the mantelshelf afire," she said. "Oh, it was a terrible blaze. I was terrified for poor Granny upstairs. That's my mother—she's bedridden and I don't know how we should ever have got her out alive if the brigade hadn't got here and put it out. It's a wicked shame that there's no gas laid on in these houses, so near the gasworks, too. Oil's dangerous. If I've said it once, I've said it a thousand times—"

She was interrupted by a high-pitched, querulous voice from the bedroom above.

"That's Granny," she said, moving to the bottom of the stairs. "What is it, Granny?" she called.

"Who's that you're talking to?" came a petulant enquiry.

"A man from the *Messenger*, dear. He wants to know all about the fire."

"Then send him up to me. Do you hear? Send him up to me."

The woman looked at Alexander. "She's a terror for having her own way, sir."

"Don't be all day about it!" came the old woman's voice.

"That's all right." Alexander smiled. "I'll go up and see her." He climbed the narrow stairs, and found himself in a tiny bedroom that was almost filled by a huge bed on which lay an old woman, her age-wrinkled face and shawl-draped shoulders showing above the crumpled sheets.

"Well? What are you standing at the door like that for? Haven't you ever been in a woman's bedroom before?" She cackled, showing her toothless gums. "So you want to know all about the fire, eh?"

"That's what I came for."

"And I'll bet she's been telling you a pack of lies. Unreliable my daughter is; always was and always will be. If I weren't bedridden I'd show the whole lot of them. Fire!" she snorted, and plucked irritably at the sheets. "Don't you believe her lies. She's made out I was in danger; that the house was on fire. Stuff and nonsense. The light fell over and caught the mantel-cloth, and a jugful of water would have had it out in no time if they hadn't run shrieking for the brigade while it burnt itself out without any damage before them clumsy machines could get here. I know what happened. I may be bedridden, but nothing's hidden from me. She's hysterical, my daughter; always was and always will be; but what I've told you is the truth. And don't you dare deny it!" She shook her fist at the woman over Alexander's shoulder.

Alexander decided that the fire was more a scare than a reality, and he wrote his report, a terse account of a few lines.

"Hullo, hullo! What's this?" cried Selway when the report came to him for sub-editing. "What little gem of précis-writing is this? Six lines, to be tucked away at the bottom of a column, about a fire which might have set the gasworks going sky-high?"

"Nothing of the kind," answered Alexander. "A light was knocked over and caught the mantel-shelf draperies afire, and it burned peacefully out before the brigade got there. There never was any danger."

Selway shook his head. "My lad," he said, "your newspaper education is far from complete. The public take a morbid interest in fires, and it doesn't do to disappoint them. This fire might have spread and endangered the gasworks—is that true?"

"It might have done, but it didn't."

"Never mind; that is justification for saying that a general conflagration was narrowly averted. And wasn't there a bedridden old lady in the room above?"

"There was—and she's more than capable of looking after herself, believe me."

"Never mind—a helpless invalid at the mercy of the flames means a shocking tragedy that might have been."

"But you told me to stick to facts."

"So I did, and so we will; but the facts in this case are that every person in that street who saw the fire-engine rush up will be looking forward to reading this account. They've been talking about it for the last two days; the thing's been growing in their minds until it seems possible to them that it was a lucky thing the whole town wasn't set on fire. We can't insult and disappoint them by putting in a squitty little paragraph like this. Our report must make a comfortable parallel to their imagination. That's where a provincial newspaper differs from a daily. The daily announces news, and by its report sets the extremes of imagination, but a provincial weekly only confirms what is generally already known, and its report has to measure up to what has already been imagined or guessed. Here you are; have another shot at it."

Selway had no complaint to make with Alexander's second article.

After a time Alexander began to appreciate his father's love for his profession and his idolatry of the *Messenger*. The paper was a hard master, but a satisfying one. The hours he worked were irregular, and tended to become more so as his shorthand speed improved. He learned the art of writing at any time and in any place, and he derived a great pleasure from the deference that was accorded to him by many people because he was a reporter. With his first week's wages he bought a pipe and tobacco, and although at first he hated the taste, he made a point of occasionally accompanying Selway to the Three Feathers to take a glass of beer with him.

Matthew watched the change in his son with a loving eye. He sympathised with his early nervousness and mistakes, and then shared the pride which grew in the boy as he came to understand the machine which had adopted him. They stood together by the press on the Thursday of Alexander's first week and saw the rollers begin to turn and the first fresh copies commence to be spewed from the press.

Matthew caught up a copy and handed it to Alexander. In it were a few paragraphs which the boy had written. "Keep it," he shouted. "One day you'll open it and read it and remember the happiest days of your life."

Alexander took it, relishing the smooth feel of the paper and the smell of drying newsprint. His father, he mused, was an incorrigible sentimentalist. But he took the paper away and laid it in one of his drawers carefully, his dark eyes shining with a new joy and his body tremulous from a new emotion.

"He's taking to it like a duck to water, sir," shouted Phipps to Matthew as they watched Alexander standing at one end of the press.

Matthew nodded. "Aye, he might have been weaned on printer's ink."

VII

A very pleasant time was had by all.

Swanbridge Messenger

For two weeks after Alexander's starting in the *Messenger* office it rained almost continually, until all the river fields were flooded, the allotments a sargasso, with the rusted roofs of sheds marking the grey water like moored rafts and the lanes around the town turned into quagmires that sucked voraciously at wheel and hoof. Then, in a night, the rain stopped, the skies cleared, and the wind went round from the south-west to the north and Swanbridge woke to find a white frost over its window-panes and a thin coating of ice on the gutter pools. For a week the nights were freezing and the days too meagre of sun to thaw the growing ice.

The Troon itself was too turbulent still with floodwater for the ice to bridle its swirling current, though in the backwaters and side-streams there were fringes of ice around the brown reed-stems. Over the flooded fields, where there was little current, the ice set hard and firm.

"Tomorrow," said Alexander jubilantly, "there will be skating."

"If it doesn't thaw," Loraine replied.

But it did not thaw, and the next day, which was a Saturday, the ice on the recreation-ground was bearing, and all those who could muster skates were on the ice in the afternoon.

Matthew sat upon the small knoll at one side of the ground putting on his skates and watching the scene. The ice was crowded; most of the skaters were contenting themselves with swinging sedately around the edge, for skating weather was not so common in Swanbridge that the townsfolk became proficient. Some of the younger people were tentatively trying their paces, urged on by the shouts and taunts of their friends. Matthew smiled as he tugged at his straps; the grey sky which might hold snow, the stained surface of the ice, and the swirl of colour over it, all gave him a feeling of happiness. They were like one big happy family, the children of Swanbridge … He might write a leader about the ice, and show how their common delight in skating brought them all closer together.

"Hullo, Dad. You're late getting down?" It was Alexander, in a windbreaker and plus fours, a blue-and-white scarf round his neck. His face was flushed with the unusual exercise.

"Yes, there were one or two things to fix up about the Old Folk's Treat. How are you getting on?"

"Oh, fine. Look, watch me!" Alexander turned and pushed off, moving away with a dignified unsteadiness that turned Matthew's smile to a grin.

"Afternoon, Matt." It was Sam Hardwick, completely at home on skates and his face redder than ever.

"Getting some of your fat down, Sam?"

Sam laughed. "This is the kind of exercise I like. You can get some satisfaction from it. When I was a boy I lived in Wisbech—up by the fens—and skating was skating in those days."

"Hullo, Mr. Hardwick." Loraine swooped towards them, graceful, lithe, and conscious that she looked lovely in a kilted blue skirt and a tightly bodiced coat. "I'll race you once round the ground. A pair of the awful silk stockings your shop sells against an ounce of whatever tobacco you smoke. Is it a bet?"

"Loraine!" Matthew stood up, stamping his skates to comfort.

But neither Sam not Loraine heeded him. "Come on then," cried Sam, and he was off, with Loraine tearing after him. Matthew watched them go, and then pushed off after them, moving cautiously for a while until he felt the old skill starting back to his limbs. After a few circuits he swerved into the centre of the field, fetched a figure of eight with a rather wide compass, and then repeated it in narrowing circles until he had complete confidence in himself.

"Good afternoon, Mr. Silverman." It was Colonel and Mrs. Waterson, skating together with their arms crossed and both dressed in the conventional winter sports outfit which marks the cosmopolitan who does most of his skating in Switzerland and never lets his friends forget it.

"Very good ice," boomed the Colonel like a cinema organ purring over a love-lyric, and giving the impression that he could always tell good skating ice by its taste.

"Very good," repeated his wife, who always echoed him, and then the two swung away and performed an intricate figure together just to show that, although they were completely democratic, there was, of course, no doubt about their superiority.

"Hullo, Uncle Matt!" This was Reginald coming up at a mad pace and circling to a stop. "Very good ice!" His voice boomed in imitation of the Colonel's and he was off, swerving and striking quickly. Matthew permitted himself a smile at the imitation. Reginald instinctively seemed to be able to master any sport which demanded speed.

Matthew swung back into the coiling circle, giving and taking greetings. He passed Mr. Cyril Markham, M.A., the headmaster of the Grammar School, his weak eyes magnified behind his spectacles, who was always quick to take any opportunity to tell how he had once been introduced to George Moore at a house-party; Mrs. Staines, the mayoress, and wife of Swanbridge's wealthy haulage contractor, a peaked-face woman, jealous of her position, and, although far-seeing in many things, blind to the fact that her favourite colour, purple, did not suit her complexion or figure; and Xavier Martell, who owned the Swanbridge Theatre and produced for his own repertory company; a competent producer, a sufferer from migraine and too much given to deploring the unxsthetic sensibilities of the rest of Swanbridge, and yet loved by all his friends for his wit and inimitable manner of telling a story. There was the matron of the hospital; even on skates she suggested a grim efficiency, and reminded Matthew of wards and operating theatres. Since the few days he had spent in the hospital for an operation on an impacted wisdom tooth, Matthew had a respectful awe of Miss Lydia Horton. And close behind her was Dr. Pimm, big-limbed, splendidly proportioned, his hair just touched with white, making him even more attractive. He was laughing and showing his fine teeth, a strong animal, about whom, Matthew reflected, perhaps only one half of the stories told in the town were true.

Matthew moved around with the crowd, happy to be with them; young boys and girls chasing each other across the ice, their shouts and laughter dying up into the grey sky. The sound of skates crisp and clean on the air, and the changing pattern of colours against the dark hedges and the row of pollarded willows that marked the bank of the Troon, all worked a peaceful mood in him. It was good to be alive in such weather. There was Alexander over there, his feet readier to the command of his brain now, and showing off before Mr. Haughton, the English master of the Grammar School, who was no skater; and Loraine in the midst of a group of young women from the Swanbridge Hockey Club, all wondering if the thaw would hold off long enough for them to fix up an ice-hockey match with Farley. And at home Mabel was waiting for him; there would be muffins for tea. He thought of his wife lovingly. She had adapted herself to his ways with a tenderness that sometimes caused him shame as he wondered whether he had not taken too much from her and given her so little. He remembered those days in 1916, when the news of his brother George's death had come. He had loved George. George had been worth a thousand of himself, and the war had taken him. Those were hateful days, and he had not lost his grief easily, and Mabel had known and suffered with him …

Round and round Matthew went, relishing the firmness of the ice beneath his runners, delighting in his old skill and proud of the strength in his body; a slightly stooped, smiling man with the cold air ruffling his iron-grey head.

Standing on the knoll, too timid to skate, yet pathetically eager to share in this winter joy, were the Misses Palmer, maiden ladies living happily on a small annuity, absorbed by, and absorbing, all that happened in Swanbridge; unofficial, tireless gazetteers recording every birth, marriage, and death, and heralding every scandal.

"There's Mr. Silverman."

"Oh, yes! Poor man—looks tired."

"Just like his father—he always looked like a washed sheet. They all work too hard."

"Not money-grubbers, though, as some we could name."

"No, and he was very nice about the advertisement when Alice strayed away."

"I always say that a man who understands a cat can understand anything."

"Poor Alice." And they forgot the virtues of Matthew in the greater and sadder contemplation of the fate of poor Alice.

When it grew dark, some of the skaters turned the headlights of their cars upon the field and continued their skating, darting from the paths of blinding light into the dark gulfs that bordered them; but Matthew did not stay.

"Were there many people there?" his wife asked on his return.

"Crowded," he replied; and then, because he knew she wanted it, he told her the names of as many as he could remember.

"Why didn't you come down, mother?" asked Alexander. "You can skate."

Mrs. Silverman shook her head. "Mrs. Staines may like to make a fool of herself, showing her old bones to everyone, but not me. Besides, I'm not sure that I could skate after all these years. It was before the war that I last did any."

"I won a pair of silk stockings from Mr. Hardwick," said Loraine.

"If the tales I hear about Sammy Hardwick are true, you're not the only girl who's ever won silk stockings from him."

"Alexander! Before Alison, too."

"Oh, that's all right, Mummy." Alison looked up from her muffin. "I heard you and Auntie Mary talking about Mr. Hardwick the other day when you didn't think I was listening."

"Alison," said Matthew, trying not to smile, "you've no right to listen to conversations which are not intended for you. If you do that, you may hear something unpleasant about yourself."

"But I have already, Daddy. I heard the postman tell Gibby that he thought I was a 'pert little miss.' Gibby said that it meant I could do with a good spanking now and then."

"And so it does, and, what's more, it means that little girls whose ears are too long won't be allowed to help at the Old Folk's Treat."

This threat silenced Alison.

Once a year, towards the end of February, the *Messenger* sponsored a Swanbridge Old Folk's Treat. The treat had its beginning in the competition between the *Messenger* and its only rival in the district, the *Farley Courier*. Farley was a bigger town than Swanbridge, and some twenty miles away, near the coast. The *Courier* proprietor had been an ambitious fellow who envied the *Messenger's* circulation, and had decided to appropriate some of it in the Swanbridge area. The war had started in Jacob's time, and, although the *Courier* had gained some ground, the sales of the *Messenger* had never been seriously threatened, and gradually the opinion had been formed on each side that there was room for both papers. The *Courier* had a large circulation in and around Farley, which the *Messenger* scarcely touched, and the *Messenger* held a prominence of sales in Swanbridge which the *Courier* could not hope to acquire.

The popularity of the *Messenger* came from its age. Its format was heavy, the front and back pages thick and dull with advertisements and its inner pages enlightened by very few photographs; but it gave news of the town and district, and that was all that was wanted, and it was always ready to open its columns for any worthy cause. Its policy was non-political, but its editorial comment, which Matthew now wrote each week, was critically liberal. Matthew was a stickler for the truth. There had never, in the whole of its history, been the faintest suggestion that the *Messenger* espoused any interest other than that of the community which it served.

The Old Folk's Treat, when Jacob had started it, had greatly enhanced the paper's popularity, and the treat had gone on from year to year until it was a firmly established event. Once a year two hundred of the oldest and poorest men and women in Swanbridge were driven, conducted, or pushed to the Town Hall and there given a party at which they ate too much, mostly of unaccustomed foods that gave them indigestion for weeks afterwards, and drank hugely of tea. After the party came an entertainment by local and professional talent, and the old folk, being of a generation which was not slow in voicing its approval or disapproval of a turn, allowed no consideration of party manners to interfere with their feelings.

There was never any stint of helpers, and it was a rule that each member of the Silverman family should do something to help. Mrs. Silverman did more than anyone else. Here were two hundred men and women to be fed. It was a task worthy of her, and she threw herself into it with a surprising vigour. She overlooked the catering; she marshalled the tea urns; she superintended the decoration of the hall; she chose the cakes and worked the bread-cutting machine; and all the while there was in her eyes a happy light as she surveyed the long tables and saw the piles of food gradually dwindling and heard the happy sighs of the full fed.

The main assembly-room of the Swanbridge Town Hall was a long, lofty chamber, with a stage at one end and entrance-doors at the other. It was surrounded by a low balcony and lighted by flanking rows of dim, stained-glass windows and three huge chandeliers like massive bronze harnesses, that hung heavily from the plaster-worked ceiling. Matthew could remember the time when the old building had been burnt and the new hall erected on its site. Then he had been delighted by the decorative scrolls and the solid trappings of the assembly-room. But as time went by he had to admit, with the rest of the citizens of the town, that the hall was perhaps rather dark.

On the afternoon of the treat the darkness of the hall was forgotten. The filtered light from the windows was swallowed in the blaze that fell from the three chandeliers and sparkled upon the scene below.

Two long tables on trestles ran the length of the hall, tables spread with white cloths that shone like snow and were almost as cold to the touch. At intervals along the boards stood dishes of cakes, plates of bread-and-butter, vases of flowers, and places for the old people, and the old people were in their places, one hundred and ninety-four of them. They had been in their places for five minutes and were beginning to feel at home.

At first they had come into the hall nervous, upset by being brought from their firesides to this chamber, which, for all the glory of the chandeliers and stained-glass windows, was cold. Then, when the trays of tea began to circulate, and the food warmed them, they lost their timidity, and slowly, like the beginning of bird song at morning, their voices had wakened, one by one, until now they were in full tumult, and with their confidence had come a certain critical attitude towards the tea. Some of them harboured the unjust suspicion that they had been brought here to be given a feed because it was supposed they never ate well at home, and some of them imagined that perhaps there was some evangelical purpose in the treat when they saw the wives of the clergy turning themselves into maids, and found sitting opposite them old enemies whom they hoped to outlive for the joy of reading the funeral account in the *Messenger*. They ate the tea, but steeled their hearts against any reconciliation of the old feuds.

93

"I been comin' to these treats for ten years, but this is the weakest cup o' tea I've ever had."

" 'Tain't the tea. I can abide that. It's the cake. I never did like shop-bought cake. If I'd ha' known, I'd ha' brought a bit of my girl's saffron cake."

"See 'im over there. 'Im with the white whiskers. I mind the time when I beat 'im in a ploughin' match at Farley Show. But he wouldn't take best until us fought for a pint after the show. Ha, them was the days. If two didn't agree they was allowed to fight them days, without fear of the vicar or a bobby comin' atween."

"Aye, and she weren't no better than the rest of them, and as for him—well, all cats are grey in the dark."

"I mind the time when there weren't a man, woman, or child around Swanbridge 'adn't 'eard of Jimmy Shaw. He could tell some o' these young uns a tale or two."

"All right, I ain't deaf. You don't have to holler, do you? Course I want some more tea."

"Am I enjoyin' meself?" A throaty chuckle from one old man, dressed in his best broadcloth, his skinny neck wrapped about with a white muffler. "This young shaver wants to know! Go on with 'ee, I'm past that kind of thing. Go on, 'tis you should be pickin' out one of these young ladies around here and enjoyin' yourself if you was half a man ..." A howl of laughter from those around him, and the young curate of St. Dunstan's, blushing, retreated hastily.

Matthew moved up and down the tables, determined to do his share, as every editor, since Jacob started the treat, had done. He was never able to decide in his mind whether the whole idea of the treat was not wrong. Sometimes, when he saw the old men and women coming rather diffidently into the hall, he was sorry for them, and indignant that they should be brought together when they probably wanted no more than to remain quietly at home; and then, when they got back their voices, he found himself hoping that theirs was a real enjoyment; that they were glad to be meeting old friends and arguing with old enemies again. It was good to think that for a few hours they were being lifted out of themselves and were perhaps recapturing some part of their past. He and Abner could never agree about the treat. Abner would take no part in it, and any discussion of it ended inevitably in a fierce denunciation of the practice by the old man, who was nauseated by what he called "this parade of senility." Matthew felt that Abner was prejudiced.

With a trayful of empty bread plates, Matthew left the hall and entered the small and hot ante-room where his wife and a staff of helpers were cutting up cake and bread and looking after the tea urns.

"My dear," he said, "you look terribly hot. Why don't you rest?"

"Nonsense, Matthew. You know I love doing this. Go away, please. I'm busy."

Matthew shrugged his shoulders, smiling, and as he turned away he bumped into Loraine, who was carrying a tray of plates.

"My God!" she moaned. "I never knew there was so much bread-and-butter in the world. They've eaten most of the cake and they've started on the bread again."

"Loraine, don't use such language!" said her mother. Mrs. Silverman started piling bread-and-butter on to the plates, filling the tray. Through the doorway came the clatter of voices from the hall.

"You'd better get Philip or someone to carry that tray," said her mother when it was loaded.

"I can manage it." Loraine took the tray and started towards the hall. At the door she had to swerve to avoid Alexander as he shot past her, brandishing an empty teapot.

"Look out!" he called, and had squirmed by her and was gone. Loraine turned to glare after him and, as she did so, her foot struck a greasy patch on the floor where someone had dropped a cup of tea, and she felt herself sliding forward. The tray mounted towards her face, and, as though she were witnessing it all in slow movement, she knew that her legs were bending and that she was going to sit down with a bump on the floor, to be liberally decorated by flying pieces of bread-and-butter. In the fraction of a second, as she fought for her balance, she knew what she would look like, her carefully waved hair sticky with butter, her blue jumper smeared, and the back of her skirt damp with tea.

She let out a cry, and was about to abandon the tray in an effort to move from under it when she felt her elbows seized firmly. Strong hands held her and restored her balance. She stood, panting and flushing from her escape.

"That was a lucky one," said a voice over her shoulder, and she was aware that the grip was still on her arms.

She moved away quickly, angry with herself for being caught so ridiculously, and found herself facing a short young man whose face was wrinkled with laughter. He was dressed in brown plus-fours, and his face was a healthy red and somewhat pugilistic, the nose squat, with wide nostrils, as though his features had been battered into hardness and ruggedness. His hair, unparted, was short and curly, and defied any arrangement other than that which was natural to it. His was a pleasant and honest countenance, but Loraine was in no mood to make notes of his good points. She saw a rather short, snub-nosed, grinning young man, obviously amused at her misfortune, and she resented his interference.

"Thank you," she said stiffly, and prepared to move away.

"Oh, that's all right. I was only too glad to be able to help. You would have looked a mess with bread-and-butter stuck all over you, wouldn't you?" His eyes travelled from her head to her feet, missing nothing and obviously appraising. "Please let me take the tray." He stepped forward.

"Don't bother." Loraine adopted her coldest manner. "I think I can manage to carry it now without—making a mess of myself." She moved off, leaving him a little puzzled, and in his eyes the reproachful, wondering look of a dog which has expected a petting rather than a beating. He waited a moment, hoping she might turn round. Loraine walked straight down the hall and was lost in the bustle about the tables.

* * *

Alexander surrendered his empty teapot and, considering that he had done his share in brightening the lives of the old people, he got himself a cup of tea and a slice of cake and wandered up on to the gallery of the hall to feed in peace. The scene below was almost medieval, the long tables crowded with men and women, the piles of food, the noise in the hall, and the gentle sound of hidden music coming from the curtained stage at the far end … He took a deep bite from his cake and settled back in comfort.

"You're Alexander Silverman, aren't you?" Someone spoke behind him, and, as he turned, a young man in brown plus-fours cocked a leg over the rail of the seat and dropped beside him.

"Mind the cup!" cried Alexander warningly. Then, as he moved it away, "Yes, I'm Alexander Silverman. What of it?"

"Nothing. Only you nearly wrecked your sister and her tray of bread and butter just now when you shot through the door with your teapot."

"Nearly?"

"Yes. I stepped in at the crucial moment and restored her balance. By the way, I'm Harold Spencer."

"Pleased to meet you," replied Alexander politely, and he wondered why it was that whenever Loraine snubbed any young man, the young man sought him out and tried to make friends with him. Did this Harold Spencer think that he could help him to gain Loraine's affection? In a few moments, he thought, he'll be asking me her second name, and when her birthday is, and if she is engaged. He took a contemptuous bite from the cake and washed it down with tea.

"She wasn't any too pleased with me. I suppose there's some Freudian reason for a pretty girl disliking a young man who's just saved her from sitting in a puddle of tea. You're a reporter for the *Messenger*, aren't you?"

"I am," Alexander admitted, not unwillingly. "What do you do?" Since there were to be no formalities, he decided to be curious as well.

Harold Spencer laughed. "At the moment I'm selling carpets, linoleum, and other household goods in Hardwick's. I'm a member of Toc H. Your father invited two or three of us to come down here and help. Do you like newspaper work?"

Alexander found his sudden questions a little disconcerting. He saw, however, that he had misjudged the other's interest in Loraine, and it was flattering to imagine that he was being sought for his own company.

"I wouldn't change it for the world," he declared. "And what about you? Do you like selling carpets?"

"I hate it!" The words were like sword-cuts, each one clear and vicious. Alexander turned to him surprised.

"You sound almost melodramatic about it."

Harold Spencer laughed. "Sorry. You see—" He hesitated, then he smiled, as though he had been wondering whether Alexander was worthy of the confidence and had found him deserving, "You see, my father owns a similar sort of a shop in Weston-super-Mare. Some day it will be mine, and I'm supposed to be getting experience. It's the most boring business in the world. You see, I want to be a reporter, like you."

"That isn't all honey." Here was battle-scarred experience tempering the lust of youth.

"I guess that. Still, it's what I want to do. The old man knows what I want to do, and I think he'd let me do it. Only once you get into one groove it's hard to get into another. Tell me something about your work."

Alexander put down his cup and began to fill a pipe. This was a new experience for him. In the office he was only a junior. Everyone knew much more than he did, and at home his position as a member of the *Messenger* staff was taken for granted. To have a stranger regard him as some form of demigod, to be eager to hear about his work, was a delicious compliment.

"It's just a job of work," he said modestly. "But it's a grand job. You feel you're working to some purpose; you're doing something tangible, not like adding up rows of figures or filing sheets of correspondence, and you come into touch with all classes. There's a great tradition behind newspapers, you know, a tradition of fighting and free speech. We deal in facts, and they are, at times, the most uncomfortable things to handle. Sometimes I wonder if you haven't even got to be a bit inhuman to be a good newspaperman; one moment you're looking at a corpse and the next laughing at a council meeting. At one time I thought I wanted to be an architect, but I changed my mind. It doesn't matter so much where a man lives, the great thing is his mind, and his mind depends largely on what he reads and upon his being well informed …"

* * *

Down in the hall the long tables had been cleared away, and the old people were seated in rows facing the stage and waiting for their entertainment. Matthew, although he would have preferred not to, always made a speech at this point. His father had always done so, and it was expected from him. He knew the wisdom of brevity, and he did no more than express his gratification at the presence of the old folk, make a polite and well-received joke about their appetites, and thank the many helpers. Then he introduced the entertainment, and slipped down to his seat in the hall with his wife and Loraine.

The first item was a comic song by a local amateur. He was dressed as a red-nosed policeman, and with a great deal of belt-hitching and truncheon-swinging sang of the joys of the crooks on his beat. The old people roared his chorus and their approval. Then came a xylophone solo by a member of a Swanbridge dance band. They sat in silence while the thin, nervous notes wandered through the hall, and when he was done there was a polite round of clapping from the helpers, some desultory clapping from a few old folk, and he decided, knowing the Old Folk's Treat, not to give his encore.

Up in the gallery, Alexander and Harold were talking, forgetful of the entertainment. They had forgotten newspapers and were arguing passionately; religion, socialism, sex, and the sterilisation of the unfit … their young and hungry souls took all topics to themselves, and they talked with an eager rapidity, laughing occasionally, contending fiercely, and utterly absorbed.

Down in the hall a young girl, dressed as a shepherdess, came on to the stage. Her white dress frilled out like a summer cloud; her saucy hat, hung with ribbons, crowned a silver periwig. The orchestra played a waltz, an old-fashioned waltz that set some of the people humming and swinging their heads, and she floated around the stage like a wisp of dandelion-down borne by the airs of an August noon. She whirled and dipped and bowed, and from the wings a shepherd-boy swung to meet her embrace, and together they waltzed. The two lost all humanness; they became the spirit of the music and were carried before it, graceful, lithe, incomparably fragile, like a memory floating up from the past to bring tears to the old eyes and a colour to the crinkled cheeks. The music stole about the hall, its charm working deeply into the souls of the old people while their eyes watched the young grace of the dancers, their thoughts flying back to the days when they had been young and eager and life had held so much for them. There was not one old man who had not been the shepherd-boy and no old woman who had not pirouetted as did the shepherdess before her love.

When the dancing and music stopped, there was a thunder of cries and clapping. The dancers came back and danced again. Four times they came back, until the conjurer waiting his turn in the wings grew angry and annoyed.

When his turn came, his anger had made him nervous. He made a slip and his trick went wrong. Instantly the hall was filled with derisive shouts.

"Butterfingers!"

"Look in your trouser pockets!"

"Perhaps you left it at home!"

The magician recovered the lost card, and, smiling bravely, requested the assistance of someone from the audience for his next trick. There was no diffidence; twenty old men made their way towards the stage, and for some time there was confusion as their claims were contested.

Loraine and Philip smiled at the magician's embarrassment. Philip Lister was a tall, slender young man, always impeccably dressed, his hair neatly combed, his face schooled to betray no emotion other than a mild disinterestedness. Actually he was seldom bored, for he had an eager curiosity for all things, but his training as an auctioneer had early taught him that eagerness and curiosity must never show themselves upon his face.

Loraine was saying, " Philip, who's the boy with the brown plus-fours and a face like a boxer who's helping here?"

"Face like a boxer?" he enquired lazily.

"Yes ... a short, curly-haired young man."

"Sounds like one of the squirts from Toc H to me. They get a choice selection up there. Very good-hearted, though, they tell me. Go up and read blood-and-thunders to the poor-house inmates each Sunday and give concerts. Looks as though there'll be a free fight before this fellow gets his man."

"They always get a bit out of hand. Toc H, you say?"

"Yes; must be one of Hardwick's assistants, I think. Most of 'em belong to Toc H. Shop-assistants either get religion or go highbrow.

Must be a kind of armour against customers. If you're religious they can't annoy you and if you're highbrow you just treat 'em with contempt."

Philip wondered why Loraine had asked him about the young man. He knew Harold Spencer fairly well, though he saw no reason why he should admit it to her right away. He loved Loraine and he was jealous for her, and he was sensible enough to make his jealousy as unostentatious as possible, realising that as yet he had little right to show any anger. It was a conviction of his that if you made up your mind to have a thing, and really believed that you would get it, then eventually it came to you. There was an old Dutch escritoire, with hundreds of secret drawers and finely inlaid with precious woods, that he had tried to buy once. The owner had refused to sell. He had wanted the piece, and eventually it came to him, because he believed that it would. He felt so about Loraine. He loved her, and knew that one day he would marry her. He believed it, and realised that it was merely a question of waiting ... He never spoke to her of his love. He was older than she, and he felt that to obtrude his love upon her youth would have been wrong. There was plenty of time. Their friendship was pleasant, easy, and unmarked by any passionate fidelities. When he kissed her, it was the casual kiss of a friend, not the kiss of a lover. Later she would waken to find him her lover, and their friendship would pass into a stronger, less youthful stage. He was content to wait.

Loraine had never analysed her feelings for Philip beyond the obvious premises that she liked him, he was good company, generally gave in to her wishes, and owned a fast sports car which he let her drive. Marriage was a distant, blue hill riding in the sky beyond the rim of a wide plateau. It was always there, and some day she would come to it. Meantime there were wooded valleys, broad rivers, and fields of sweet-scented flowers to explore.

* * *

"If only people would realise that Shaw's advocacy of an equality of incomes is the real panacea for which the world is longing ..." Alexander sucked at his cold pipe dejectedly. "It's terrible," he went on, his voice dull with the misery of the dreamer who finds his dreams evaporating like a September brume against a strong sun, "to think that there the solution is, and no one has the sense to grasp it firmly."

"That's true. But socialism is not a political credo. It's not entirely an economic doctrine. It's a religion; a new way of life. Look at all those people down there—" Harold flung out a hand and indicated the old folk. "They've come to the end of their tether. In ten years most of them will be dead, and what will the sum of their lives have been? Misery, struggle against hunger and baseness, some sins, and a few passing hours of happiness. So much beautiful human material gone waste, scattered like sunflower seeds."

"That's a good alliteration," said Alexander appraisingly. "Scattered like sunflower seeds. You know, you've got a good command of words. You shouldn't be wasting your time in a lousy store."

"What else can I do? It's no good tilting at windmills these days. I tried to get on a newspaper in Trowbridge, but they wouldn't look at me. I worked there for a while."

Alexander did not reply at once. He was thinking. He liked Harold Spencer. Here, he felt, was a man after his own manner. Someone who saw through the shams of life and who did not appear to be afraid to speak his mind. The world needed such people, and the *Messenger* needed them. The *Messenger*. What a name! What it could come to mean! A messenger of sanity and peace, exposing and denouncing … When he was editor … His father was hopeless. Stuck fast in his own generation, guileless. An honest, plodding editor, content to follow the conventions of his forefathers and stopping his ears to all new influences …

"What would you say," he said slowly, "if I were to offer you a job on the *Messenger*?"

"You wouldn't?"

"I would." Alexander was a king giving a royal command. "At least, I'd see that you got it. One of our chaps is leaving, and there'll be a vacancy. I could get the old man to let you have that. What's your shorthand speed?"

"About eighty words a minute. You see, I've always kept up my practice, hoping for something like this …"

"Um. You'll have to improve a lot on that before you can take on anything really big. Still ..."

"Do you really think you could get it for me?" Harold kept a tight rein on his enthusiasm. He was attracted by this dark, vivacious, wild youth; but he guessed that Alexander occasionally, in the delirium of his words, lost touch with reality. Harold had the same dreams. His age gave him discretion. He could talk with a paradisaic wantonness to Alexander, but he knew how to suit his conversation to any company. He worshipped the same gods, only he was accustomed to be more reticent in the parade of his feelings.

"I'm sure," said Alexander. "I'll speak to the old man and let you know when to see him. He's a sensible old boy, and he'll realise that this will be a good thing. But when you see him, keep a soft pedal on the Red Flag tune and speak reverently of the *Messenger*."

* * *

The rain clouds had lifted and the night turned clear with stars. New-washed, the Great Bear sprawled its length above the river, and over the banked masses of trees Orion straddled the western horizon. The Thames swept by, busy with flood-water from the hills, and George watched the play of lights across the ripples. He had taken the bus to Sandford and walked back along the towpath to settle his thoughts.

He had come up full of energy, ready for work, and now he was dissatisfied with himself. Just when he felt himself getting into the heart of things, his mind shied and he found himself staring into the fire, his thoughts wandering. At first he had been angry. Then humiliated. He had sought relief in prayer, but prayer refused to exorcise his devil. And now he was worried ...

He perched himself on the arm of a small bridge that carried the path over a contributory stream and frowned at the night. This thing had to be faced now and for ever. He had never been like this before. There was nothing wrong in it. It was, he comforted himself, a healthy, human desire, the finest thing that ever happened to most people. The trouble was its strength; brushed aside as silly and childish, it came back with a potency that began to frighten him. In his first year he had felt himself falling in love with a waitress in Stewart's Café.

Stubbornly he had convinced himself of his stupidity and had never again entered the café. For two days he had been miserable and then the pain had gone. This thing was different. A couple came down the path, arm in arm, and as the man drew hard at his cigarette the red glow showed their smiling faces, a touch of intimacy in the darkness of the river night.

George knocked his pipe out viciously against the wooden rail. There was a sharp click, and he realised that the stem had broken short. He heard the bowl drop with a deep *plop* into the river.

He stopped the expostulation which rose from his heart, and then turned towards the city. The pipe had decided him. Unless—he saw the allegory clearly—unless he acted right away, the time would come when he would break, brittle as the stuff of a pipe stem. There was a comfort in allegories. He walked on past the grey ghosts of the barges on his right, up St. Aldate's and across Carfax.

He switched the light on in his room in Beaumont Street and, sitting down at his table, began to write a letter.

VIII

WANTED: young man, good
appearance, assistant draper's
and outfitter's. Live out. Apply—
Hardwick's, Swanbridge.

Swanbridge Messenger (Advertisement)

Matthew pushed the book from him, ran his hand across his hair, and then picked up his pen. Once a week came this moment, and never did it fail to impress him with a sense of responsibility. This that he wrote now was not news. It was Matthew Silverman— not one Matthew Silverman, but the thousands of Matthew Silvermans who were the thousands who read his editorial in the *Messenger*. "An editor is not one man, one personality; he shares some part of every man, woman, and child who reads him." That had been a favourite remark of his father, and it was a precept which Matthew held very dearly, and he carried it into practice by writing what he felt was right and hoping that, in his words, each one of his readers would find something to commend and nothing to hurt unjustly.

He sat for a moment or two listening to the buzz of traffic outside his window. Then he wrote in a precise, slow hand:

> *Like as the waves make towards the pebbled shore, So do our minutes hasten to their end.*

He stopped and looked at the words. That, he felt, would not do! It was too solemn; it brought the vision of death too close and it would upset people. No one, with spring coming, wanted to be reminded of these things. He turned the leaves of his reference book a while, biting the end of his pen and humming gently to himself. Through his specctacles his grey eyes probed the book. His face in repose had a smile.

He wrote again:

> *The world is young today*
> *Forget the gods are old,*
> *Forget the years of gold*
> *When all the months were May.*

That was better; it had a happier note. It was important to get the spirit of his writing from the quotation which always headed the editorial. He went on, happy enough:

> "Truth has its own ebullience, its own gaiety, and a grand contempt for age. The young measure their age in years, but their elders accept only the measure of the spirit which is in them. To be young is to live in the present, denied the joy of memories. Memories belong to the old, and last Friday the memories of the old made them youthful, and what is annually known as the Old Folks' Treat turned itself into the jolliest party of youngsters that the Swanbridge Town Hall has ever known …"

He broke off as there came a knock at the door. Alexander came in. Matthew frowned as he saw him. He did not like being disturbed when he was writing his leader.

"Could I speak to you for a moment, sir?"

"What is it? I'm busy."

"It's about a young fellow I met at the Old Folks' Treat." Very quickly—for he could guess his father's irritation at the interruption—Alexander told him about Harold Spencer. He said only that Harold was keen to get on a newspaper and that he, Alexander, had promised to speak to his father about him.

"What makes him think there's a job here for him?"

"I told him that Barnes was going."

"Um!" Matthew pulled at his chin. He was not sure that he altogether approved of Alexander taking the step he had done. He guessed that Alexander had probably promised more than he could fulfil. "We want an experienced man in the place of Barnes."

"I know, sir. But I've worked it all out. You see, if you take Spencer, that means that you've got now two people, myself and Spencer, in the place of Barnes, and I'm sure we can make up for him."

"So you've worked it all out, have you?"

"I mean that I've thought about it in my own mind. I know, of course, that everything depends upon what you say. I was merely trying to help him. He seemed a nice, eager chap." The tone of Alexander's last remark did not escape Matthew. The boy was generous. It was good to see this desire to help others.

"All right, son. Tell him to come in this afternoon and I'll see him."

He returned to his writing. He wrote slowly for half an hour, occasionally erasing a sentence. When he had finished, he read it through carefully, and then, folding it, walked from his room through the works to the linotype room.

"Send a pull of this down to me as soon as you can," he said. When he had gone, the foreman, a sturdy, efficient man, sat down and, opening the paper, began to read it slowly, sucking his lips as though it were a long drink he was relishing. When he had finished it, he pulled out his stubby pencil and corrected a misspelt word which had escaped Matthew and handed it to an operator. "Here's the weekly sermon," he said. "Let's have it soon."

* * *

That afternoon Harold Spencer called to see Matthew. He was not nervous, though he wondered whether he was not taking a lot of trouble to ascertain what he knew must happen. No newspaper would want him with his inexperience.

"My son tells me that you want to get a job on a newspaper, young man. Is that correct?" Matthew, firmly ensconced in his chair, surveyed Harold as though he were a general reviewing his troops. Without waiting for a reply, he went on: "Every young man thinks

107

he wants to be a reporter these days. They go to the pictures and see absurd American films about newspapers, and get their heads filled with a lot of adventurous, romantic twaddle. Reporting isn't like that. It's just another job, and it can be as dull as clerking; a deal duller at times." Matthew did not believe this last statement, but he saw no reason why he should not make it. It was effective. "What makes you think you'd like to be a reporter?"

"Well, sir, I've always wanted to be. I suppose it's just something inside me. Perhaps I ought not to have come bothering you … only your son was kind enough to suggest that you might … well …" Harold looked up and grinned suddenly. He would not get the job, he felt. He could not expect it, but he had tried. "You see, sir," he said frankly, "when you feel a thing in your blood, the only sensible thing, it seems to me, is to try and satisfy it. You're very kind, but I can see that you don't want me. That doesn't matter, only I'm not disappointed in the real sense of the word. Some day I shall get what I want, and that's all that matters. I know I shall get on a newspaper. I believe it. Some people don't know what they want until they get it—then they love it. I'm the other way round. I know what I want and I love it, and some day I'll get it." He stooped for his hat on the floor by his chair.

At first Matthew had been uninterested in this young man. For Alexander's sake he was seeing him, and he had hoped to discourage him, not harshly, but with the mild wisdom of an older man. Now he found his tolerance changed to a respect for the youth. He had spoken to him in a quiet voice, and every word had come cleanly from him with a force and decision that meant more than the words themselves, though the words were true enough. Some people—he was thinking of Alexander—did not know what they loved until it was given them, and this boy knew what he loved but could not get it. Here was a passion which he had known, a passion which his father had encouraged … There was something in this lad that forbade Matthew from accepting his mild withdrawal.

"Wait a minute," he said. Then, because he wanted time to think, he picked up a book from his desk and handed it to the puzzled Harold. "We don't usually review books in our columns, but this is the latest novel of Mr. Austin Swing, who is coming down here to address a meeting, and I feel a review would be a complimentary gesture to him. I was going to do it myself. Now I've decided that you can do it. I want to see if you can write good English. After that we'll have another chat."

Harold looked first at the decorated wrapper of the novel and then at Matthew; his eyes were brilliant with hope, the wild hope of the unexpected.

"Mr. Silverman."

"Now I'm very busy." Matthew stopped him sternly. "Two hundred words to be in this office by tomorrow evening. I expect you can find your way out."

When Spencer had gone, Matthew shook his head and rang the bell for Mr. Sharples, the advertisement manager. "I must be getting softening of the brain," he mused as he waited. "Soon I shall be fair prey for any lavender-seller." He deprecated his sentiments while at heart he was glad he had done as he did. The face of old John Silverman looked down upon him from its canvas, serious, no smile, the face of a man accustomed to adversity, yet in the eyes Matthew imagined there was a suggestion of approval. He remembered one of his father's sayings. He never had difficulty in remembering his father's pronouncements, for James had lost no opportunity of hammering home an axiom. "If ever I sit in my chair here and the sight of the pictures of my predecessors makes me feel uncomfortable, then I know I've done wrong." Matthew felt very comfortable as he waited for Mr. Sharples.

When the man came in, his mood dropped quickly from him.

"Now then, Mr. Sharples," he began sternly, "what's all this talk about the inefficiency of our sales department? Have you and your minions been letting the *Courier* steal some more of our customers? What you don't seem to realise is that newspapers have to be sold like any other commodity, and selling means competition. I know, I know." He raised a hand and stopped Mr. Sharples's protest. "You're going to tell me that you've done your best, that it isn't your fault. I don't want to hear that. My father wouldn't have listened to that talk, nor his father before him, and I don't mean to. Take the facts. The *Messenger* is a better paper than the *Courier*, it has a larger popularity around here—and yet you tell me that you are losing sales. And I tell you that it's all nonsense. If the sales go down, it means only one thing—somewhere in your department there's slackness."

Mr. Sharples sighed and let the flood pour over him. He was so used to Matthew's outbursts that he wondered the old man had not recognised long ago how useless that had become. He had served on many provincial newspapers, and, wherever he was, he gave his best, and accepted the inevitable responsibility of taking the blame for any fall of sales when the fault lay in the caprice of scores of Toms, Dicks, and Harrys.

"Now, then, let me have a look at those figures." Sharples recognised the tone. The tide had run its course; Matthew was approachable.

* * *

"Did you ever have to keep a secret, Gibby?" Alison, back from her holiday with Aunt Adelaide, was being put to bed.

"Maybe," answered Gibby non-committally, in a voice which indicated that, if she had, it would have been quite safe with her, and that she would not have begun to talk about it when it was time to be in bed and asleep.

"I've got a secret. Only nobody knows I've got it."

"I know you've got it."

"Yes, but you don't know what it is. It's nice to have a secret. It's like"—her small face was screwed up as she sought to define her feeling in words—"like going to have a present and not knowing what it is."

Gibby switched off the light and ended Alison's philosophy by darkness. She stopped at the door, smiling to herself in the darkness, and called back gently:

"Mind you don't talk in your sleep. You may give it away."

* * *

Harold Spencer read Mr. Austin Swing's novel, disliked it, and wrote a sober review calculated to give pleasure to all those people who liked Mr. Swing's works. He was far from a fool. Personally he regarded the book as pernicious, but he was wise enough to know that his own feelings were not those of most people.

"This," said Matthew as he read it through, "is quite good, quite good indeed." He made a few alterations for the sake of his prestige as an editor, and then looked up smiling at Harold. He had been thinking about him overnight and he knew what to do. It gave him a sense of fulfilment to feel that he was the means of gratifying an ambition which Harold had cherished so long. It was the age-old joy of power. He had the power to thwart or aid.

"As soon as you can leave Mr. Hardwick's shop there's a job waiting for you here. I'm doing a rather unusual thing in taking you, but I believe that it is a wise thing. I hope you won't disappoint me."

"I shall never be able to thank you enough, Mr. Silverman. It's almost too good to be true."

"All right. Let me know when you can start, and meantime you'd better be working hard at your shorthand. You must be faster than you are."

He picked up the review as Harold left, and read it again. It was a sound piece of work. Matthew was no skilled literary critic. The article, to him, seemed to supply all that was necessary in a review. It told the reader something about the story, but not enough to make the reading of the book a supererogation; it quoted a pleasant passage and left a desire for more, and it was quietly complimentary without being condescending. And the boy, he noticed, had had the good sense to work in a reference to the coming meeting.

His door was opened and, without any announcement, Uncle Abner came into the room, followed by Pelang. The Alsatian walked heavily to the rug by the fire and collapsed with a dull grunt, eyeing the pair with a sad regard which seemed to say, "Now then, carry on, but no nonsense."

"Good evening, Abner. What brings you out at this hour?"

"Who," demanded Abner brusquely, "was that young fellow I passed on the stairs? Haven't seen him around here before."

Matthew pushed the article from him and looked at Abner. The old man was dressed in a closely buttoned, high-collared suit of pepper-and-salt mixture. Covering his shirt-front was a black cravat sprigged with tiny white shamrocks and pierced by a pearl-headed pin. In one hand he held a long umbrella, and he wore a hard, square-shaped hat of ancient design. He kept his hat on, not from any disrespect for conventions, but from a fear of catching a cold in the head.

"His name's Harold Spencer, and until a few moments ago he was a draper's assistant at Hardwick's."

"And now, I suppose, he's just discovered that he's a prince of the royal blood, been left a million pounds by his father, and wants you to make an announcement of the facts in the *Messenger*? Why does it take you so long to get to the point? What's he doing here?"

"I've just engaged him as a reporter in the place of Barnes." Matthew went on quickly before Abner could interrupt: "He's had no experience of newspaper work, his shorthand is not good—but nevertheless I've engaged him. I trusted my instinct."

For a moment Abner seemed to contemplate an outburst, a protest against Harold's engagement; then, as so often happened with him, he realised the uselessness of trying to effect a change in Matthew's plans.

"Instinct!" He spoke scornfully. "You talk like a woman. They're always fussing about the place, talking about their instinct and their intuitions, and a messier lot of managers than most women I've never seen. Instinct is something that belongs exclusively to birds and animals. An editor should rely upon his common sense."

"Well, fundamentally, instinct is common sense."

"Only so far as building birds' nests is concerned; after that the two separate. Still, you've done it now. All I know is that I shouldn't have done it. I suppose you've written a wishy-washy editorial about the Old Folks' Treat? A disgusting event, making a parade of age, as though they were some circus animals."

"You're prejudiced."

"Nonsense. I'm seventy-five, and I wouldn't go back a year or barter a moment of my life for anything in the world, and when the time comes for me to die I hope I shan't be reluctant to go. Only young people and the middle-aged are afraid of dying. I shouldn't wonder if the thought of it makes you uncomfortable at times, and it was probably the same thought that started George towards the Church. And that reminds me what I've come here for. How's Alexander getting along?"

Matthew told him, describing his son's enthusiasm.

"He's too keen," said Abner. "It's a pity George ever left."

"The keener he is, the better. Why, he's absolutely forgotten all about his architecture, and he's happy here."

"That's the trouble. If you had more common sense than instinct you'd understand that. You can feed a young hawk on gravy-soaked bread, but when its wings get feathered nothing can keep it from flying after game."

Matthew lifted an eyebrow. "You're talking in parables, Abner."

"So I may be—but it's one worth thinking about. There's more sense in that than in a dozen of your editorials. Good-bye, and think it over."

He was gone, with the dog trailing after him.

Matthew laughed and dismissed him from his mind. Periodically Abner descended upon the office, spent anything from five to fifty minutes lecturing or cavilling, and then went—and experience had taught Matthew not to take too much notice of him.

IX

Mr. Austin Swing has once again demonstrated his profound knowledge of the intricacies of feminine psychology.

Swanbridge Messenger (From a review
of *Child of the Heart*)

Mr. Austin Swing dropped his *Daily Express* to the floor of the compartment and stared out of the window. The train was just pulling into Swanbridge. Across the sets of rails showed the untidy back yards of small houses, yards that held an accumulation of human rubbish, tin baths, rickety fowl-sheds, meagre patches of earth, and one or two clothes lines holding limp washing, grey in the fading light of the afternoon. Beyond the houses, surprisingly rotund and red, was the bulk of a gasometer, a wisp of steam rising at its foot from an engine-house—incense fire before an altar. Next to the gasometer was a four-storeyed building of ugly grey brick; some sort of factory, Mr. Swing guessed. On the other side of the line a long hoarding hid the town from his view. He could tell what it was like. Bustling with its own importance, intolerant of outside influences, with its local cliques, its patches of squalid slum that gave the churches an opportunity to indulge their Christianity, the select neighbourhood where the professional and tradespeople lived, the two cinemas, and perhaps a draughty, barn-like theatre, empty, or warmed some weeks by cheap variety. He knew exactly what it was like, for he had been born in such a town, and the memory gave him little pleasure. Tomorrow he would leave it (he was a fool to have promised to stay overnight), and until then he would have to hide his boredom, and he was very good at doing that.

Mr. Swing, thought Matthew, as he drove him in a taxi from the station, was just like his photographs—a little theatrical, a little flashy, yet somehow solid and sympathetic. He had a keen, questioning face; the nose superbly aquiline and the lips perhaps a little too full, a knowing, worldly face, the face of a famous novelist. His body deserved his face, for it was athletic—the shoulders square because his tailor knew how to pad, and his figure abundantly trim and regular because he wore an elastic belt. Matthew guessed nothing of the belt or the padding. He was joyous from the honour which had come to him.

"It's not a large town, Mr. Swing, but there will be an enthusiastic audience."

"That's the only qualification I insist on in an audience—enthusiasm. It makes everything else so easy." He spoke pleasantly and charmingly, slightly deprecating by his tone everything he said.

Mrs. Silverman decided at once that he was a "nice" man. When she told him how much she had enjoyed *The Golden Fortress* he had made a half-bow towards her and smiled, as though the compliment coming from her meant more than any other. Generally she distrusted people who were too well-mannered. Mr. Swing captivated her right away, and set her in bonds by eating heartily of the cakes she had prepared for tea.

They were, he told himself, a comfortable family, friendly, secure, and proud to have him. Their proudness did not embarrass him; he was so used to it. The father was a pompous busy-body who liked to have a finger in every pie; the mother a good-natured soul without a deal of intelligence; the son—he sensed at once that Alexander did not like him, and the boy's unspoken antipathy amused him while it irritated him—was very quiet, and probably a devotee of Erskine Caldwell and the sex-without-sentiment school of fiction; and the daughter, Loraine, was obviously about to fall in love with him. He sighed inwardly as he watched her. All the symptoms were there. She had been very quiet when he was introduced. She had said little during tea, and every now and then he had turned to find her eyes upon him, and, when he spoke, he knew that she listened to the sound of his voice more than to the sense of his words. Sometimes he got tired of being Austin Swing. To have your hosts' daughters falling in love with you was like a recurrent fever ... though sometimes the delirium of fever brought pleasure.

Loraine watched Mr. Swing covertly. There was, she thought, something magnetic about him. All her male friends were very ordinary, commonplace people; she knew all about them. This man was different. He was famous, and yet so charming and unaffected by it. He must be used to far grander houses than theirs, and yet he moved and took his place among them as though he had been accustomed to their ways all his life. When he looked at her, was he, she wondered, making mental notes to use in some future novel? His heroines, she mused, a little disturbed by the thought, were always young and pretty, and she knew she was pretty. It was rather exciting to be sitting close to a man who wrote so well about love, and who described with a brief but unforgettable poignancy the consummation of desire. "Her corn-ripe hair ... eyes ultramarine and fathomless as the sea, holding all its mystery ..." Was he thinking of her like that? She raised an empty cup to her lips and, discovering it, pretended to drink so that none should notice her lapse.

"I do think the League of Nations is such an admirable thing, don't you, Mr. Swing?" said Mrs. Silverman in the same tone she would have used to commend a new soap-powder. "May I fill your cup for you?"

"And I'm sure a lot more people will think so after they've heard Mr. Swing's speech tonight," declared Matthew gallantly. He did not want this celebrity to think they were uncouth, and unused to entertaining the intelligent. Provincial they might be, but not unenlightened.

"You flatter me, Mr. Silverman"—with a deprecatory shake of the head. "All I can do is to put the facts of the case. Sanity can dictate only one solution to our problems, the problems of the world: the brotherhood of the League, the ultimate decency of mankind. You remember what Stevenson once said: 'I believe in the ultimate decency of things; aye, and if I woke in hell, should still believe it.' "

Stevenson in the mouth of Swing, thought Alexander. It was enough to make a dog vomit. That was how he wrote for the Sunday papers: "All things bright and beautiful; all creatures great and small."

"It seems to me," Alexander said, doubting the wisdom of doing so and remembering the adage about pearls before swine, "that the League of Nations represents nothing more than a convenient form of conscience-money paid by the larger capitalist countries to excuse their tyrannies upon the smaller ones."

Matthew laughed with a little too much heartiness and shook his head. "Don't take any notice of Alexander, Mr. Swing. He's a rabid anarchist."

Mr. Swing smiled indulgently, and said in a tone which he knew would infuriate Alexander: "I know. Youth must always be anarchistic, setting up gods to destroy them …"

How simply, thought Loraine, he had put Alexander in his place; and a good job. He was too cocky at times.

"Aren't you going to have another cress sandwich?" Mrs. Silverman enquired anxiously of Alexander, noticing his frown.

* * *

An hour before dinner, Swing went up to his room. He had to change, and wanted an opportunity to glance over the notes of his address. He sat for a while looking out of the window at the dark filigree of trees against the star-bright sky. Blast the Duchess of Len for getting him to address this meeting! The League of Nations was all right. It had been the means of earning him many a fat cheque. Only he wished that he had not come to this dull little town when he might be idling in his St. John's Wood flat. He threw his cigarette-stub into the fire, and was about to open his case for another when there came a knock at the door. It was a gentle, almost timid knock; the knock of someone whose fist had half hesitated.

"Come in," he called lazily, and then, as the door opened, he rose to his feet. "Miss Silverman?"

Loraine smiled at him. She was being a little fool; still, she had done it now.

117

"Am I interrupting you?" she asked nervously. He shook his head and beckoned her into the room. "No one would mind being interrupted by you, I'm sure, Miss Silverman. Is there anything I can do for you?"

"I … I …" Loraine felt herself getting into a panic. For a moment she was conscious only of her body trembling and the tremendous noise of her heart in her ears, swelling into a tumult as it did when you were given an anaesthetic. He moved towards her, and suddenly she was in control of herself.

"I came to see if everything was all right. Is there anything you want that I can get for you? Gibby—that is the maid—sometimes forgets …"

When some women blushed they were ugly. Loraine's blushing emphasised her prettiness. It was like … Swing sought for the words as an exercise … like the flush of a dipping sun over snowfields. He was aware of the vitality of her body, the blossoming that was taking place; and the contrast between his tiredness and her eager, rushing spirit made him curiously tender. One day some oaf in this town would take all that loveliness as though he were buying a packet of tea. It demanded reverence … He pulled himself up, recognising a weakness which had been with him longer than he cared to remember, this merging of his self into the part of one of his own heroes.

"No," he replied briskly. "I'm perfectly happy. It was nice of you to come and ask, though." His smile warmed Loraine and encouraged her.

"I didn't like to ask you downstairs. Would you … would you be kind enough to sign? … I hope you don't think it's too bad of me." She was holding out towards him the copy of his latest book which she had got from Matthew's table in the library.

Swing took it and, laying it on the table, unscrewed the cap of his fountain-pen. "Not at all."

He signed his name and soberly scored it with a flourish, noticing, as he handed the book back to her, that the flyleaf was marked with a stamp—"With the publisher's compliments"—and guessing how she had come by it.

Back in her room, Loraine looked at the signature. She was happy. Not just the happiness that comes from pleasure in doing or receiving;

her happiness came from inside her, as though it had been there for a long time, a tight bud, which some new warmth, some sweet dew, had touched and broken into flower.

* * *

In his tower room, Alexander was putting on his dinner-jacket. Whenever there were guests the Silvermans dressed for dinner, and Alexander, who regarded dress suits as a mark of the capitalists, a bourgeois symbol, and a damned imposition, was in a bad temper. He would have to sit through dinner and listen to Swing larding everybody with his compliments and fancy phrases, and after dinner he would have to sit in the Town Hall and watch eight hundred men and women regarding Swing with glazed, hypnotic eyes ... *The Golden Fortress*, and what was the latest?—*Child of the Heart*— why, if he couldn't write a novel like that with his hands tied, his eyes blindfolded, and holding the pen in his mouth, he'd ... he did not know what he would do. He glared into his mirror and pulled savagely at his tie.

"What," said a voice behind him, "is a pernicious hypocrite?"

He swung round, and beheld Alison, who had come softly into his room. She was in her nightdress, and it was obvious that she had slipped away after Gibby had put her to bed.

"Who's been talking to you about pernicious hypocrites?"

"You were."

"I was?"

"Yes, when I came into the room just then. You were saying, 'Of all the pernicious hypocrites ...' "

"Did I?"

"Yes. What are they?"

Alexander made a grab at her and hoisted her into his arms, pinching her bottom as he did so and making her squeal delightedly. "They're the first cousins of the maggots you find in apples. Come on! Gibby'll slaughter you if she finds you out of bed."

He carried her down the stairs into her room. He bounced her on the bed and covered her up. "Now then, go to sleep."

"Bounce me again," she pleaded, and Alexander found himself doing as she said.

"Children," he said to himself when he left her, "make a man sentimental." But he was smiling at the memory of the delight in Alison's eyes as she squealed with pleasure. He continued to smile all the way down to the dining-room. At the door he composed himself, and went in with a studied air of abstraction, a martyr immolating himself.

* * *

After dinner they all walked to the Town Hall for the meeting, where Mr. Swing was safely delivered to the local officials of the League of Nations Union. From the body of the hall the Silvermans heard him make his speech, a reasoned, competent plea for a greater interest in the League, a few jokes at the expense of chauvinists, and a final subtle burst of eloquence to send everyone home thinking more of Mr. Austin Swing than the League of Nations. Mr. Swing bowed to the applause, and made a mental note to say something about the enthusiasm of provincial audiences in the causerie which he did for a Sunday paper.

"I can't help thinking that the Japanese have made a great mistake," said Mrs. Silverman, "a great mistake. But, then, what could you expect from people who live in paper houses—or is it cardboard? And those chopsticks … how do they manage?"

"He was wonderful, wasn't he, Philip?"

Philip looked down at Loraine, disturbed by her tone; then he remembered that she was a great Swing fan.

"Pretty good. In fact, very good. He should have been an auctioneer."

"That's exactly what he is," said Alexander gloomily, depressed by Swing's undoubted oratorical brilliance. "He sells his talents to the highest bidder in any cause. Peace happens to pay more than warfare, but they tell me he was a red-hot jingoist during the war."

"You're a jealous little beast," said Loraine simply.

"The trouble with you is that you're in love with him," replied Alexander calmly. "Anyone could see it."

"Indeed!" Loraine was indignant.

"Now then! Now then!" Philip interposed with a great show of humour. "No quarrelling in public, please." Loraine, he could see, was fighting to hide her embarrassment.

"Who is fighting in public?" asked Matthew, coming up at that moment.

"Your children, sir. Had I not been here, I fancy they would by now have been gouging each other's eyes out or slashing with razors!"

Matthew laughed at the fancy. "They are a little savage at times," he admitted; "but, then, they have a family tradition that blood-letting is healthy. The medical profession discarded the idea years ago. What a speech, eh? What a masterly exercise! Alexander, my boy, when you can talk or write like that you'll have something to be proud of."

"And he didn't once look at his notes. That is what I think is so wonderful," said Mrs. Silverman; and then added, as though she ought to be fair all round, "Still, some people have such good memories."

At this moment Swing came up to them. The hall had cleared.

"If you don't mind," he said, as they moved towards the door, "we'll go out the back way. There'll probably be some autograph fiends out there, and I don't feel like signing tonight."

He looked across at Loraine as he said this, and a tiny smile passed between them, the ghost of a smile which seemed to isolate them for a second.

Swollen-headed pup, mused Alexander, and he did not alter his decision when half a dozen experienceded autograph-hunters pounced on Swing at the side door and thrust their open books before him.

"Can I give any of you a lift back in the car?" asked Philip. His car was parked outside. There was only room for four. "There's scarcely room for all."

"That's all right; we'll walk." They all made the noble gesture demanded of them, though Mrs. Silverman did not at all want to walk.

"We'll walk, thanks, Philip," said Matthew. "The air will freshen us after the closeness of the hall. It was close in there, didn't you think, Mr. Swing? I'll have a word with the boilerman when I see him next."

"Coming, Loraine?" Philip looked at her.

"I think I'll walk tonight, Philip," she said, hating him for the moment because he had shown such a proprietorial interest in her.

121

"I'll come with you," Alexander said, sliding into the seat next to Philip. "She wants to walk with Swing," he confided as they drove off. "He's put you right out of the picture, hasn't he?"

"Maybe," answered Philip, pulling up his collar against the wind. He changed gear with a roar that defied conversation for a time.

"Funny, that," mused Alexander aloud. "Damn' funny ... but understandable. My God! You went pretty close to that!" cried Alexander, as the sports car roared by a bus, the brightly lit vehicle lumbering above them.

"Yes, I tried to. Don't you find it funny?"

"Sorry," said Alexander, who liked Philip. "I didn't mean to annoy you." And then, because he knew Philip did not care for such songs, he began to sing *Gefoozalum* softly.

* * *

Swing never decided whether Loraine knew that he was still in the room when she came downstairs to fetch a magazine. He had imagined that all the family were in bed, except Matthew, who had excused himself and gone into the library to answer a few letters which needed his attention urgently. He himself was thinking of going up to his room when he could effectively overcome the attraction of the fire, his armchair, and the whisky decanter at his elbow.

"Please don't get up," Loraine cried as he made to move. "I've only come to get a magazine I was reading. I can't sleep unless I read a while." He looked tired—probably the effect of his speech.

"Can I help you find it?" he asked as she hunted around, turning the cushions up from the settee and flipping over a pile of papers in her search.

"No, I can. Oh!" Loraine stopped suddenly and blushed.

"What is it?" She was standing before him, prettily confused. One day, his thoughts went back, some oaf would take all that and rudely waken within her ... like the sun over snowfields.

"I've just remembered," Loraine said, "I left it in the chair you're sitting in. Please don't—"

"If that's all—" He was on his feet and had retrieved the magazine from the back of the chair. The covers were warm from his body. He held it out towards her. Loraine did not take it. She was looking at him, and he was reminded of something a long time back in his life. She was wearing a dress of dull blue material, rising high to her young throat, the sleeves falling away in soft folds to leave her shoulders bare. Through her half-parted lips he could see the whiteness of her teeth, and her breasts, tight little worlds, strained at the stuff of her bodice.

"Loraine." The sound was like the gentle stir of a tide turning back over warm sands.

She moved towards him, and his hands, dropping the magazine, went out to her, holding her shoulders, slipping across the smoothness of her back to rest firmly about her body. He was kissing her.

Loraine never knew that his lips were hurting her. She was aware only of his overpowering masculineness; she was wrapped up in it, lifted from herself and lost. Within her roared that stirring which troubles the mind and body when consciousness begins to fade and she knew that when she woke in the quiet, dreamy aftermath nothing would be the same; colours would be fresher from her changing, frost on dead piles of leaves would have a different light in the morning, her fingers across the wood of her hockey-stick would be aware of a strange rhythm. ... She let herself go, let herself sink into the darkness, hoping it would never pass and knowing that it must, to leave a great longing, a dissatisfaction.

Swing let her go. She stood before him, her head bowed a little, as though the vertigo in her brain would not let her raise her head quickly. Then slowly she looked up at him, and from her lips came a faint protest.

"My darling." He was angry with himself, but he wanted to tell, her... . Damn, how could you tell a woman anything when she was all emotion? At his words Loraine shook her head. She did not want him to speak. She stooped mechanically and picked up the magazine, and before he could stop her she was gone.

He stared after her for a while. Then he sat down and poured himself a whisky, and drank it neat. The bite of the bare liquid on his throat pleased him with its sharp pain.

He looked up as the french windows swung open and Matthew came into the room from the garden terrace. And now, thought

Swing, seeing Matthew's face, here comes the indignant father of the outraged girl to make it a real old-fashioned melodrama, a Toole burlesque.

Matthew closed the windows carefully and jerked the heavy velvet curtains across them. He was terribly upset. He told himself he must not show it before this man, who would not understand a decent emotion.

"I should have thought, Mr. Swing," he said with an exaggerated calmness, "that you might have taken the very elementary precaution of doing that." His head moved very slightly towards the swinging curtain.

"I suppose I should say I'm sorry."

"Do you—usually?"

Swing laughed uneasily. He had no reply that Matthew could understand. He was, to Matthew, Tarquin. Suddenly the conventional situation enraged him.

"Come, let's be sensible about it. I know I shouldn't have done it. I was weak; but it's not so serious as you may imagine."

"It may not, in the unfortunate circle which accepts your company, be considered serious, Mr. Swing. That, however, is not my view."

"Please, Mr. Silverman." Swing rebelled against this bickering. "I am terribly sorry. I can see that it is no good trying to explain myself to you. You couldn't understand. To you, I have abused your hospitality. Very well, I will go now."

"Oh, no, you won't!" Matthew spoke curtly. "You will stay here as arranged tonight, and catch an early train in the morning. I am being sensible, as you requested. Good night! I must finish locking up."

Matthew did not sleep for a long time. In the darkness he could see the yellow square of light which had confronted him as he had walked up from the orchard. Fuller often left the orchard door unbolted, and he liked to feel sure of it. It was hard to readjust suddenly all your conceptions about children. George had gone away from him, demanded his freedom, and he had given it to him. He had struggled to keep him and then let him go, impelled by his own good sense. And now Loraine was gone. Living so close to her, it had been easy to forget that she was growing up. Always she had been a girl; first an awkward schoolgirl and then a rather elegant young miss, but still a girl, his child. Now that was changed. She was no longer a girl; she was a woman. It had been his fault not to have recognised sooner that it must come. A man as he grew old tended to get himself into a groove and, because he was firm and stable, to imagine that the things and people around him were so; but things and people had an unfortunate habit of changing. When he went down to breakfast in the morning the Loraine who would face him across the table would be a different person, complete, and farther away from him. The ties had to be cut. You could go on loving them, helping them, all your life, and they would love you … Only there was that part of them which closed itself from you, shut you out even as you had been compelled once to shut out other people … He could even be a little sorry for Swing. It was hard for a man like that … What a silly little fool Loraine had been! He kicked savagely at the sheets for a moment. All his body wanted to go into her room and spank her, and then his mind stepped in and said, "Don't be a fool, Matthew. That won't do any good." And it wouldn't do any good. He knew that. An old-fashioned father might have done it, said something to her. He wasn't so old as all that. She wasn't a child any longer. She was Loraine Silverman… .

* * *

The following morning Loraine did not appear at breakfast, sending down a message that she had a bad head. Mr. Swing was his jolly, attentive, amusing self, and, after a good breakfast, he made his apologies for having to rush off and his thanks for being entertained, and went.

"What a nice man," said Mrs. Silverman when he had gone. She was alone in the breakfast-room with Gibby.

"No nicer than any of the others," answered Gibby curtly.

"Why, Gibby!"

"Well, he took it."

"Took what?"

"The cake of soap from the guest-room. They all do the same."

Mrs. Silverman laughed and shook her head. "That's just absent-mindedness," she said.

"That's not what I call it."

Matthew said nothing to his wife or Loraine about Mr. Swing. He kept his own counsel, and wrote an editorial for his paper about the League of Nations meeting, and he was scrupulously fair to Mr. Swing in it, although he refrained from dubbing the speech brilliant and named it able. After that he did his best to forget Mr. Swing; there were many other more important affairs to occupy his mind.

X

Mr. A. Silverman also spoke.

Swanbridge Messenger (From a report
of an Open-Air Anti-Fascist Meeting)

"There are various ways of disposing of an olive-stone, my boy.
You can remove it in your handkerchief while pretending to wipe
your mouth and then dispose of it when you are alone. Or you
can genteelly take it from your mouth, inspect it delicately for a
moment to see that you have removed all the meat from the bone,
and then flip it casually over your shoulder with an expression on
your face that indicates a cultured indifference to manners. You
can—and some shy people do—swallow it to avoid yourself present
embarrassment, or you may—and I am of this school—spit it
violently and openly into the fireplace." So saying, Mr. Jolly Roger
Selway spat his olive-stone into the fireplace of the Three Feathers'
bar and took another from the free dish on the counter. "You were
saying?" he gurgled, rolling the fruit obscenely in his mouth before
biting it.

"I was saying," said Alexander, a little irritated by the constant
interruption of Selway, "that the whole edifice of capitalism has
become top-heavy, its machinery cumbersome, and the time not far
distant when it must collapse willy-nilly."

"I know," put in Selway, "and when that time comes you will
set about establishing the pretty little Utopia you have already
sketched out for me. Two more bitters, please, miss. You will want
some help to do that. I suppose you are a member of our local
Socialist Club?"

"Socialist Club?"

"Yes. But I see that you are not. Surely you have heard of the Swanbridge Socialist Club?"

"No. Are you a member?"

"In a way. Come, I will lead you to it. If I introduce a paying member, that will in some way compensate for my own free membership. You see," he explained to Alexander as they left the hotel, "it pays for a reporter to be a sort of *ex-officio* member of all the town's clubs and organisations."

And that was how Alexander became a member of the Swanbridge Socialist Club, and became known to some people as Comrade Silverman.

The meetings were held in a small room above a newsagent and tobacconist's shop at the back of the station, and the leading light of the club was the secretary, Comrade Burnside, a tall, cadaverous man, pale-skinned, with dark, heavy eyes, who gave the impression that he was eaten out by fierce fires of passion, and aided the impression by smoking a pipe almost incessantly. When he had recovered from his surprise at the announcement that Alexander was the son of Matthew Silverman, he was almost exuberantly glad to welcome him into the great brotherhood.

Alexander served his novitiate nobly. He liked the members, most of whom were railwaymen from the works, and he attended regularly at the weekly meetings of the club. The chief exercise of the club, apart from the private conversions worked by the members in their homes and on their friends, was the fortnightly open-air meeting held in the small square at the back of the Town Hall. At this meeting members of the club got upon a platform and let off the steam which still remained after their arguments in the clubroom. It was an admirable safety-valve, and did no one much harm, if it did but little good. To speak at one of these meetings became Alexander's ambition, and, although the competition for ten minutes to tell the world what was wrong with it, and make suggestions for putting it right, was keen, Alexander got his chance.

"Comrade Silverman"—Burnside addressed him formally one evening in the club— "the Selection Committee have decided that you shall be given an opportunity to speak at the great Anti-Dictatorship rally which we are to hold. You will be wanted to speak for ten minutes on the effect of Nazism on the Press, and to compare it with the effect of Socialism on the Press."

Alexander so far forgot himself as to let out a wild hooray.

* * *

The vocalist stepped forward from the band and began to croon something about love in bloom, and the players settled to their instruments with well-fed, seraphic smiles about their lips, as though they had just enjoyed a good dinner and had no fear of indigestion. The lights in the hall died to a glimmer, and on the dance-floor the couples moved around in a coloured whorl, like a mass of spring petals caught in a gentle whirlpool. A spot-light, probing, rude, went stiffly, jerkily across the floor, stopping now and again as it caught a couple and then following them for a while as though it were a lonely white shadow longing for a sponsor.

"This," said Loraine suddenly, and in a louder voice than she intended, "is the stupidest, dullest dance I've ever been to."

The remark not only shocked Philip, her partner, but it shocked the one or two people who heard her. Their first reaction was to hush at her for her sacrilege in breaking the spell of the sentimental moan that was filling the hall, and their second to contradict her, for this was the night of the annual Swanbridge Rugby Football Club ball, and what dance was ever gayer in Swanbridge than the Rugby ball? Loraine herself had often said it was the brightest dance of the year, and the police, who were only occasionally wanted, seemed to be attracted to it, constable after constable, from eleven onwards until three—until, in fact, the bar closed down.

Philip did not immediately show his surprise. As Loraine dropped her arms from him and began to leave the floor, he followed her.

"What do you want to do? Shall I get you an ice?"

"No—thank you. Get my wrap, will you, and let's get outside and have some fresh air."

Philip accepted the rebuff meekly, for when Loraine refused an ice he knew she could not be herself. "What is the matter with you?" he enquired gently, as they went down the Town Hall steps. "You've been terribly moody lately, haven't you?"

"Have I?"

"Yes, I think you have."

"Then I have. So what?"

"Nothing. Only I just wondered why. After all—"

"Oh, shut up, Philip. Why do you keep on?"

"I wasn't keeping on. After all—"

"There you go again. Don't keep saying 'after all.' "

"All right." He was silent, keeping pace with her and wondering why she looked straight before her, never giving him a glance. Lately—it was undeniable—she had changed. She was more imperious; at times she was rude to him; and once or twice when he had called for her by arrangement he had been told that she was out. Where she went she never said.

"You're fine company," Loraine said after a time. "Why don't you say something? Things are dull enough as it is without you trying to make them duller."

"What do you want me to do?" He spoke sharply, forgetting his habitual tolerance.

"Oh, what do I want you to do?" Loraine was exasperated. Really, Philip could at times be the dullest of people. "Do something, say something. You just walk about with me, answering 'Yes' and 'No' to my questions, and doing what I tell you as though you were some little slave-boy looking after an African queen. I don't know; you don't seem to be alive to me."

"Oh, come. That's a bit strong, Loraine. After all—"

"Philip! If you say that again I'll go straight home. In fact, I think—"

Loraine stopped speaking as a loud voice came booming across to her. In their talk they had wandered round to the Town Hall Square, and she saw that on the other side a meeting was in progress. It was the voice of the man addressing the meeting which had attracted her attention. It was Comrade Burnside.

"And now, fellow workers, comrades and ladies"—this last was for the gratification of a few young girls, and an elderly lady who was slightly deaf and was there under the impression that it was a meeting of the Anti-Vivisectionists' League—"I will call upon my very good friend and comrade, one who will tell you what he tells you because he knows what he speaks about, a man not used to mincin' his words, and one who ..." Comrade Burnside hesitated; then, realising that the sentence had got the better of him, he announced in a voice that echoed all over the square: "Comrade Silverman!"

There was a husky mutter that might have been taken for approval, had it not been obvious that a great many of the spectators were Fascists. Loraine saw Alexander, flushing with pride and some trepidation, step on to the platform, his hair deliberately a little tousled and his dark features riding above a brilliant red tie.

Alexander cleared his throat, looked as many of the crowd as came within his direct vision squarely in the eye, and said, "Comrades and others ..."

"Well, I'm——" Philip turned to Loraine. "It's Alexander!"

"Yes, it's Alexander," she said, and at the sight of Alexander's eager young face, his wild, happy eyes as he addressed the crowd, she found herself filled with a swift hatred of him and herself, a hatred that passed almost at once and left her remembering Swing talking from the hall inside. "Come along," she cried, taking Philip by the arm. "I don't want to stop here, listening to him make a fool of himself." And, although he would have liked to remain to hear Alexander, Philip allowed himself to be pulled away. For one moment he found himself wondering, in a spasm of disloyalty, whether Loraine wasn't more blasted nuisance then she was worth.

* * *

Mr. Samuel Hardwick was an Alderman of the Swanbridge Borough Council, a jovial Rotarian, a fairly wealthy business man, and, at heart, a very good fellow; but none of these honours or qualities could afford him the forgiveness of the censorious head waiter of the Three Feathers when he pushed his chair back from his table and, after wiping his mouth with his serviette, belched refinedly.

"No, Jack," he said to his companion. "I think you're on the wrong tack. If you insist, I'll do it for you. But I say I think you'd be wiser to leave well alone."

"Fiddle-de-dee, Sammy, my boy. I've knocked about a bit more than you have, and I know the world. Yes, it's a rummy place, but no one has ever been able to say that James H. Brown ever found it too much for him."

"Talking about being too much for one reminds me of the story about the honeymoon couple that went to the Lake District for—"

"Yes, I know, Sammy boy, but you tell me that after you've telephoned for me. Go on now, or I'll make you pay for this dinner."

Mr. Hardwick, his laugh the deep note of a bass violin, heaved himself from his chair and waddled like a duck from the room, while his friend carefully trimmed the end of a match-stick into a point and pierced the end of a cigar. He sat beaming at the ceiling and blowing clouds of smoke, and it was easy to see that he was contemplating some satisfying prospect of business done, or about to be done, successfully.

After a while Mr. Hardwick came back.

"Well?" Mr. Brown came out of his reverie.

"He wasn't at his house," explained Mr. Hardwick, puffing into his chair. "They said he was working at his office, so I took the liberty of ringing him there."

"And what did he say?"

"He said he didn't usually see people so late. I explained about your going off early and only having popped down for a few hours, and he said all right. He'll see you in an hour's time. You know, Jimmy, I think you're going to unnecessary—"

"Not again, Sammy boy. Not again. Here, waiter, bring us two more brandies. Now then, you behave."

Mr. Hardwick withdrew his protest, contenting himself with the thought that it was really not his business.

* * *

Matthew looked around the door of the reporters' room and saw Harold Spencer working at his table. "Will you be here for some time yet?" he asked. Harold looked up from his work and nodded.

"Good. There's a Mr. Brown coming to see me here in about an hour's time. I wish you'd let him in when he knocks."

"Certainly, Mr. Silverman."

"Thank you, Spencer. By the way"—Matthew halted—"I'm glad to see that you're settling down so well to things here. I suppose you don't want to go back to the drapery business now?"

"Not me, Mr. Silverman. Now I'm in I'm stopping in until the last possible moment. My dad would like me to go back, though."

"Your father?"

"Yes." Harold hesitated. He knew from Alexander a little about George and Matthew's desire to have an elder son in the *Messenger*, and he wondered whether he ought to say anything about his own father. Then he looked up at Matthew, saw the mild grey eyes, his scholarly stoop, his half-frowning, kindly face, and he knew that Matthew would understand. "Yes, you see, Mr. Silverman, he owns a big drapery business in Weston-super-Mare, and he wanted me to go into business."

"Did you leave Hardwick's against his wishes?" Matthew put the question tersely. This young man had made him the instrument, he thought, of his own desires, bad used him to wreck parental wishes. Harold's answer reassured him.

"No, sir. He had always said I might go if I could get a job on a newspaper. Though, of course, he would have preferred me to stay in the business, and I know that if ever I wanted to I could go back … but I shan't."

"Your father is a very generous and wise man, Spencer. You're lucky to be his son."

"Yes, I think so, sir."

"Don't forget to let Mr. Brown in." Matthew was gone, leaving Harold staring at the proofs of a charity subscription list.

How stupid, thought Matthew, as he sat down in his chair. How very stupid I have been. Until then he had imagined that he was the only father who had seen the wisdom of giving way to his son. He had been so immersed in his own trouble that he had not realised that it was a trouble common to many fathers. There was something almost ruthless about young men these days. They wanted a thing and got it, and anything in their way had to be swept aside, even a father; and the disturbing fact was that the fathers deserved to be swept aside. Did they? Yes, he decided they did, unless they had the very good sense, as he had, to step aside. And Mr. Spencer? He tried to picture him;

perhaps wandering about his deserted shop at night, wondering why he bothered to carry on with all the work and worry when it was to so little purpose. And there was no younger son there to take the place of the elder.... And he, Matthew Silverman, had been the means of doing this to Mr. Spencer. He had helped bring upon another man the same misfortune which had fallen to him. Harold Spencer was going to be a good journalist, and, if the *Messenger* turned him out, some other paper would one day take him. He sat back in his chair and carefully packed his pipe. What a pity, he mused, what a pity George had decided that he wanted to enter the Church. Although he would have disowned it, at the back of his mind Matthew held the common enough opinion that those who became preachers were often enough those who felt themselves incapable of the moil and toil of a harder life. They sought the Church as a refuge, and grouped themselves under its standard, not defiantly, but diffidently. It seemed impossible that George could wish to be like that ... George would not be like that, of course.

When Harold Spencer knocked on the door to usher in Mr. James H. Brown, Matthew's pipe was still unlit and he was regarding the painting of John Silverman with a fixed, unseeing stare. The entry of Spencer brought him back to earth.

"Thank you, Spencer," he called as Harold left them. "Now, Mr. Brown, if you'll please take a seat."

"That's good of you, sir. Very good of you."

"Not at all. As an editor it is my duty to be available whenever I am wanted."

"Still, I guess a man is entitled to some time for himself, eh?" Mr. Brown laughed, and fished in his pocket for his cigar-case. "Smoke, Mr. Silverman? Oh, I see you've got a pipe. Never could stand one myself; always going out. Guess you're wondering who I am, and why I've come bothering you at this hour."

"Mr. Hardwick said that—"

"Ha, Sammy Hardwick. Nice fellow, capable business man, and, between ourselves, a bit fatter than he ought to be for his age. Good living and not enough exercise. Always believe in exercise, myself. May surprise you to know, Mr. Silverman, that I was born in this town. Yes, I lived the first eleven years of my life here. Remember the *Messenger* and your father very well. Went to London from here, and since then I've been all over the place. Yes, James H. Brown has travelled since those days."

Matthew, slightly amused at the other's manner, wondered if he knew that he talked something like a film business man.

"Well, what can I do for you, Mr. Brown?"

"Now that's what I call a blunt question, and a good question. No beating about the bush with you, I can see that. What can you do for me, eh? And what can I do for you, perhaps, eh? Now, let's get down to business. You know that the council are planning to build a lot of new houses in this town—a new estate, in fact—to house most of the factory and railway workers who are living down behind the gasworks."

"I do know it," put in Matthew quickly. "Those slums behind the gasworks have been a disgrace, a pollution in this town, too long already. In fact, it was largely because of the strong attitude taken by the *Messenger*, and the efforts of one or two councillors, who are my personal friends, that the scheme was instituted."

"Good. There speaks a man of action. When you see a thing that wants doing, you go for it bald-headed. I like a man like that; you know where you are. I think those slums are pretty awful, too. I remember—but we won't waste our time telling stories. The point is—where is that estate going to be?"

"Where is it going to be?" As he repeated the question, Matthew found himself wondering what it mattered to Mr. Brown where the site would be, and why he should think that he was the proper person to seek the information from. If he wanted to know, why did he not go to the council? "Well, that rather depends upon the council, doesn't it?" he suggested.

"Yes, it does. It depends entirely upon the council. Listen, Mr. Silverman; there are only two places where the estates can be built, and you, and every man in this town, know where they are. In the first place, there is the suggested site on what is known as Pennyquick fields to the north of this town on the London road, and the other suggested site is on the two large fields now used as a children's recreation ground and allotments which lie off to the left of High Street on the way to the river. You know it well, of course, because your orchard wall comes out to the back of the ground. Your wife would be pretty pleased, I imagine, about having a council housing estate at the back of her house?"

"Nothing of the kind will happen," exclaimed Matthew indignantly.

"But it might. The council own that land, and there is nothing to stop them putting up houses there."

"Oh, yes, there is, Mr. Brown. There's the weight of public opinion in this town, the feelings of a good many of the councillors, and the power of this paper to stop them. The only site is the Pennyquick one. Look at the situation fairly. This town is growing; in another fifty years there will have been more than one estate built around it, and by then those fields, in what is almost the centre of the town, will be a godsend for children and grown-ups."

"That may be so, Mr. Silverman. In fact, it is so; but you forget that there is a considerable body on the council who look at it from the financial point of view. They own the recreation ground. To build there will be an economy; because to build at Pennyquick fields means they must first buy the land. Now listen, Mr. Silverman. This is where two smart people like ourselves may be able to do one another some good. For all your high-sounding talk I know you don't want that housing estate at the back of your nice house. It would depreciate its value and make things uncomfortable for you. And I don't want it there because I happen to own Pennyquick fields, and should be glad to sell it to the council at a fair price." Mr. Brown winked roguishly at Matthew and waited. Here, he could see, was a man who understood life, a man who could put forward a nice platform speech about the position of a housing estate, giving every reason but the one in his heart, and who would, for a consideration—this would have to be arranged in a nice way—see that his newspaper went all out for an estate at Pennyquick fields. Some people—extraordinary folk, mused Mr. Brown—found life a complex affair. Personally it had always treated him well, so long as he had obeyed the rules. Mr. Silverman was all right.

Matthew looked at Mr. Brown. It was as though he were seeing him through the wrong end of a telescope, a minute, bug-like figure squatting at the end of a long tunnel. Then the bug-like figure swam down the tunnel towards him, growing larger as the perspective decreased, until Mr. Brown was sitting before him in the office chair.

"Bribery and corruption, eh?"

"Come, come!" Mr. Brown started back, his whole sense of dignity and propriety outraged. "You can't say that."

"I can't say that? I—I, Matthew Silverman, the editor of the *Messenger*—can't say that to you, when you come into my room and deliberately insult me? Why, man, if I weren't naturally of a pacific nature, and this didn't happen to be the twentieth century, I should have been justified in throwing you out into the street. Do you realise what you are suggesting?" Matthew began to forget his pacific nature and, striding round to Mr. Brown, stood threateningly over him. "Do you realise that you have been trying to bribe me? Presumably you judge all men by yourself. Trying to bribe me!" The statement of the offence quickened Matthew's anger. "This is the *Messenger*," he declared, "and for nearly a hundred years the editors of this paper have been above suspicion. What we have considered good for this town we have advocated, not letting our private feelings or personal desires halt us in any way, and now you come wriggling into my office and suggest, because you own the land at Pennyquick fields and because I may not care to see council houses behind my house, that I use the power of the *Messenger* to make sure it doesn't happen. How much were you going to offer me to do this?" The last question came coldly and shrewdly, and Mr. Brown, still trying to make up his mind, grasped it hopefully. He was, he decided, dealing with a very astute man.

"Gosh, you had me fooled for a moment. I thought about fifty—"

"Guineas," snapped Matthew. "That's a hard bargain."

"Fifty guineas, and write the cheque now."

"Now?"

"Yes, now!"

"All right, all right," Mr. Brown said soothingly, and he drew out his cheque-book and made out the payment.

"Thank you," said Matthew, taking the cheque and sitting down. He felt calmer now. "Now attend to me a moment, Mr. Brown. I want you to listen carefully. You see that painting up there?" He pointed to John. "That was my great-grandfather. He founded this newspaper and died for it, and the others with him; they put all they knew into it. In this town the *Messenger* has a reputation which no one has ever questioned, and no one is ever going to question it, not while a Silverman has anything to do with it. This town wants a new estate, and that estate is going to be at Pennyquick fields—but not for the reason you think. Pennyquick fields is the best place, and if it possibly lies in the power of the *Messenger* to make them have it there, then we shall do everything we can towards that end. But if the recreation ground behind my house were the best place, and if it meant that my house would be isolated in a sea of council houses, the peace destroyed, its value deflated, I should still, as editor of the *Messenger*, do all I possibly could to see that the estate was built on the recreation ground. You want the estate at Pennyquick fields because you own the land and would make a nice profit from the sale, and you came here tonight hoping to persuade me into espousing your cause—for a consideration." Matthew waved the cheque. "You could have saved yourself time and money by stopping away, for I had already intended to support the Pennyquick fields estate. I shall pay this cheque into the Swanbridge Hospital as a charity donation, and the receipt will be sent to you in due course. And now, Mr. Brown, you will oblige me by leaving this office as quickly as you can, and, if you ever come inside it again, I promise you that, although I am an old man, I shall do my best to kick you out. Good night!" And Matthew, partly to cover his own embarrassment and partly as a last defiant gesture, strode to the window and opened it, letting in a cold sweep of night air.

When he turned round, Mr. Brown had gone, for he was not altogether lacking in sense. Matthew sat down at his table, wrote a suitable note to the secretary of the hospital, and put it, with the cheque, in an envelope.

"You might," he said to Spencer as he went out, "drop that at the hospital as you go by on your way home." He handed the letter to the reporter.

Although he had managed to control his first outbreak and speak calmly to Mr. Brown, Matthew felt the whole of his being was jangled and vibrant from his passion, and he knew that the only thing to quieten himself was a walk in the fresh air. He put on his hat and slipped across the road, intending to cut behind the Town Hall and hit the path by the river and walk home by a roundabout route. The first thing he saw as he rounded the corner of the Town Hall was his son, Alexander, standing upon a platform before a mob of people, shaking his fist in the air and uttering violent cries.

The only public speaking which Alexander had ever done was in the mild debates of the Swanbridge Grammar School Debating Society, which lengthily involved itself in such turgid arguments as "Should Women Work?" "Does Civilisation make us any Happier?" and "Should Games be Compulsory?" In these Alexander had thought himself brilliant. He had exploded the theory that women should not work, tempering his wisdom by referring offhandedly at times to Huxley's essay on "Emancipation—Black and White." The aggregate of human happiness, he had maintained, against considerable opposition, was static, and unrelated to any advance in the civilisation of a race and, although he had not at the time read them, he had managed to bring in Samuel Butler and William Morris to help him; and as for the debate on school games, he had loftily refused to participate, declaring that none but an idiot would ever want to make games compulsory.

He prepared his speech for the open-air meeting with a great deal of care, and studded it with a liberal jewelling of statistics. To the audience of Alison he delivered it for practice in his room at Khartum, and was considerably embarrassed the following morning when Alison, catching at a remark of Matthew's as he scanned the paper, had said proudly, "Hitler and Mussolini are no longer buffoons escaped from a …from a comic film. They are foul, devouring monsters." Loyally she would not, despite a momentary inquisition, divulge the source of her political knowledge, and Matthew had gone to his office a little worried by the child's precocity. At the back of his mind was an old-fashioned notion that precocious children died early or turned out to be very dull adults.

"Comrades, and others!" Alexander, his stomach melting from him and his tongue thick and heavy in his mouth, forced the words out, and the crowd, realising from his tremulous voice and youthful appearance that this was probably his first public speech, accorded him the respectful silence which was due to an unknown quality. Alexander took their silence and respectful attitude to come from the spell which the magic of his voice had put upon them; at his first wild clarion call they had been forced to acknowledge the domination that flowed from him in a form of personal magnetism.

For the most part they were a peaceful crowd; the old lady who thought it was an anti-vivisectionist meeting; the young girls who scarcely heard the speakers but kept their eyes on the youths; a good sprinkling of Socialists and Labour men who needed no conversion to the point of view of the speakers; an equal sprinkling of Fascists who had come to see that the fair name of Fascism was not sullied without some remonstrance, vocal to begin with and physical if it proved to be necessary; one or two impartial spirits who could find virtuous elements in both parties; three small boys who should have been in bed but whose mothers were at the pictures, ignorant of their sons' crepuscular freedom; and a handful of sturdy sceptics who loved a meeting, derived their chief joy from heckling, and preferred an M.P. explaining away the Means Test to a soft seat and two hours of Hollywood flim-flam.

They all, even the small boys, recognised the novice, and maintained a respectful attention for a while. Alexander felt his stomach at last establish friendly relations with the rest of his body, heard his voice take a firmer, even deeper note, and delivered himself evenly of the fine sentences and staggering statistics which he had prepared.

"… and that," he said, "was the state of affairs in Italy and Germany before the Fascist and Nazi regimes. But today, what do we find?" He paused to let the sentence, this turning-point in his speech, this herald of his diatribe, sink home.

"Dunno," came the voice of one of the sceptics, recovering his manhood again. "Suppose you tell us; you're doing the speakin'."

There was a titter at this, and one of the Socialists shouted, "Shame! Give the man a chance!" Alexander took no notice, other than to turn a withering smile on the interrupter.

"Right, I will tell you," he cried, and proceeded, with the help of more statistics, to explain just what the position of newspapers was under Hitler and Mussolini. The picture he outlined had Grand Guignol qualities, and after a time he found himself wandering from statistics, losing track of his own mental notes, and speaking straight from the heart with all the impassioned sincerity and bias of youth expounding an ideal.

"Today, in those countries, no man dare speak what is in his mind. The Press is muzzled and the people ignorant of the true facts. That's dictatorship! There are your fine Hitlers and Mussolinis, men afraid of the voice of public conscience, men who have to put their own flesh and blood, their own countrymen, in bondage to bolster up the weak edifice of their own pomps and vanities."

"Hear, hear," cried one of the impartialists. Hitler and Mussolini, after all, were foreigners.

"Today those men are no longer platitudinous buffoons escaped from some Silly Symphony film—"

"Listen to him! He's swallowed the dictionary!" cried a Fascist, whose motto was the old one of sticks and stones may break bones but hard words never hurt. And Comrade Burnside, fidgeting beneath Alexander because the boy had exceeded his ten minutes and there seemed no way of stopping him, thought that this use of long words was wrong, not fitted to the audience. But Alexander, the bit well between his teeth, plunged on.

"They are no longer comic figures exciting our laughter and pity; they have become monsters—uncouth, gigantic monsters—devouring their own kind and wallowing in rape and pillage—"

"No rape for Hitler," yelled a sceptic, determined on fair play, but Alexander turned him like a fisherman heading a salmon from deep water.

"... the rape of public confidence and the pillage of honourable institutions." Comrade Burnside breathed freely once more. Sex was a dangerous topic since the Russian Revolution.

"And now," went on Alexander, "England begins to follow the way of these dictatorship countries. There is a Fascist Party today in England. At the moment it is in the first stage of all such parties; it is still a comic film, its leaders and followers the prancing puppets of their own misshapen destinies—"

"Who says they are?" The question came, united, from several of the Fascists. With true British equanimity they had heard Hitler and Mussolini maligned—after all, this was a country of free speech—but when it came to their own party, honour demanded a protest.

"I say they are!" Alexander shouted back.

"And he's right!" This from a squat, hirsute railway worker whose favourite trick when the fair visited the recreation ground on Bank Holidays was the cracking of coconuts in his bare hands.

"Well, I says he bloody well ain't right!" came back the challenge from an equally burly Fascist, his chest thrust forward, pouter-pigeon fashion, under his black shirt.

"The time has come for all honest, free-thinking citizens to rise and demand the extermination of these pests like rats ..."

"Rats!" The Fascists could stand much, but not that last insult, and their anger broke out in a roar. The crowd surged, and the nut-cracking Socialist, seeing that the time was ripe for all good men to come to the aid of the party, calmly swiped the leader of the Fascists on the jaw and, as he fell, jumped on him. Comrade Burnside, who above all loved the arts of peace, cowered back under the shelter of the rostrum, but an enraged Fascist, who had come prepared, took advantage of the clear target offered by his melanic profile and slung a mildewed orange at it. The fruit, well decomposed, disintegrated over Burnside's face, and he forgot his pacific intentions and leapt into the fray, muttering to himself.

At his feet, Alexander watched the orderly crowd change into a milling mob. The Socialists attacked the Fascists, the sceptics marooned in the melée took the very wise course of punching indiscriminately at all within their reach, while the impartialists, who saw some good even in the worst elements, danced around the outskirts yelling unheard but excellent advice to the combatants.

Alexander deprecated the fight. It showed a lack of intelligence, he thought, an illogical irritableness with just criticism. He raised his voice to call the elements to order.

"Friends! Comrades! Let us not squabble like children."

What an earnest young man, thought the deaf lady, edging away from the crowd; such an excellent thing to find one so young defending the rights of poor dumb creatures; but why were all the men fighting like that? It was rude when the boy was speaking.

The crowd took no notice of Alexander. They had forgotten him. The conflict became a pancratium; some couples sparred in professional pugilistic fashion, determined, it seemed, to keep a decorum even in their brawl; others hung in groups, wrestling, kicking, and rolling ...

Alexander eyed them, fascinated; a surge of pride rising within him as he realised that he had precipitated this brawl. Then he decided that this was the time for action, not words. He crouched on the platform, taking advantage of his elevated position, waiting for one of the milling Fascists to come within reach. A blackshirt swam out of the welter, eddied below him, and Alexander sprang. The man moved at the last moment, and Alexander missed, landing on all fours from the impetus of his jump. He straightened up and dashed forward towards the mob, and as he did so a heavy hand fell upon his shoulder.

"Eh!" He swung round, aiming a savage blow. A hand caught his arm restrainingly, and he found himself looking into the round, plump face of a police constable.

"Now, now, Mr. Silverman," the policeman chided him gently, like a mother remonstrating with a pettish child. "Don't you go striking the law. Come on now, you don't want to get mixed up in that unmannerly business. What would your father say?"

"Damn my father!" snapped Alexander, wriggling to get free. The policeman held him firmly and laughed. Already from the Town Hall other policemen had appeared and were wading into the fight, plucking out the fiercest contestants and shaking them quickly into quietness.

"Oh, no; you come with me!"

Alexander was borne off, protesting, indignant, and yet half pleased that he was going to be arrested. For the first time, he felt, he was really in the heart of the working-class movement; this was the beginning of the uprising of the masses.

Without a word the policeman conducted him past the Town Hall and across the High Street towards St. Dunstan's Church.

"Hey, this isn't the way to the police station."

"Quite right, me lad. This is the way home—for you. Now go on." They were not far from Khartum. "Go on—skip off and get to bed." The policeman released him and gave him a push towards the house.

"I'll be damned if I'll leave my friends!"

The policeman laughed. "They'll be all right, Mr. Silverman. Now go on, go on." He shooed him away—a cottage wife herding geese— and Alexander realised that he stood no chance of getting back to the square.

"All right, all right, you big slop. But one day you and the ruling classes who employ you will regret this." He strode off, muttering to himself, and was annoyed to hear the jovial laugh of the policeman behind him.

The policeman turned and walked back towards the High Street. On the corner he met Matthew. He stopped and touched his helmet to him.

"Did you get him, constable?" Matthew asked. "Yes, sir. He was annoyed, but I took him home and sent him to bed like a good boy."

"Thank you, Grimes." Matthew smiled at the man, and added, "He's very young yet, you know, and all youngsters go a bit wild at times. I didn't want him mixed up in that crowd."

"Oh, that's all right, sir. There ain't no harm in him. Just high spirits. Got a boy like him myself, sir. If there's a fight going on anywhere, he just has to join in. He gets it from his mother, I'm afraid. She's Irish. Glad to help you, Mr. Silverman. Good night, sir." He hitched up his belt and walked off.

Matthew went on towards Khartum. He had forgotten Mr. James Brown; all he could remember was a vivid impression of Alexander waving a fist in the air, shouting, "Rats! Rats!" while a hundred men squirmed and fought around him. Somehow the picture was not so disquieting to him as he imagined it should be. It was youth, he supposed. His own youth had not been like that. In those days people had seemed more contented; they worked hard; they had no over-reaching ambitions, and saw themselves less as young gods and more as raw youngsters, a little afraid of life and eager to learn. He smiled and then frowned, telling himself this was no time to smile. In the morning he would talk to Alexander. As he entered the drive, he looked up to see a light in Alexander's room. After he had locked up, he stood at the bottom of the stairs that twisted to the room, debating whether he should go to the boy. A faint, intermittent tapping of a typewriter stopped him. He could guess what Alexander was doing, and he smiled again to himself and went happily to bed.

XI

Largest Net Sales in the County.

Swanbridge Messenger (Advertisement)

Miss Adelaide Silverman was a very active woman. She allowed none of her seventy-two years to interfere more than she could help with her activities. "Age," she often said—and when she said it there was a great deal of her brother James in her voice—"is no excuse for incompetence." She was a small woman, with a great deal of dignity and a certain likeness in face and figure to Queen Victoria, of whom she had been, and still was, a great admirer, regarding her as a human pandect of the spartan Victorian virtues that made happy families and contented empires.

Alison, while she had been staying with her, had found that she had a very lively sense of humour and a very proper opinion of the place of children in a household. She stood no nonsense about fundamentals such as the time for bed, eating one's food, and respect for elders, yet she was a daring player of charades, a convincing teller of somewhat moral stories, and very good company. Alison liked her, and when she told her so, Aunt Adelaide was not in the least surprised, and had replied that it was no more than she had expected, since she tried never to do anything which would make people dislike her, and that if Alison wanted to get any happiness from life she had better adopt the same altruistic principle. Miss Peters liked her, too, only she wished she would not cheat at piquet, which they played every evening. Miss Peters often wanted to cheat herself. A strong sense of rectitude stopped her from doing so, and she privately thought that Aunt Adelaide ought also to control her wicked desire. But custom had turned to habit in Aunt Adelaide, and she could no more help herself from cheating at cards than she could prevent herself from quarrelling with Uncle Abner.

"I am going," said Aunt Adelaide primly over the knitted tea-cosy one morning, "into Swanbridge to see Matthew. Would you care to come with me for the drive? You can amuse yourself by doing some shopping for me while I talk to him, and then we will have lunch with Mabel at Khartum. I shall telephone her after breakfast and, no doubt, stampede her into her kitchen in the flighty way she has when I announce my coming. For the daughter of a vicar she has surprisingly little poise. *Mais si elle n'est que bonne ménagère il y a d'excellents traits dans son caractère.*" She held it that every woman of breeding should be able to point a sentence with some French.

"I should like to come with you," said Miss Peters, who recognised that she was wanted to go to Swanbridge. The word "drive" as used by Aunt Adelaide meant no lordly progression in a private motor-car. She had no car of her own, saying that she had not enough use to warrant its expense.

At ten o'clock they caught the local bus outside the village post-office. They took their seats unobtrusively, but when the conductor came for their tickets Aunt Adelaide paid him the money and said, "I want no recurrence of the dangerous driving which happened on my last drive to Swanbridge, conductor. You will please inform the driver of that. I have, as you know," she turned to Miss Peters and added, "no objection to these self-propelled carriages, but they should not be allowed to become instruments of death."

"You'd better go easy until we get to Swanbridge, 'Arry," the conductor warned the driver.

" 'Ow's that?"

"Got Miss Silverman be'ind. You know what she is!"

"Ho!" The driver waved a small car on with the utmost courtesy, and edged elaborately around a pedal-cyclist. He knew Miss Silverman all right.

Matthew was not exactly pleased to see Aunt Adelaide. It was press day; he had a lot to do; and when she entered his room unannounced he had been about to send for Alexander to lecture him on his disgusting behaviour of the previous evening.

"Why, good morning, Aunt Adelaide. This is a pleasant surprise," he said, rising from his chair and piloting her to a seat near the window. He knew of old that it was fatal to seat her near his desk;

otherwise, the whole time she was talking she would be fiddling and playing with the papers on the desk, asking the most absurd and irrelevant questions.

"Then it will be the first time you have been pleasantly surprised by me, Matthew Silverman. Why don't you speak the truth these days? You know you aren't glad to see me. You know it's press day, and you have probably not got half your pages made up, and even if it wasn't press day you still wouldn't be glad to see me—and you know why." She paused for a moment, fixing him with a severe frown, conscious a little of her regal attitude, her black gown spread out about the chair, her white hand very firm on the handle of her umbrella. "What is all this I hear?" she questioned coldly.

"All what, Adelaide?"

"Don't procrastinate, Matthew. I have been hearing the most disquieting rumours."

"My dear Adelaide." Matthew pulled the proof of one of the sports pages towards him and pretended to scan it. He knew what she meant, but he resented her coming to him in this inquisitorial frame of mind, though she seldom visited him in any other. She was the head of the Silverman clan, and he, to her, was a small boy entrusted with the care of an elaborate and expensive business, which, if her sex had been different, she would have been running. "Rumour is a lying jade."

"Don't try to fob me off with your silly quotations, Matthew. I've often told you how I dislike them in your weekly chit-chats." She hoped that this slighting reference to his editorials would rouse him.

But Matthew was not to be drawn. "My dear Adelaide, you do seem to have a most preposterous view of my editorials. Surely they are the most valuable contribution to the paper?"

"We're wandering from the point, Matthew. Since you lost your head and let George go into the Church you seem to have developed a most surprising lack of initiative. There almost seems to be something furtive in your manner. The Silvermans may often have been uncommunicative, never furtive. What I came here to find out is—"

"And what did Aunt Adelaide come here to find?" They both turned at the voice. Abner was standing in the doorway, at his heels the huge Alsatian.

"Some people take the trouble to have themselves announced," said Aunt Adelaide coldly, forgetting her own entry; "and almost everyone would have the natural good manners not to intrude upon a private conversation. *Il est évident que vous n'avez pas de savoir vivre.*"

"*Tu parles français comme une vache espagnole. Il donne la comédie aux gens,*" smiled Abner genially. At some time in his life he had lived long in Paris, and he was always pleased when Aunt Adelaide opened her attack thus, for it gave him an immeasurable advantage. He walked over to the table and took a chair; the dog couched itself on the rug at his feet.

"I hate dogs," said Aunt Adelaide. "Can't you leave that smelly beast outside?"

"Why"—Matthew felt it was time he interfered— "must you two always quarrel like this whenever you meet? It is scarcely civilised, you know."

"Hold your tongue, Matthew. I was not quarrelling. I was making a perfectly reasonable request."

"Pelang stays here," said Abner. "In some company one needs a bodyguard." Abner patted Pelang's head. Aunt Adelaide looked at it with loathing. She regarded a kennel as the proper place for dogs; this practice of bringing them into the house was nauseating.

"The dog's all right," Matthew tried to conciliate her.

"Never mind the dog," said Abner. "No one has answered my question about what Aunt Adelaide came here to find out."

"She hasn't told me yet."

"You know perfectly well what I came about, Matthew," snapped Aunt Adelaide; "and Abner there knows as well, unless he's a bigger fool than I take him to be. I've been hearing nasty tales about the *Messenger*, and I came to see if they were true. Not that I believe they are, but these rumours were serious enough to justify some investigation. After all, Matthew, you are the editor of the paper, and, except for one unfortunate period during the war"—she smiled sweetly at Abner as she said this—"have been for the last twenty-four years, but I am as much interested in it as you are. I am a Silverman, and as long as there are Silvermans the *Messenger* must be their concern. Abner here, of course, may not appreciate fully our natural family concern for the paper—"

Abner started to protest, but Adelaide went on:

"Even he, distantly related as he is, obviously feels some alarm at the rumours. That, I presume, is why he has come here today."

"Yes, that is why I have come. What did you expect me to do? Sit at home twiddling my thumbs? Listen to me, madam. When I married your sister, my dear wife, God rest her soul, I became part of this family, and I watched Jacob breaking his heart and body to make the *Messenger* a fine paper. I found him at the bottom of those stairs on a day I shall never forget. And I helped James when he took over, and no man could have been sorrier than I when he went and did that damn-fool trick of standing in the rain and catching his death. Matthew here knows that when I was wanted I helped him, and for all your base insinuations, madam, I ran this paper during the war years as well as it has ever been run before or since, and I was a proud man to be asked to stand godfather for young George, thinking of the day … Still, that's beside the point. What does matter is that anything which threatens the *Messenger* threatens a vital part of my life. And I know how to deal with threats, madam!"

Isobel, thought Aunt Adelaide, had been helpless against this man. Even now he was powerful, and in those, his young days, few girls could have withstood his headstrong determination.

"And the rumours are that the sales of the *Messenger* are falling off? Is that it?" asked Matthew, knowing it was so.

Aunt Adelaide understood his tone, and a warm feeling of sympathy for Matthew thawed the harshness from her manner for a moment. "Now, Matthew, no one is blaming you for that."

"Of course not!" Abner thumped his stick on the floor, and the dog looked up at him, its ears pricked.

"Nevertheless, they have fallen off," Matthew went on. "I haven't said anything to you before because I didn't think it was serious. Even now it is not so serious as you are probably imagining. Our peak circulation is roughly thirty-five thousand. That was in 1932. Since then it has fluctuated between that figure and thirty-two thousand. Never below and never above. The district we serve has become more populous in places, and we have shared that increase with the *Courier*."

"A cheap, nasty rag," barked Abner, and then, for the benefit and mystification of Aunt Adelaide, he added, "*Une feuille de chou!*"

"For the last two months," Matthew went on, "our figures have shown a gradual trend downwards. At first I thought it was only a phase; that we should pick up. Well, to be frank, we haven't picked up. It's distressing, but there you are. Our circulation now is about thirty thousand. That isn't ruinous. Our production isn't affected alarmingly. The only unpleasant aspect is that advertisers naturally want value for their money, and you can't go on charging the same advertisement rates for a circulation of thirty thousand as you can for a circulation of thirty-four to thirty-five thousand, and you know that advertisements are our life-blood. The shares of the paper are held entirely by the family, and the majority of them by you two, so it is right that you should know the exact position."

"We're not thinking of that, Matt. The question is—why?"

"Why?"

"Yes, why have the sales gone down? I can see that it isn't bringing us to the point of bankruptcy. It's a question of prestige. The *Messenger* has always been the best paper around here, the only paper. And now it looks as though you're going to have to take second place—and the *Courier* takes our place, although it isn't even printed in the town."

"Where have the sales fallen off most? In any particular district?" asked Aunt Adelaide.

"No. I've analysed the figures, and the falling off is very evenly distributed. Frankly, I can't understand it. Nothing has happened to the quality of the paper. We still give all the news. We haven't changed our policy."

"And the *Courier* has taken our sales?"

"That I can't say definitely. You see, I know their figures—they produce them for their advertisers, as we have to. Undoubtedly they have increased lately, increased a lot. The reasons for this are not clear-cut. Farley has grown much lately; it's a fruit-growing district, and there are three canning factories in the town now which weren't there a year or two ago. Their sales have gone up with their increased population, but they have pretty certainly taken away some of our customers ... a good many of our customers. The question is, why? As Abner says."

"Well, it's your job as editor to find that out, Matthew."

"I know. I haven't said that I can't. I haven't even admitted defeat and settled down to content myself with a circulation that would always be a reproach to me."

"The trouble is that people are too damned fickle these days," snorted Abner. "And the daily papers churn out such a spate of sensational stuff that they haven't the patience to read a good local newspaper. Well, we shall have to do something about it. I'm not going to see the *Messenger* play second fiddle to an illiterate rag like the *Courier*. You print bad enough bloomers in the *Messenger* at times, and sometimes things in bad taste; but the *Courier* …!" He stood up with a gesture of annoyance and prodded Pelang with his stick.

Adelaide sat, tight-lipped, watching the two men. She had a great confidence in Matthew, although she never cared to show it entirely and, admitting her own ignorance of the technical side of the paper, she believed in his ability. Abner, too, though she would certainly never admit it to him, was able enough. Between them they ought to be able to put things right.

"I'm going," she said curtly, "and I expect to hear what you propose to do. I may be only a woman, but I do not care to be disregarded …"

"Of course, my dear Adelaide. Are you going round to see Mabel?"

"I'm lunching at Khartum."

"Good," exclaimed Matthew, and decided that he would be too busy to go home for his lunch. He would have something sent in from the Three Feathers.

* * *

Although Aunt Adelaide and Uncle Abner had not even implied that the trouble of the sales was in any way his fault, Matthew felt that they somehow regarded him as the author of the misfortune. His was the ultimate responsibility for the whole newspaper, and—the thought saddened him—he was failing the *Messenger*. Perhaps he was getting old and losing his grip. After all, a man could not go on all his life with the same vitality, the same keenness of mind … Perhaps he was losing touch with the feelings of the people who had read his paper… . Perhaps …

He rang for Alexander.

"Ha," breathed Matthew, when his son entered, and his face lost its tired lines. "So here is our infant Karl Marx, our young Maxton, our budding Cripps. Well, and how does it feel to have the whole weight of the cares of the proletariat upon your shoulders?"

Alexander stared at his father, not fully understanding him. Matthew was amused at Alexander's bewilderment. Looking back to the escapade, he found little about it to concern him deeply. If Alexander needed an excuse, then his youth provided it, and Matthew realised that one had to make allowances for youth, and perhaps even wider allowances than usual when the youth was Alexander. Nevertheless, he considered that, for the good of the boy's morale, he should reprimand him. He found it distracting trying to hold the balance between his regulatory duty and his natural toleration and understanding.

"No reply, eh? A heart that's conscious of its guilt! Do you remember that in the first day you came into this office you stood where you now stand and I impressed upon you that one of the most important things in your life from that moment was that you should do nothing to bring the *Messenger* into disrepute?"

"Of course, I remember it, sir. What about it?"

"What about it!" Matthew raised his voice, because this he felt was the correct moment, and proceeded to tell Alexander what about it. He explained to Alexander his surprise at seeing him so far lost in decency as to become embroiled in a vulgar brawl with low associates in the public square of Swanbridge, and finally be borne away by a policeman who had fortunately followed the dictates of his good sense rather than his duty. "What do you mean by it?" he finished.

Alexander sighed to himself. What did he mean by it? He should have thought that it was obvious what he meant.

"Surely I have a right to lead my own political life?"

"Rights! Every young irresponsible hot-head quotes that word today as though it were some shibboleth that would pass him wherever he wanted to go. Rights! A man has no rights today, not the slightest, to do stupid, childish acts, any more than anyone has at any time had such rights. Wake up, my boy, wake up! You're living in a world of hard fact, not in a pretty paradise of your own creation. The sooner you learn that brawling in the street is not considered dignified or decent the better."

"Surely a man is allowed to express his opinions freely?" Alexander started his defence, and then broke off, conscious that nothing he could say would persuade Matthew to see his side.

"Think of others, Alexander. Imagine the feelings of your mother if you had been arrested for creating a public disturbance, her feelings and mine. I know that you young people like to think that the only responsibility parents have is the biological one of producing children. Unfortunately, it seems, most parents don't just have children—they love them; and that complicates all your modern logic. And now"— Matthew's eyes held more laughter than indignation as he went on— "now I'll have the report you have written of the meeting and do it myself. I fancy it would be better written by an impartial observer rather than by one of the principals of the incident!"

Alexander made no reply. Everything Matthew had said sounded so just that he knew it would be a hopeless task trying to state his case, and he had a shrewd idea that his father was laughing at him and would not be interested in any justification.

"How art thou fallen from heaven, O Lucifer, son of the morning," Selway greeted him as he came into the reporters' room. "For a while the thunder roared and the lightning flashed, a combat worthy of St. Michael and all his angels. The battle was short, brother?"

"Very short," Alexander grinned, beginning to recover his spirits. "This account will probably be shorter, though." He took up his report from the table. The two knew of his adventure.

"What did he say?" asked Harold.

"Actually he was very reasonable; so much so that, although I can't see why, I feel just a little ashamed of myself."

"The old man always makes one feel like that," sympathised Selway, "even when he is in the wrong."

"He must have seen you at that meeting. I wish I'd been there. You didn't tell me you'd joined the club even."

"Yes, he was there all right, and I can understand now why the policeman was so fatherly towards me. The old man must have warned him off to keep an eye on me. Even the police are corrupt in this town." He pulled a letter from his pocket. "I got this prose gem from

Comrade Burnside today. He sent it around here." He read dolefully: "At a special meeting held late last night it was unanimously decided by all present to ask you to resign your membership of this club, it being considered you were the means of bringing it into disrepute for the first time in its long and honourable history."

"Two years, that is," said Selway. "Did they return your subscription?"

"Seems as if I've brought disrepute—that seems to be a favourite word of the old man's, too—on the *Messenger* and the club."

"Fate, my boy. You're what the Americans so succinctly term a jinx. You bring bad luck to all you touch."

Alexander threw the letter into the fireplace.

"Did you," said Spencer, trying to turn the conversation, since he could see that Alexander was, for all his nonchalance, hurt, "see that Miss Peters who came here to wait for Miss Silverman?"

"As lovely a creature as ever I set eyes on," Selway finished for him. "If you ask me, the visit of those two love-birds this morning wasn't altogether an accident. They probably went at the old man about the circulation figures—and there, if you really want something to think about, is a pretty problem."

"Are things really going so badly, then?" Alexander looked up.

"Nothing tragic, my young Lochinvar, nothing tragic. You won't be on the streets begging just yet."

"Be serious, Selway," said Harold.

"All right. It's serious enough to have Sharples worried and the advertisers asking awkward questions, and the old man doesn't feel any too rosy about it. If you want exact figures you had better apply to Sharples; he'll welcome you with open arms. He's so snowed under with figures these days that he'll be glad to get rid of a few. Hey, where are you going?" He looked across at Alexander, who was making for the door.

"To see Sharples, of course!" came the reply.

"You made him shift pretty quickly," said Harold as the door slammed.

Selway laughed quietly. "You don't know your Silvermans yet, young man. This paper is their god—a very wise god to have, too—and they don't sit around when anything threatens it, not even the young uns like Alex."

XII

It is anticipated that there will be a gratifying response to the request for helpers willing to render service at the forthcoming hospital fête.

Swanbridge Messenger

Loraine's eyes went up to the green back of the downs, a bare line against the drawn spring sky, and a phrase from the book in her hand swam into her brain: "When proud-pied April, dress'd in all his trim, hath put a spirit of youth in everything." She did not feel very youthful, although it was April. The winter wheat was bright green, geometrical, across the chocolate fields at her feet, and a handful of rooks swirled into the air above the downs, like flying scraps of tinder from some huge bonfire behind the ridge. From the foot of the downs the tree-pooled valley stretched away toward the blue mist which overhung the coast.

Spring was come again, she thought; lovely, sad spring. Everyone was looking forward to the months ahead, the warm joys of summer, their holidays … She wished she could feel like that, but her heart would not let her. Two cock blackbirds began to fight around a holly-tree at the side of the path. She dropped her eyes to her book and read the words again. When she had first seen them they had sent a deep pang through her, a delicious, agonising, breathless pain; not because they were beautiful, but because she was alone and so sad.

> *Art thou gone so far,*
> *Beyond the poplar tops, beyond the sunset-bar,*

Beyond the purple cloud that smells on high
In the tender fields of sky?

"Oh, come thou again," she prayed to herself. He wouldn't come; no one would ever come. She would have to go on, hiding her sadness and smiling bravely at the world, pretending a part she hated. Poetry was lovely. It was with a little glad surprise that she discovered she could say that and mean it. At school she had hated it; lines and lines about nightingales and larks and continually having to look up in the glossary who Apollyon was and the relation of Thea to Hyperion. She knew now that, whatever she had thought then, poetry had been waiting for her until this moment when she would want it ... *Art thou gone so far, so far* ... And Philip was so dull. Oh, dear, how had she ever put up with him and his stuffy ways so long? A walk with. him after church on Sunday evening, perhaps the pictures on Monday evening, supper at his or her house in the mid-week, and a dance on Saturday ... anybody would think they were engaged. And when he kissed her after the pictures or a dance it was always a gentle kiss, as though he were afraid she would break ... And the things he talked about—furniture, furniture, furniture and houses. He seemed to think that houses were built only to put furniture in. He didn't even take an interest in the fast car he had; let Reggie look after it for him; never opened the bonnet and seldom drove it all out. What—she posed the insoluble question to a puff of feathery cloud that had floated over the downs, like a young boy venturing into deep water for the first time, and was now moving adventurously towards the horizon—what was the sense of having a car that would do eighty-five if you never did more than fifty-five or sixty? Oh, dear.... *Beyond the poplar tops.*

A rabbit scuttled along the bottom of the hedge, the thud of its feet punctuating the air. Loraine raised her head and found herself looking into the face of Harold Spencer. She had been so occupied with her thoughts that she had not seen his approach until the rabbit had warned her. He smiled down at her, a frank, anxious smile.

"I didn't expect to find you up here, Miss Silverman. Isn't the view lovely?"

Loraine knew all about him now; her father had spoken of his work for the paper, and once or twice they had met in the office and passed polite exchanges.

"Yes," she said without a thought. "I often come up here and sit watching."

"Watching what?" he asked.

Loraine paused for a while, then said: "Oh, just watching things ... life down there—"

"Ah." He took her up quickly. "Watching life. You're a philosopher, Miss Silverman; sitting up here like a goddess on Olympus, watching the play of mortals down there."

"Oh, do you think so?" She was not sure which she liked better, being compared to a philosopher—no one else had ever thought of that—or to a goddess on Olympus. He was not such an awful little squirt as she had imagined. She leaned forward, her light navy-blue overcoat slipping open to show the blue-and-white jumper and the young vigour of her body. The book slid from her lap, and Harold bent to retrieve it.

"Hullo," he said pleasantly as he picked it up, "an anthology of poems. I say, I didn't know you liked poetry. I thought—" He stopped, confused.

Loraine felt no anger towards him. She had thought as he did until a few weeks ago. "You thought I was like all the other girls in Swanbridge," she said easily, smiling at him to banish his awkwardness; "fond only of dancing and having a good time."

"No, please!"

"Yes, you did—confess it now!" Her eyes held him to her until he smiled and nodded his head.

"Perhaps I did. I was mistaken, though." His eyes had left her and were on the book, whose pages he was turning slowly. He held a page open and read slowly:

When I consider how my light is spent
E'er half my days, in this dark world and wide,
And that one Talent which is death to hide
Lodg'd with me useless ...

He went on, and Loraine listened to him happily. He could read well, and the low power of his voice wrapped her about like a cloak and shut away all the unhappiness which she had known.

"*They also serve who only stand and wait.*"

"That's lovely."

"Milton. Some people don't like it. I'm glad you do."

"It's wonderful."

"Have you ever read his *Comus*? I'll lend it to you, if you'd care to have it."

"Oh, I should—and I'd be ever so careful with it." She was not quite sure what *Comus* was, but she guessed it was a book, and when people lent books it was well to make a promise of care. She wriggled stiffly on the grass as a preliminary to rising. He held out a warm hand, and she took it.

"Thank you." His hand held hers for a second or two after she was standing, and the contact was like the feeling of the sun hot upon one's cheek for the first time after a hard winter. They walked off together, Harold swinging the book and talking happily, and Loraine walking silently, her face half turned towards him, her eyes wide.

* * *

Reginald Cartwright was Abner's grandson. He had considerably disappointed Abner, and shaken his belief a little in heredity, when he showed that he had few of the intellectual characteristics of his father. When he died, Peter Cartwright was the senior partner in a Farley firm of solicitors, a county councillor, the author of an interestingly erudite book on the history of Swanbridge, and he had before him the ambition to become chairman of the county council, an ambition which Abner, and all those who knew him, realised would come to him eventually. A German bullet had killed him quickly and cleanly. His wife, Mary, although she lived on for the sake of her son, became no more than an insubstantial figure, negative, unobtrusive, living only for Abner and her son.

Abner wanted Reginald to take the place of his father; all Peter's ambition should become Reginald's. But Reginald had made that impossible. He had not rebelled from Abner's authority. He was always obedient, and it was Abner who realised first that Reginald must go his own way. He had one ambition—to become the proprietor of a garage; the size, affluence, importance of the garage

158

meant nothing, only the proprietorship and the freedom to spend his hours with motor machinery attracted him. His literature was the motor journals; his relaxation grass-track racing; and his delight a contented motor. Where Mrs. Silverman would fuss with a soufflé he would fuss with valve-timings, and the pride she took in her polished brass was nothing to the joy in Reginald's heart as he polished and lapped in pistons.

Between Philip and Reginald was a curious intimacy. Both of them loved their work, idealising it, and, recognising each other's ability, they found a friendship that never became exuberant or weighty. They were neither of the type that enjoys exposing confidences to any sympathetic listener, yet with each other they discovered a comfort that occasionally led them to the expression of intimacies they would have held fast from all others.

"Don't you love anything else but cars?" asked Philip one day, when Reginald was attending to his car.

"Motor-cycles," replied Reginald.

"Is that all? Haven't you ever been in love?"

"Once," said Reginald, straightening up. He was a short, broad-chested young man who stood as though he were inviting you to punch his stomach to see how he could take it without flinching. His face, beneath the oil and grime, was pleasantly freckled. "You know, Philip, you ought not to run this car with only three plugs firing. You should stop and change the dud one. You wouldn't try to hunt a horse that could only use three legs."

"I don't hunt."

"A good job, too. You'd probably be as bad a horseman as you are a driver."

"When was it?" asked Philip, going back to his first question.

"Oh, a long time ago. When I was younger and had just started this business." He began to screw a sparking-plug into the cylinder head.

"What was she like?"

"Hot stuff! She really belonged to a commercial traveller, but he used to bring her with him and leave her here for a few days while he did business in the town."

Philip was surprised. "This sounds a bit …"

"Yes, it does, doesn't it? She was a peach, though. And she had a lovely figure; class. Told me that he got her cheap from a fellow in Ealing who'd got tired of her—three hundred he gave for her. There was only one thing about her which I didn't like; she had an outside gear-change, which is a nuisance in wet weather."

"Ass!"

"Not at all. I was in love with her. When he went I used to be miserable for days."

"Have you noticed Loraine lately?" The question came up from the depths, hurriedly; a diver too long kept under.

Reginald straightened his back, laughed, and then went round to the other side of the car and slipped into the driver's seat.

"I nearly killed her the other day. I was taking Colonel Waterson's Flying Veda out to his place, and she was walking in the middle of the road reading poetry."

"Poetry?"

"Yes, poetry. She didn't even know I'd nearly killed her. I gave her a lift, and she read some of it to me—a bit about a girl called Sabrina. Know it?"

"No. But I'm worried about her. She's been very funny lately."

"Loraine's all right." Reginald started the engine, and the crepitations shook the thin roof of the garage, making the tools on the bonnet dance. Then the notes died away to a soft purring, as though the engine knew and respected Reginald; an obedient, gentle beast. "You want to marry her, don't you?"

"I'm going to one day."

"One day!" Reginald made the car roar noisily. "Why not now? You can afford it."

"She's too young. It wouldn't be right to ask her ust yet."

"Poppycock! What Loraine wants, if I know anything about girls—and I don't spend all my time in this garage—is for someone to take hold of her and spank her good and hard. Then set her on her feet, give her a good hard kiss—no party peck—and tell her that she's got to get married right away. You'd be surprised!"

Philip laughed indulgently and shook his head.

"You can't treat a woman like that, Reggie. Any more than you'd treat a machine like that."

"I don't know," mused Reginald, switching off the engine and rubbing a dirty finger across his nose. "I had a wristlet watch once that defied all the care and love I lavished on it. So I threw it across the room. I'll admit it broke the watch-glass, but after that it went like a bird. I'm wearing it now. Some cars are like that, too. I remember—"

Philip was gone. When Reginald began to remember cars, it was a sign for those who knew him to go away.

* * *

Alexander yawned, uncrossed his legs, and switched off the wireless.

"Well, mother," he asked, "how did you like that little talk? You now know exactly what your legal position is if you invite Mr. and Mrs. Hardwick here and the ceiling falls on their heads while they're eating."

"I know, dear. Isn't it terrible?" said Mrs. Silverman, who wasn't really listening. There was such an interesting crossword that had come with the butter, and it wasn't very difficult; some of the clues were already filled in. Of course, it was an advertisement. Yet someone had to win the five hundred pounds. It would be such a surprise to say one morning at breakfast, "Well, my dears, what do you think has happened? I've just received a cheque from the Blue Cow Butter Company for five hundred pounds. The first prize in their crossword competition. No, no, Matthew. This is my money, and I'm not going to bank it. I'm going to spend it all." And she would spend it. A really expensive coat for herself—mink, perhaps; her musquash was looking a bit frumpy now, and Matthew was in no mood these days to be talked to about fur coats. Matthew—she would give him a new desk for his room; a big desk with plenty of drawers to keep his papers in, so that Gibby didn't grumble; a shaded lamp that you could adjust ... Her mind ran on in the pleasant occupation of spending five hundred pounds.

"I don't think it's terrible," said Alexander. "It would do Hardwick good to have a chunk of plaster fall on his head."

Mrs. Silverman nodded, musing to herself, "A star which was wrecked ... beginning with Hes and ending with s. A wreck? Hes ... There was the wreck of the Hesperus. Yes, and that fits the spaces. Is it a star? Probably one of those fancy names they give to stars." She looked up, about to ask Alexander if Hesperus was the name of a star. No, she must not do that; it was to be a surprise. There was an encyclopaedia in Matthew's library.

Alexander watched his mother get up and leave the room. He smiled tenderly to himself. Then he looked across at Loraine.

"Has mother got another of those crosswords, Lot?"

Loraine did not answer. She had not even heard him. She was bent over a thin book, her brows frowning, her lips moving quietly:

> *I sat me down to watch upon a bank*
> *With ivy canopied, and interwove*
> *With flaunting honeysuckle, and began,*
> *Wrapt in a pleasing fit of melancholy,*
> *To meditate my rural minstrelsy ...*

Well, at least, she could understand that part. Somebody had sat down to think. Why did they have to be so tortuous about what they thought and did, making it so hard to follow?

"Alexander!" She was on her feet, her eyes flaring and her hands groping for the book he had snatched from her. "Give that to me. You pig! How would you like someone to take your book?"

"Ho-ho! Master Milton's *Comus!*" jeered Alexander, dancing safely out of her reach. "And you were actually reading it? What's the matter with the library these days? Haven't they got any books by Swing?"

"It's not a library book. Give it back." Loraine advanced on him, and he took cover behind the settee.

"No, I see it isn't." Alexander was looking at the fly-leaf. "Harold Johnson Spencer—so that's his middle name. And how do you like Milton, my little sister? I have been mistaken all these years. I thought your development had stopped prematurely, but I see it was only arrested. Under the benign influence of Milton—and Harold— you are flowering like a late rose, luscious, full-scented, and, I hope, thornless. Tell me, what do you think of Ezra Pound and Auden?"

"You superior little worm!" Loraine was surprised at the vehemence of her feeling. Had she a knife she would have willingly plunged it into her brother.

"*O brother, 'tis my father's shepherd, sure,*" quoted Alexander from the book, mockingly. "Yes, it is my father's faithful shepherd, Harold. He's too nice a lad for you to seduce. Hey!" He was too late.

Loraine vaulted the settee and was upon him. Her hands went for the book and found his arms. For a while they struggled, panting, and then, enjoying the tussle, Alexander tripped her, and they fell to the carpet, rolling and kicking like a pair of puppies fighting for the joy of movement. A flying arm hit the fireside table and tipped it over, scattering a cloud of ash from a tray into Alexander's hair.

"Give me that book!" Loraine was as strong as her brother, and her rage made her stronger. Her fingers were tight upon his wrist, one sharp nail digging into the flesh and drawing blood.

"Children!"

They knew the voice, and they stopped fighting at once. They sat up, panting and absently jerking at their clothing to tidy themselves.

"It was my fault," said Alexander, brushing the ash from his hair. "I annoyed her." He added hopefully, wondering if Matthew would make a point of it. "She was reading Milton."

"Well, that's not the effect Milton usually has on one. Loraine—do your skirt up at the side." Matthew repressed a smile as he turned and left the room.

The two watched him go. Alexander licked his hand where it was bleeding from Loraine's nail.

"I'd better go and wash this," he said.

"I hope it turns septic," said Loraine pleasantly.

"Maybe it will," replied Alexander lightly. "I'm only glad you didn't bite me or I should have had to worry about hydrophobia!"

"Some day, I suppose," said Matthew, going into the library and finding his wife there, "these children of ours will grow up."

"What's Alison been doing now?" asked his wife. "I thought she was in bed?"

"So she is. I mean Alexander and Loraine. They were fighting on the floor when I went in just now."

"Dear me, how extraordinary. I've only just come from the room, and they were quite peaceful then."

"It must have been a sudden storm," smiled Matthew, putting his arm affectionately around her shoulder. He seldom showed any sign of their intimacy except when they were alone. It was, to him, a tender, reverent affection, which could not be shared or demonstrated before others. Through the window the garden was purple with heavy dusk; over the tips of the flowering fruit-trees the night sky held its great shield of stars, dark and polished. A stiff row of tulips carried themselves rigidly in the light from the room. The beam of a car climbing the hills beyond the town threw a great arc across the night, a bar of gold that wavered for a while and then was gone, leaving the black night blacker.

His wife was happy. The weight of his arm upon her was a comfort, and Hesperus was the name of the evening star. Perhaps it was one of the stars shining out there now. Standing at the window, watching the night, with the smell of damp grass, where Fuller had cut the lawn, in her nostrils, she was reminded of the evening when she had stood with Matthew above the town, on a spur of the downs that ran downwards to the river, and he had asked her to marry him. She would always remember the moment—his halting yet determined words and her trembling, mounting joy that it was all happening to her, that he should want her. She could feel again the silky touch of a moth across her cheek and the whistle of wind through the pinions of some night bird overhead, and above all the smell of the earth, of young things breaking into life, of the whispering grasses and the hedges full of hawthorn blossom. The memory touched her, and she felt happy tears move behind her eyes. God had been good to her ...

"What kind of young man is this Harold Spencer?" she asked after a while.

Matthew knew why she asked. "He's a nice fellow, steady and excellent at his job. Reminds me of Barnes a lot. I think I was wiser than I knew in taking him on. Why?"

"You know why," said his wife slowly. "Loraine's most casual with Philip these days, and she's been out quite a lot with Harold Spencer. I just wondered ..."

"Don't you worry, my dear. Loraine's young. Philip's a good fellow, and so is Harold. We mustn't interfere. I don't suppose I was the first young man who ever made eyes at you when you were a girl, was I?"

"Well ... no ..." It was a sweet lie. There had been no trail of young men to her father's vicarage. It was like Matthew to think that there had been.

Away to the right the Town Hall clock began to strike eight, each note flooding the night with deep vibrations, disturbing the darkness into an almost tangible flux. Matthew dropped his arm from his wife's shoulder.

"I must be going, my love. There is a hospital fête meeting tonight."

* * *

The hospital fête meeting was held in one of the committee-rooms of the Town Hall, and was attended by the few people who concerned themselves each year with the organisation of the fête. It was an honour, not lightly bestowed, to be a member of the committee. Matthew, by virtue of the publicity which the *Messenger* accorded the affair, was always the chairman, although each year they went through the formality of electing him. The hospital secretary performed the same duty for the fête, and was given an insubstantial honorarium for his services; the other members were Dr. Pimm and the matron, representing the hospital; Xavier Martell, who looked after the dressing and decoration of the fête; Mrs. Staines, who as mayor's wife gave a civic flavour to the proceedings; Colonel Waterson, who held a watching brief for the retired gentlefolk of the town; Samuel Hardwick, who personified the tradespeople; and Mr. Cyril Markham, the Grammar School headmaster, to whom any matters of doubt in good taste were submitted. The Church had her spokesman in the person of the Reverend Giles Todd of St. Dunstan's.

Matthew was the last member to arrive. He took his seat hurriedly, murmuring: "Sorry to keep you waiting, ladies and gentlemen, but a newspaper is a hard master, and we cannot always break away when we would. Right, Mr. Secretary. Perhaps you would proceed."

Mr. Secretary did proceed—a thin man with a large Adam's apple that seemed to move like the bubble in a spirit level as he swayed in and out of the perpendicular. Mr. Secretary read the minutes of the last meeting, and they were confirmed and then signed by Matthew.

"And now will Mr. Secretary tell us what has happened about the various affairs that were suggested at the last meeting?" This was Mrs.

Staines, her head crowned by a green toque, intolerant of official procedure and determined not to be pushed into the background.

"Quite, Mrs. Staines. Everything in its place." Matthew did not intend to let her run the meeting. Later on, he knew from experience, order would disappear; but for the moment he was in the saddle, and meant to stay there as long as he could. "Now, Mr. Secretary, perhaps you would satisfy the consuming curiosity of the members by making your report."

Mr. Secretary rose, coughed importantly, rustled the papers in his hand, and began to report.

"Item number one. His Worship the Mayor of Swanbridge has kindly consented to open the fête"—Mrs. Staines's head rose even higher above her stiff lace throat-band—"and the town council have kindly allowed us the use of the recreation ground, and have offered the services of the town road-sweepers to clean up the ground when the fête is over. Item number two. Messrs. Brown & Coates have agreed to look after the catering on the terms already settled by the committee."

"I know it is not in order for me to raise the point at this stage"— this was the Reverend Giles Todd, his voice mild and soothing, his eyes dark-shadowed from reading—"but it seems a sad thing that the catering for this, so essentially a town affair, should be done by a Farley firm."

"But, my dear vicar"—Colonel Waterson brought his battery to bear upon the interrupter—"we have gone into that. If none of the catering firms in this town will do it, then we must let in outsiders. The tenders we did have from the firms in Swanbridge were too ridiculously high."

"And remember, quite a lot of Farley folk come to the fête," put in Martell impartially.

"I'm sure some of our ladies could perhaps run the catering, then?" suggested the vicar. "We have enough volunteers."

Matthew could see that an old argument was going to be re-opened unless he came forward and stopped it.

"Mr. Todd," he said firmly, "I appreciate your feelings, we all appreciate your feelings, but the matter unfortunately is beyond our control. Our ladies could not possibly run the catering by themselves. It needs experts, and, as it is, the ladies have all their work cut out helping the experts. I think I'm right in saying that they are almost the hardest worked of all the helpers."

"Very good. I withdraw." The vicar smiled gracefully.

The secretary coughed to bring attention back to himself, and then went on: "The magistrates have granted a licence for the sale of intoxicating liquors at the fête, and the catering for this has been given to Mr. Jordan of the Three Feathers Hotel on the terms already settled with the Troon Brewery Company."

"I hope no extension of the licence beyond the normal hours is intended?"

"No, Mr. Markham," Matthew was quick to answer, for this drink question yearly divided the committee into two camps. "The refreshment marquee will be closed for the sale of anything but soft drinks after half past ten."

"It's a pity that people coming to the fête to help the hospital should have to be enticed by the lure of drink!" observed Mrs. Staines tartly. "I shall always deplore it."

"Hospital fêtes are thirsty affairs, Mrs. Staines," suggested Martell. "You wouldn't deny a man his drink?"

"Not healthy drink, Mr. Martell, of course not; but spirituous liquors …" She shook her toque defiantly.

"Lips that touch liquor shall never touch mine, eh?" boomed the Colonel heartily. This drink problem never bothered him at all. "Come, don't let's be narrow-minded. Those that want a glass of beer ought to be able to get it, and those that like lemonade shouldn't grudge it to them."

"Hear, hear!" Sam Hardwick thumped the table jovially.

"Mr. Jordan is a very discreet man," said Dr. Pimm. "He can be relied upon to stop serving anyone who is getting a little the worse for wear."

"If you mean drunk, why not say so?" declared Mrs. Staines, who believed in frank words and hard hitting.

"My dear Mrs. Staines," interposed the vicar gently, "surely Dr. Pimm's euphemism is most charitable?"

"Faith, hope, and charity, and the greatest of these … eh, vicar?" Sam Hardwick thumped the table again, and, in the pause while the combatants were recovering their arms and preparing for another attack, the secretary took Matthew's hint and read on quickly:

"Mr. Matthew Silverman has kindly agreed to print and present free the placards of the fête, and the proofs of these have already been passed by Mr. Martell, and they are to be sent to the billposters at the end of this week."

"I think the committee might have been allowed to see the proofs. These bills are very important, and a turn of wording or the form of design means a lot." Mr. Markham took off his glasses and rubbed them vigorously to emphasise his protest.

Xavier Martell was on his feet in a moment.

"Mr. Chairman, may I be allowed to reply? Thank you. The posters of this fête have been left to me because in the past this committee has proved incapable of reaching a common decision about lettering or colouring, and as for design ..." He shrugged his shoulders expressively. "I did not ask for the responsibility; it was conferred upon me, and I took it gladly. I may remind the committee that in the past—happily when I was not a member—the posters have been laughed at for their design even by the undiscerning people of this town."

"Please"—this was Matthew, worried that some slur might next rebound upon the printing of the *Messenger* plant. "I think we can rely upon Mr. Martell. Now, the next, Mr. Secretary?"

"Arrangements have now been definitely made with Universal Amusements Ltd. for the hire of all the necessary stalls and side-shows, the hire charge to include delivery and collection after the fête and to cover insurance against the usual risks." He paused to draw breath and got no chance to proceed, for this was the moment many of them had been waiting for.

There was a great jealousy for the charge of the various shows, and their disposition was not made easy by the fact that the members of the committee shared the jealousy. Each year a small cup was awarded for the show which took the most money, and last year the Misses Palmer had astounded everyone by winning the prize. Usually Mrs. Staines won it on the quoits or Mr. Hardwick on the coconut shies. The Misses Palmer had been given a show where one threw a penny on to a platform covered with a metal discs, and if the penny covered a disc a bell rang and an indicator marked a winning of anything from twopence to a shilling. It was a new stall, and no one had suspected that it would be so popular. This year the Misses Palmer stood no chance of getting the stall again; Mr. Hardwick and Mrs. Staines had marked it for their own.

"I think that this year there should be a general reshuffling of the shows," suggested Mrs. Staines.

"Good idea!" agreed the Colonel. "I should like the shooting-gallery for a change. Bit of a comedown, what? Shooting bottles after one has had to deal with big game. Still, the hospital the great leveller."

"I think he's making nasty remarks about the efficiency of your hospital, Dr. Pimm," said Martell with a smile.

"Never mind, we'll have him on the operating-table one day; eh, Colonel? Then you'll wish you'd been more polite."

"You're a blood-thirsty Apache!" roared the Colonel jovially. "Never get me on your table. Sound in wind and limb as yet!"

Very carefully they went through the list of helpers, assigning stalls and assistants. The Colonel got his shooting-gallery; Martell was given the Aunt Sally. Dr. Pimm and the matron took the coconut shies, and Mr. Markham accepted the dart-throwing show for the Grammar School to run, and the various other applicants, sponsored by various committee members, were awarded shows.

"And what about the electric penny show? The Misses Palmer did well with it last year. I think we ought to let them have it again, eh?" This was Matthew, fond of the Misses Palmer and appreciative of the joy that came into their lives from this brief fame.

"Oh, no, Matt. We've agreed on a general reshuffle," put in Sam Hardwick.

Mrs. Staines leagued with him, and the Misses Palmer were given the hoop-la to look after.

And then Mr. Hardwick and Mrs. Staines began to do battle for the electric penny show. Sam suggested that he would have it draped and decorated by his assistants to resemble a fruit and flower shop, and dress four of his prettiest girls as the four seasons of the year. Mrs. Staines laughed at his romantic notion, and said that it was obvious that an electric penny show must be modern, and promised that she would get her husband to make it look like a miniature BBC and have girls wearing earphones, dressed in stiff skirts of metallic cloth, and have neon lighting put wherever it was possible.

"The omphalos of the fête," murmured the vicar.

Gradually, as their partisanship increased, Matthew began to see that there might be bad feeling about the electric penny show. The committee began to take sides. The vicar was with Mr. Hardwick; he liked the idea of the four seasons. Markham sided with Mrs. Staines—her husband was a governor of the Grammar School and he enjoyed dining with them—and the Colonel supported her because he disliked her less than he did Mr. Hardwick. Dr. Pimm and the matron were for Mr. Hardwick because they thought Mrs. Staines was a busybody who got her own way too often. Only Martell and Matthew retained any impartiality, though Matthew could guess that if it came to the vote Martell would vote for Mrs. Staines because he liked her decorative idea better than he did Hardwick's. That, thought Matthew, leaves me with the deciding vote, and that is not what I want.

He took a penny from his pocket and, looking down the table, said: "It is quite impossible to decide this question on merits. Both Mrs. Staines and Mr. Hardwick would do equal justice to the stall, and their respective decorative ideas are good. I suggest that the only solution is to toss for it?"

They accepted his wisdom, and the coin fell in favour of Mrs. Staines.

"My wife will never forgive me for coming home without that electric penny stall," Sam moaned to Matthew as they walked together down the road. "These women are more worrying than a business sometimes."

"Never mind, Sam. You couldn't help it. After all, a coin is a coin, and sometimes it falls heads and sometimes tails. There's a destiny in these things."

"I'm not grumbling, Matt. It's just that that Staines woman gets my back up at times. Her husband's a fine fellow; I like old Staines; one of the best business men in this county. By the way," he added jokingly, his good spirits coming back like the return of a wave, "what's all this I hear about the *Messenger* going bankrupt?"

Matthew did not like the joke. He did not tell Sam that he found the joke distasteful, for Sam was an advertiser, and he gave no hint that the falling circulation of the *Messenger* had caused him any worry.

"When the *Messenger* goes bankrupt, Sam, you can lock up your shop, for there won't be anyone in Swanbridge to buy goods from you."

They laughed pleasantly together, and then parted for their homes; Sam to explain his defeat to his wife, and Matthew wondering just how general the feeling was about the *Messenger*.

XIII

That the Council have decided against any alteration is a matter for congratulation. It must not be supposed, as some of the councillors would have us believe, that any change, no matter what, is desirable. We have said before, and we say it again, that no support would be given to a change in the existing scheme unless it were first proved a change for the better.

Swanbridge Messenger (From an Editorial)

Matthew allowed the circulation to worry him more than it should have done. The Silvermans were accustomed to worry about their business, but their anxieties were usually concerned with increasing the sales, not with meeting a falling circulation. He said nothing to his family, but they knew of his trouble and were silent, not only because they knew he would not want them to talk about it, but also because they had no very helpful suggestions to make.

"Daddy is upset about the *Messenger* sales, isn't he?" Loraine asked her mother when Matthew had been particularly silent during a meal.

"Yes, dear. But don't say anything to him about it. He likes to think that we don't know."

"All the town knows that the *Courier* are pinching his sales. I call it a dirty trick. But, then, the *Courier* people are like that. The editor's daughter plays hockey for Farley, and if she's a sample—"

"Now, Loraine, it's not kind to be like that. After all, there's no need to worry so much. All these things come right in the end. It's just part of a great plan, as your grandfather used to say, a great plan." She began to clip the stems from a bunch of roses before putting them in water, loose petals falling from the blooms to the table, where they rested like fragile coracles.

Alexander alone of the rest of the family was not content to let his concern ebb. He was a Silverman; he worked on the *Messenger* and had accepted its traditions, its prides, and all the glory that belonged to it, and he discovered that he was readier to fight for it than to praise it.

His worry did not affect him in the same way as it did Matthew. Matthew sought for the cause of the fall in circulation somewhere in the intricate machinery which he controlled. He never questioned the *Messenger* itself, only the production of the *Messenger*. He harried the advertisement and circulation manager, criticising his distribution methods, and questioning the efficiency of his sales methods. Everyone felt his keen tongue. Reporters were rated for missing news, for bad writing—and his eyes searched the building for evidence of waste. All he did, all he could do, was to tighten up the internal economy of the works and then to admit to himself alone that the trouble lay, must lie, in the people who had bought the paper for years. It never for one moment occurred to him that the *Messenger* itself might be the cause of the fall in the circulation.

Alexander approached the problem from a less reverent standpoint, and in a slightly different spirit from his father, and he thought he saw at once where the trouble was. A good many people who worked on the *Messenger* might have told Matthew, if they had had the courage to do so, what was wrong with the *Messenger*, but it takes a brave man to tell a mother, doting over the beauties of her child, that it happens to be squint-eyed, crooked with rickets, and club-footed. Alexander saw the trouble and he saw the difficulty. The difficulty was not merely to alter the *Messenger*, but to get Matthew first to see that alterations were needed and then to make them.

He and Harold discussed it between themselves one evening, alone in the reporters' room. Although he teased Loraine about Harold, he had never said anything to his friend about her.

"The thing's obvious," said Alexander. "This paper has been going on in the same way for years. It's old-fashioned, and Dad doesn't know it. For years they've published it in the same old way, expecting the public to like it. Well, the public don't like it any more. They like the *Courier* better, and I don't blame them. What we want is stuff to brighten up the paper—not necessarily cheap trash like the *Courier* uses. A paper can be bright without being vulgar. Just look at the *Messenger*. It has few pictures; only weddings and cattle shows. We ought to have flashlight photographs of groups at dances, and an occasional interest picture of some village green or an old house. In fact, we ought to run a page of pictures."

"That's it," put in Harold. He had been thinking about the problem. "We could have a photograph taken each week in a different village High Street, and give ten bob to the person we mark with a star."

"Dad'll never do that. Too much like a daily picture paper."

"He's got to do it. It's a sure way of making folk buy the paper. Then we should have a weekly, chatty column about local personalities. You know the kind of thing: 'Have you heard that a Swanbridge young man well known for his cricketing prowess was seen, or may probably …' etc. And it wouldn't hurt the paper to have a few book reviews. Your dad gets enough review copies sent by publishers to make up a column each week. I could do the reviewing. Then there's the films. We could have quite a snappy lot of notes about the local shows, and get advance pictures and publicity paragraphs about what Greta Garbo has for breakfast. And open up the correspondence columns more. We only print about three letters a week. We want more—get a real raging fight going between correspondents about the best way of stopping foot rot and that kind of thing."

"Then there's the make-up," suggested Alexander. He did not want Harold to think of all the improvements. "Our make-up is terrible. The type is all right, and most papers of our size use minion for the general news, but we could get better cross-heads, make the page more attractive. After all, it isn't our job to touch national news. But that's no reason why local news shouldn't be given headlines—they're as important to Swanbridge as the news of a Government defeat is to the nation. And perhaps a serial story—that makes 'em come again. Gosh, I didn't realise fully how dull the *Messenger* was until this moment. There are lots of things we could do to give it a push, if only—"

"If only what?"

Alexander grinned, and knocked his pipe out in Selway's waste-paper basket. "If only we can make the old man see our point of view. You know what he thinks about that kind of thing. Classes any catchpenny idea as vulgar. I doubt whether we can do it."

"You've got to, Alex. Don't you realise what'll happen if it isn't done? This paper will die … Oh, slowly, of course, but eventually it will die. This is its centenary year. There aren't many papers can say they've been going as long as that. It would be a pity if this year were to mark the beginning of the decline. If a paper is to grow lustier with age, then it stands to reason that it must change with the years. It would be a grand thing if the centenary year saw the birth of a new *Messenger*, a handsome organ, meeting the needs of a changed public … Why, I almost feel as though I could convince the old man myself."

"Don't worry, my young orator, you're going to have a chance. We'll tabulate all our reforms and go to him. We'll back one another up and make him see sense. Come on, let's get these points down!" They went to work on them eagerly, with all the high courage of youth.

* * *

Matthew had lunched, on the day they went to him, at the weekly meeting of the Swanbridge Chamber of Commerce. The luncheon club—for that was what it was—met once a week in a private room of the Three Feathers, and most of the prominent tradespeople and a few of the professional men were members.

Matthew always enjoyed the luncheon. They were jolly, masculine affairs, where all the men were devoid of nonsense; plain, sensible business people whose chief aim was the interest of Swanbridge and their own fortunes—and the two were very much wrapped up in each other. The food was good; rich brown soup, boiled beef and carrots, and a sweet—familiar to Matthew at home under another name—frequently served by the hotel and aggrandised by the title *pouding de cabinet*. Everyone drank beer and made themselves too sleepy to care much for work in the afternoon. The guest of honour had been a spruce, colonel-like gentleman who represented a company which was building a cheese factory in Swanbridge; the rates in the town were low, there was plenty of cheap labour, and the district could supply all the milk needed. Swanbridge cheeses—one portion per person—no table complete without it—would be making the town even more famous within a year, he had declared.

They had cheered him, and asked one another in whispers whether the name was Henson or Hitchcock. Matthew, as chairman for the week, had welcomed him and replied to his speech. He privately considered that his speech was much better than Mr. Hancock's. One part of it stayed in his brain despite the babble of talk and the food and drink—"Mr. Hancock in the course of his speech has said that necessity is the mother of invention. Let me go further into the genealogical table and say that invention has become the father of progress, and we in Swanbridge today welcome progress. This is no idle backwater, but a busy, thriving town, adapting itself to changing times, proud of its past and hopeful of its future ..." They had cheered him loudly, and then Henry Wilton, the manager of the corset factory, had taken up Matthew's phrase, "adapting itself to changing times," to talk about corsets, a subject on which he enlarged at every opportunity; but Sam Hardwick had cut him short by shouting that it wasn't the times corsets had to adapt themselves to, and the meeting had degenerated into a merry, hearty party of joking men taking a holiday from cares.

Sam Hardwick had walked up the street with Matthew afterwards. Sam was a little maudlin from drink and inclined to regret his lost youth.

"Y'know, Matt, I wish I'd had the chance to be better educated when I was young. I miss it now. That was a damned fine speech of yours. Specially that bit about the father of progress—smart, that was. I wish I could say things like that, straight off the reel. I'd give something to be young again." He patted the curve of his waistcoat, and waited for Matthew to reciprocate and compliment him about his corset joke. But Matthew merely said, " 'Tisn't the education of the mind that counts; it's the heart, Sam." Sam had taken courage from this and gone back to his emporium. Catching a male assistant flirting with one of the young girls in the hosiery department, he had given them a stentorian lecture, much to their embarrassment and the amusement of the other assistants and the few customers, and then gone to his office, put an engaged notice on the door-handle, and settled himself for a sleep; and the male assistant, knowing Sam's habits after a Chamber of Commerce lunch, had gone back to the girl assistant.

* * *

Matthew did not sleep that afternoon. As soon as he was settled in his room Alexander and Harold came in to him. He was not pleased to see them. He had earmarked the afternoon to write his editorial commending the council's foresight in selecting the Pennyquick fields estate for their new houses, determined to add a salutary caution to the effect that the houses had better justify the estate. He wanted no jokes about Swanbridge council houses.

At first Alexander was the spokesman. He put forward their ideas, as simply and as quickly as he could, and, when he had finished, Harold as quickly made an appeal to reason and an avowal that the scheme could not possibly go wrong.

Matthew did them the honour of listening without interruption. He even took Alexander's scheduled list of suggestions and glanced through them. This was youth, he thought, headstrong youth, razing mountains to the ground, iconoclastic; and he was touched at their sincerity. At this moment he was more sure than ever of the wisdom he had shown in bringing Alexander into the *Messenger*. He was his son, ready to fight for the paper, identifying his spirit with the life of the paper. He was, for all his awkward modernisms, a Silverman. And Harold Spencer—here was an instance of the spell which the *Messenger* could throw over those who worked for it, of the eager loyalty it could evoke from its servants. Loraine might do worse than marry him.

"Thank you," he said quietly. "I appreciate this a great deal. I don't have to say why. But I can't do it. This is the *Messenger*, not a touting daily paper. My father would not have done it; his father would have thrown you out of the room at the suggestion; and if I did it my conscience would be uneasy for the rest of my days. Apart from all that, I don't think the solution of our difficulty lies in the direction you suggest. This is a phase—it will pass." As he said that, he doubted his own words.

Alexander started to protest. Matthew stopped him and, seeing that they could do no good, the two withdrew and Matthew began to write his editorial. But he could not concentrate. He could hear the earnestness in Alexander's voice, and see the hopeful look of Harold's eyes. He shook his head angrily to dispel the memory. His telephone rang, and although the business was trivial, he was glad of the interruption. He started to write again. After a time he found himself staring before him, his pen idle, his eyes fixed on the portrait of John Silverman over the fireplace, and the other editors. Then the sight of their stolid, secure faces sent a wave of irritation over him, and he got up from his chair and paced to the window, where he stood looking out on the movement of the street, pulling his chin with one hand and playing with the window-cord with the other.

He felt the closeness of the walls; the sound of typewriters and of men and women working closed in about him, filling him with a great discontent, a longing to get away from the place. Over in the printing room, where he had been making an adjustment to his machine, Phipps started the press rolling to check his work. The rumble echoed through the rooms, reaching Matthew's office and beating in tiny waves at his eardrums, a tinnitus that, growing louder as the machine gathered speed, became unendurable. He turned, picked up his hat, and made for the door. As he moved, his eye caught a sheet of white paper on the table. It was the list of suggestions. Scarcely knowing why he did so, he picked it up and stuffed it into his pocket.

Some time later he entered Khartum, asked his wife to send a strong cup of tea into the library, and shut himself in. Mrs. Silverman took the tea in herself. One glance at Matthew told her that it was folly to attempt any conversation. She left him his tea, and Gibby removed the cup some hours later. The tea was untouched, a brown film over the surface.

"Some people seem fond of making other people go to a lot of fuss to get things they don't in the end want," she commented.

XIV

In short, the Clerk of the Weather, the
stallholders and helpers, and those on
pleasure bent, were in their best humour,
and it is confidently expected that the
proceeds of this year's fête will surpass
all previous records.

Swanbridge Messenger

Uncle Abner was angry, and he felt that he had reason to be angry. It was a hot day at the end of June—just the kind of day, he thought, that everyone said was so good for a fête—and he had to admit, despite his bad temper, that hot days were good for fêtes. Nevertheless, that did not make him like fêtes. Stuffy, overcrowded affairs, where he was jostled by people who looked old enough to have acquired some dignity yet acted like children ... that was what they were. Yet he had to go. He was one of the hospital board, and a place had been reserved for him on the platform from which the Mayor of Swanbridge was to declare the fête open, and after that he would have to accompany the Mayor and his party around the fête while some irreverent pup of a reporter from Matthew's place took photographs. He could see the captions in his mind now: "His Worship the Mayor tries his hand at the coconut shies."

It was his opinion that hospitals should not have to rely upon the money raised at local fêtes and by charity. A sensible Government would have nationalised them long ago. And then there was his letter which *The Times* had not printed. A letter about the drought was needed to wake the authorities up, and he was almost an authority on the water-supplies of the county and his literary style was impeccable; the information he had given was of obvious importance and interest; then what could account for its absence from the correspondence columns other than direct discrimination? The position of honour had been given to a lengthy, ambiguous screed about the little owl which any country schoolboy could have confounded. And after lunch he would have to sit beside the Mayor and listen to an almost illiterate speech.

"I've a good mind to drop *The Times*," he snapped across the luncheon table.

"Hullo." Reginald recognised the complaint. "Haven't they printed one of your letters?"

"They have not!" replied Abner with dignity, his old cheeks twitching and his grey eyes, sharp as a squirrel's, defying Reginald to make any cheap witticism at his expense.

"Well, they've got to give their other contributors a chance!"

"Nonsense. I've lost faith in their judgment. Seems a different paper since they made that mistake about the Parnell letter."

"That was an awful long time ago, wasn't it—in Gladstone's day?" said Mrs. Cartwright gently.

"So was the American War of Independence a long time ago," came Abner's answer; "but it was a mistake none the less, and the effects are still felt."

"Do you mean that *The Times* thought your letter might be a bogus one?" asked Reginald innocently, and then slipped from the room before Abner could reply.

* * *

As Abner sat beside the Mayor he was less angry than he had been. Although he disliked fêtes, he could not stifle his love of colour and movement, and the fête gave him these without stint.

It was Swanbridge's half day, and the recreation ground was crowded. There were young men in open-necked shirts with their sweethearts, whose bright dresses hid the green of the grass; fathers and mothers in their Sunday finery, with children whose faces shone at first with cleanliness and later with excitement; young men in fancy tweed jackets and well-creased grey trousers out for a spree, and girls in cool summer frocks who eyed the young men and wondered which they would dance with when night came and the floodlights were turned on the roped arena at the top of the ground; labourers, doctors, railwaymen, nurses from the hospital, clerks, shop assistants, and busloads of excursionists who had come from Farley and other places.

The moment the Mayor had finished his speech and declared the fête open the crowd broke into movement and the stalls were beleaguered.

Mrs. Staines, her stall like a hall of mechanical marvels at an exhibition, shook her satchel of change and invited patronage; Mrs. Hardwick, on the skittle alley—"Four down out of five and you win a packet of cigarettes"—rattled the balls in her crate and held two aloft temptingly; Colonel Waterson, his daughter dressed in a cowgirl suit, loaded the rifles on the shooting gallery and offered advice on marksmanship—"Hold it firmly but gently, boy. Remember, shoot when you see the whites of his eyes! Ha, ha!"; and the Misses Palmer, with coloured handkerchiefs about their heads, hoping that they looked like gypsies, waved their sticks, beringed with quoits, so sweetly that it was hard to refuse their offers to buy three for tuppence and try to ring one of the nickel-plated watches mounted on the tiny plinths that covered the stall, and, when an attempt failed, the look of disappointment in their eyes matched the expression in the eyes of their unlucky customer.

Matthew took Alison round the fête systematically, for he knew that he would have no peace until it was done. Alison, with the excuse that it was all for the good of the hospital, would let him burke no show. He won her a coconut, got three skittles down of the five, smashed five bottles at the shooting gallery, and had to let Alison try until she, too, held by the Colonel, had broken a bottle, and on the hoop-la stall their efforts were so prolonged and determined that it was almost as much as the younger Miss Palmer could do to prevent herself from surreptitiously pushing one of their quoits over when they were not looking; only honesty had to be served. With Mrs. Staines they were lucky, and won tenpence for threepence, and then lost it all at the darts.

"I'm thirsty, Daddy, after all that," said Alison when they had done their round. Matthew took her to the refreshment tent, where Mrs. Silverman served them with lemonade.

"Why, my dear, you look properly exhausted."

"It's all the throwing," explained Alison. "It makes Daddy hot. But look, we won a coconut." She held her prize aloft.

From outside came the noise of laughter and the cries of the stallholders, and mixed with it the unreal voice of a broadcast gramophone record. The voice, booming and penetrating, worked its way over the fête, a constant unintelligible background for all the other noises.

Matthew left Alison with her mother and went out to get some fresh air. It was hot inside the marquee.

To one side of the ground was a row of tall elms, gigantic trees grown past safety, that dropped great branches in the winter storms, and even in summer cast a tribute of small twigs in any breeze. Matthew sat beneath them on a seat and made a note that he must again bring up the question of having the trees lopped.

He sat quietly looking across the field with its white stall tops, flying ribbons, and moving crowds. All this had sprung from the writing of a few letters, some committee meetings, and a great deal of organisation by various people. Tomorrow it would be all gone, and the hospital would be so much the better off for all the money that was being spent now. Matthew was wandering off into a gentle speculation about the power of accumulated pennies, driblets from the pockets of thousands of modest people, when a voice broke in upon his thoughts.

"Nice turn-out, Mr. Silverman. Ought to do the hospital a great deal of good."

Mr. James Brown had seated himself at the side of Matthew.

"Didn't expect to see me here, eh?" Mr. Brown went on.

"I wouldn't say that," said Matthew, eyeing Mr. Brown, who was rigged out in white flannels, a blue blazer, and panama.

"Cautious!" was Mr. Brown's comment on this. He bore Matthew no ill will from their previous meeting, and, such was his nature, he did not believe that Matthew bore him any. "But you can be too cautious, you know. Still, you're not exactly pleased to see me. I don't bear any malice. I got that Pennyquick fields business, so why should I?"

"So I understand. And, having got that, I presume you will have finished with Swanbridge?"

"Oh, no! Not so fast, Mr. Silverman. You seem anxious to get rid of me. But you forget that I'm as much a Swanbridge man as you are, and when I come to look around me it strikes me that it wouldn't be a bad little town for a man to end his days in. I'm seriously thinking of retiring here for good. Does that disturb you?"

"Not at all." Matthew smiled. There was an infectious optimism about Mr. Brown that forbade anyone disliking him for long. "As long as you behave yourself we shall be glad to welcome you."

"Ha, that's a good one! Behave myself! I understand; no trying to talk nicely to editors, eh? Perhaps you're right. Perhaps you're right. But it wouldn't be the behaving that would worry me. No, it's the retiring part I can't face. I've been thinking about that. If there was some little business in the town I could interest myself in when I retire I would be happy. A man must have something to do."

"I agree," said Matthew seriously, who had no intention himself of ever retiring. "Without work some men are unhappy."

"That's right—and that brings me to the question. I didn't come along casually and begin talking to you for the fun of it. That's not Mr. Brown's method. I had a purpose. Always have a purpose; that's the way to get on in life."

"And what was your purpose?" asked Matthew politely. "If I can help you I shall be only too glad."

"You can help all right. What I want to do is to buy a controlling interest in the *Messenger*."

A hawker went by selling popcorn and the gramophone voice was singing, "You ought to see Sally on Sunday." From where he sat Matthew could see Aunt Adelaide's arts and crafts stall, where she was selling articles made by her villagers. His eyes travelled upwards from the stall, over the roofs of the houses beyond the ground to the blue sky, where a patch of rooks, disturbed from the elms by the fête, swung circling.

"Do you mind telling me what makes you want to do that—and why you think you might be able to do it?"

"Not at all, Mr. Silverman. You see, I've always had a kind of hankering to run a newspaper—boyhood dream, you know—and I thought in my old age I might treat myself to the dream. And I chose your paper because—well, very frankly, Mr. Silverman, there's some talk in this town that you aren't doing so well, and I thought if it was from lack of funds then my offer would be acceptable, and if it wasn't from lack of funds then my ideas would be worth having. The least I could do would be to brighten the paper up. It's a dull twopennyworth, you know. That's probably why you aren't doing so well. Got to make it snappy for folks these days. What do you say?"

Matthew did not say anything for a moment. He could not be angry with Mr. Brown, because the other's offer had been perfectly straightforward and businesslike. Yet he was distressed and hurt, though Mr. Brown got no hint of it. In the town they thought he was bankrupt—even a comparative stranger like Mr. Brown came to know it soon enough—and they thought the paper was dull. It was too solid for them; they wanted something snappy, as Mr. Brown called it. That was what Alexander and Harold had told him, and he had tried not to believe. Now a stranger was telling him and he still found it hard to acknowledge that the slow, weighty days of Jacob and James were gone; found it hard to admit to himself what he should have admitted long ago—that he had failed to move with the times. And he knew Swanbridge; he knew the power of gossip.

The sales had fallen—and they said he was bankrupt; and that meant people would lose faith, and it would not be long before the rumour of insolvency became a fact. Suddenly, as he sat there on the elm bench, surrounded by the gaiety of the fête, Matthew had a harrowing vision of the *Messenger* offices empty, of the great plant with dust thickening on it, and of himself with nothing to look forward to but a barren old age; and in that moment he was afraid, encompassed by a fear that he had never known before. It shot through him, physical and nauseating, until his head swam and he was thankful for the warm, comfortable presence of Mr. Brown at his side. Then he pulled himself together, and he had made up his mind. Thank God, he thought, he had not been left to wonder until it was too late to do anything.

He turned to Mr. Brown and shook his head.

"I'm afraid you've come to the wrong man, Mr. Brown. The *Messenger* doesn't want more money, and I fancy that any new ideas can easily be supplied by the staff. In a few weeks' time you will understand that your offer was not altogether an appropriate one, though I thank you just the same. Good afternoon!"

He was gone, leaving Mr. Brown, a little mystified, on the bench. "Funny cove, that," mused Mr. Brown, wiping his head with a handkerchief, "and, if I know human nature, a deep one!"

* * *

Matthew found Uncle Abner seated outside the refreshment tent with a glass of water in his hand. Matthew lost no time. He told Abner that the *Messenger* was out of date; that the service it gave was adequate in the days of his predecessors, but not adequate for these days.

"What I am saying is the cold truth. We have got to alter the *Messenger*. Swanbridge and the people who read the paper have changed vastly since the day my father took over the editorship. A paper should never lag in the rear of civilisation: it should march abreast of it—and that is what the *Messenger* is going to do! We must infuse its old veins with new blood. We must modernise it, in order to live on."

"The paper's all right as it is. You must be touched by the heat, Matthew. You're talking more like Alexander."

"Then Alexander is right—and he is right; he's tried to point this out to me before, but I was stubborn."

"You're mad, Matthew. Go into the shade. I suppose you're going to fill the pages with pictures."

"I am."

"Intelligent people don't want your pictures."

"And we're going to have a serial story."

"Why don't you turn it into a magazine? No"—this to the popcorn vendor, who had halted before them—"I don't want any popcorn. What is this, a lunatic asylum? People trying to sell me popcorn, you talking unmitigated nonsense, and that damned gramophone blaring away and drowning everything."

"The things you and I hate, Abner, have come to stay, and it's our duty to accept them, though there will be no need to countenance the kind of vulgarity that some papers practise. Competitions—"

"Abominations! Stupid rebuses and crossword puzzles!"

Matthew went on. He knew Abner would not agree, yet he told him everything.

"We shall have a column of book reviews, give more prominence to news of films and plays, break up our columns by boxes and make the lay-out of the pages more attractive."

"At this moment your father is turning in his grave."

"Would you like a piece of my coconut, Uncle Abner?"

Alison, a large section of coconut in a dirty hand, came up and offered it to Abner, who took it absent-mindedly.

"We shall run a short gossip column and other attractions. We must give the public what they want. The Silvermans have always served Swanbridge, and they will continue to do so. If necessity is the mother of invention, then invention is the father of progress, and we must not let our invention stray behind that of rivals, otherwise we cease to make progress."

"This is the death-knell of the *Messenger*!"

"Mind you chew it well, Uncle Abner. Gives you indigestion otherwise."

"Chew what well?" exclaimed Abner indignantly, staring down at Alison.

"The coconut, of course."

Abner discovered the coconut in his hand and, with an expression of disgust, gave it back to Alison and pushed her away.

"I'm sure Adelaide will see my point of view."

"I'm sure she will," Abner interrupted quickly, "as soon as she hears that I'm against it. Well, I can't forbid it, but no one shall ever say that I countenanced these blasphemies. Now I'm going to leave this bedlam before I go mad as well."

* * *

It was a hot afternoon, and the little space in her stall made for stuffiness, yet Aunt Adelaide was cool and unflustered. Before her on the sloping boards was the handiwork of her villagers, handiwork which had been made during the last twelve months for sale on this one day, and it was a boast of Aunt Adelaide's that the kettle-holders, barbola-worked boxes, and painted cork mats, and the host of other useful articles that came from Hurlden, seldom went back. Aunt Adelaide knew all about salesmanship long before books began to be written about it.

"No, I'm afraid we haven't a sewing-bag with a rose design; only hollyhocks and birds. Let me show you. There, isn't that lovely? Blue birds they are. Queen Mary bought one of exactly the same design at the British Industries Fair. I thought you'd like it. Yes, three and sixpence. Thank you."

Matthew came into the stall and stood beside her. "May I interrupt your labours and talk to you? It's very important."

"Certainly, Matt. Though I shan't interrupt my labours. I shall hear you. Yes, aren't they lovely baskets, madam? Troon withies, picked by our villagers themselves and dyed in the same way as the Ancient Britons dyed their basket-work. Go on, Matt. What is it?"

Matthew began to tell her, very simply, what he had already told Abner.

"Excellent idea," said Aunt Adelaide. "I was going to make the same suggestion myself. Go ahead, Matthew. I'm with you. No one shall say that the Silvermans can't adapt themselves to changing conditions. No, I'm afraid that one is not for sale. It's already sold. But there's one here. Of course Abner wouldn't agree. You should have known that. But he'll come around. There! Talking to you I've given the wrong change to that lady. Excuse me, Matt, I must run after her." Aunt Adelaide slipped from the stall in pursuit of her customer.

Matthew smiled as he watched her. A voice broke upon his thoughts. "I suppose you haven't got a green one like this?" A young girl was holding up a pincushion.

"What? Oh, a green pincushion. Let me see... ." He began to rummage happily amongst the tidy piles of Aunt Adelaide's merchandise.

* * *

The fête passed off very pleasantly. In the evening, after the fireworks display, there was dancing on the grass in the marked area, and Loraine danced all the time with Harold.

Alexander drank a little too much with Roger Selway, and took the skin off his elbow trying to come down the helter-skelter without a mat, and Reginald and Philip spent most of their time between the dart-throwing stall and the shooting gallery. The only unhappy person was Mrs. Staines, for at half past six, when the crowd was getting thick and the spending fastest, something went wrong with the electrical economy of her stall. The indicator bells refused to ring on four of the eight sections of the stall, and Reginald, called to her aid, reported, after he had crawled under the stall, that the batteries supplied by the contractors must have been very low and were now run out. For the rest of the evening, since no new batteries were available, Mrs. Staines's stall functioned on four only of its eight sections, and the drop in her revenue was appreciable and she found the sight of the happy faces of the Misses Palmer on the next stall irritating to her. And the faces of the Misses Palmer remained happy, for, although they sympathised with Mrs. Staines's plight, they knew now that they would again win the stall prize.

Mr. Phipps spent a substantial hour in the refreshment bar and then, when the lights of the fête were paling the dark sky in a red underglow, he proceeded to the darts stall, where, insisting upon using his own darts, which he carried about with him in a little case, with a skill worthy of Abaris he won for Alison five different prizes before Gibby found them and put an end to the conspiracy.

* * *

The following afternoon—for Matthew intended to waste no time—he called a conference of his staff and explained the revolution which was to take place in the *Messenger*. Since they had come to his room with their proposals he had said nothing to Alexander and Harold. They heard him now with amazement, trying to find reasons for his volte-face and finding none. Very carefully he expounded his ideas, and delegated new work to them. Selway was to do the gossip column; Spencer had the book reviews; Alexander was to look after the films and plays; the foreman printer was to see to the new pages ... one by one he went through the details, missing nothing, and towards the end he said:

"These ideas are, of course, not entirely mine. They have been done, and are done, by many newspapers already. Experience has proved them good, and we must never burke the lessons of experience. That the *Messenger* has wanted new life of this kind has, I imagine, been evident to most of us for some time. The trouble was to shake free of some of our more ponderous traditions."

He then made a handsome acknowledgment to Alexander and Harold for the part they had taken in attacking the heavy conservatism of the *Messenger*.

"When do we start with this new make-up?" asked the advertisement manager.

"At once. You've got just over a week to get out preliminary publicity. After that, I think I am justified in saying that the only publicity this paper will want will be itself."

Harold looked at Alexander as they left the conference and winked. "Well, we won, after all."

"What a victory! That's just like the old man. Even when you beat him he manages to make it his own triumph."

The first number of the new *Messenger* had some startling results. Phipps printed thirty thousand copies, and for three days he and the circulation manager were on tiptoes hoping that Matthew would not discover that they could have printed another thousand copies and sold them. Matthew did find out, and was so pleased at the news that he forgot to rebuke them. The new paper also brought Abner hot-foot to the office, complaining of the puerility of the serial story, which was being supplied by an agency, and found him giving grudging praise for the undoubtedly better make-up, and insisting that he be allowed to write a letter in reply to one in the correspondence column about the preservation of village greens.

XV

The greatest lesson to be learned from the past is that nothing can afford to stand still, and a paper, more than anything else, must march in the van of progress. To our readers, then, we dedicate this new *Messenger*, in the confident hope of their approval.

Swanbridge Messenger (From an Editorial)

Loraine was in love with Harold Spencer. She never called it being "in love"; though Alexander did as often as he was given the opportunity. At first Harold had lent her *Comus* and she had struggled through it, getting very little pleasure from it; but because she knew he would think the more of her if she did so, she pretended to him that she had enjoyed it. Then he had lent her Norman Douglas's *South Wind*, which she had liked in parts, although she could not understand why Harold thought it was so good. Her admiration for him and his cleverness did not suffer because she could not take the full measure of it in the way he wished. She became a skilled dissembler and, as long as she listened and made careful, occasional remarks, Harold would do all the talking that was necessary. He told himself that at last he had found an intelligent woman, when he meant that he had found a woman who would listen and not make stupid interjections; and Loraine told herself that at last she had met a man who was not stuffed with commonplaces like Philip, someone who was alive and interested in things. The plural noun "things " had a vague, satisfying application to all the emotions which were stirred within her by her discontent. To begin with, she read his books loyally and liked him. When he took her to see Spencer Tracy at the Swanbridge Regal Cinema, and proved that he had enough catholicism to appreciate films as well as Milton, she knew she was right, and when he kissed her before leaving her at Khartum the same evening she wondered how she could ever have disliked him so much on the afternoon of the Old Folk's Treat. Secretly Harold's pride was satisfied by the thought that Matthew Silverman's daughter should find him good company. He liked Loraine, he thought he divined in her the glimmer of the spark of true appreciation, and he did his best to fan the spark to a blaze. He deliberately set about cultivating her mind. He plied her with good books, read poetry to her, discussed politics and national questions with her, took her to see the shows of the Swanbridge Repertory Company and, when culture tired them, made love to her with all the healthy enthusiasm of a young man who believes in bringing a passionate sincerity to everything he does.

They made bicycle and omnibus excursions to places of interest around Swanbridge, and with the help of a guide-book traced that part of the Pilgrims' Way which ran along the downs.

One day they went to Maltsey Castle, a gigantic ruin, overgrown with ivy, inhabited by daws, and, from a charge of sixpence for admission, bringing a comfortable income to the descendants of the noble Norman who had built the castle in the eleventh century.

"Funny to think people once lived in this place," Harold said as they climbed the rickety stairs that led to the top of the one perfect watch-tower. He took Loraine's hand and helped her up the last few steps, and they stood on the tower top.

Below them was an open square of gravel, used for a car-park. To one side of the castle ran a half-moon of moat, its surface covered by spreading lily-leaves and marked into dark channels along which moorhens thrust their way. On a tiny island in the moat a swan was nesting, while her sire sailed slowly along the edge of the water taking the titbits thrown by the visitors who had gathered in a group to feed the birds and watch the nest. Beyond the castle a wood ran towards the sky, the trees in leaf, a green army of giants pouring down the hillside upon the ruin.

"Lovely, isn't it?" said Loraine, looking at him and catching his arm to steady herself. She was not very good at heights, and it was a sheer drop to the ground.

"Grand. Did you notice all that lozenge-work decoration on the windows?"

"Yes, wasn't it very Norman? And the attendant, he was funny, I thought."

"Some of the walls are twelve feet thick. They built to last in those days."

"You know, Harold, my uncle—Reggie's father, who was killed in the war—he was frightfully keen about Normans and things like that."

"He wrote that book about Swanbridge, didn't he? I'll bet it was interesting to listen to him talk."

"Oh, it was; he used to go on for hours … sometimes you just couldn't stop him, no matter what you did. Not," she added hastily, "that I'd have minded, but Mummy told me that Daddy used to get irritable at times. There are a lot of people here, aren't there?"

"Saturday," he said. "You know, there's a place near Weston called Worlebury where there's an old English camp. It's on top of a hill in a wood, and …" Something told him that Loraine was not listening. He looked at her and saw that she was watching the people feeding the swans; but hers was no casual interest, her brow was puckered and her eyes intent. "What's the matter, Loraine? Here—" He pulled her away from the parapet, fearful that she had been seized with a giddiness and might fall.

"Stop it!" she cried. "It's all right, Harold. I'm not giddy; but I think I'm seeing things. See those two people at the edge of the group? There, the man's just thrown something to the swan!"

"Well, what about them?" Harold could see them very plainly; a tall, well-made man, hatless and with a scarf dangling loosely round his shoulders. The woman was neater, and dressed in a smart dark-blue suit, and she too was hatless.

"What about them?" Loraine cried, wondering at his stupidity. "Come on, follow me!" She turned and was running down the stairs at a dangerous pace. Harold followed her, hoping that she would not slip and break her leg or neck. They were held up at the turnstile leading from the castle by a party of schoolgirls pushing their way in.

"Oh, dear!" Loraine danced impatiently. Then she was through the turnstile. She ran swiftly across the gravel, but when she reached the moat the pair had gone. "Well, I could have—" She broke off as she heard the note of a familiar horn, and turned to see a small car bounce across the ruts in the square and pass out into the main road. She had a glimpse of a girl in a blue suit and then the car had gone.

"What's the matter? Do you know those people?" Harold asked.

Loraine nodded her head. "I do; at least I know the car, and unless George has sold his, that's whose it was, and I'm pretty sure that was George with the scarf. Now who the devil could that girl be, and what is he doing here when he should be at Oxford?"

* * *

"Very well," said Loraine, "then call me a liar and have done with it."

The Silvermans were at breakfast, and Loraine had just told the family how she had seen George with a girl at Maltsey Castle the previous day. Alexander had looked up from his eggs and bacon and told her that she had been dreaming:

"No one is calling you a liar, Loraine," said Matthew pompously. It was Sunday. morning, and he was attired for church in pin-stripe trousers, a black coat, spread-eagle collar, and a cravat that was as splendid as the day and his wife would tolerate. "I hope none of my family would have the indelicacy to apply such an epithet to another member of this happy household."

"But it was his car."

"There are plenty of cars like George's," said Mrs. Silverman.

"I remember when I was a girl going to Maltsey Castle. Father took me. He wanted some of the water-weeds from the moat for his microscope. This new coffee is nice, isn't it?"

"Excellent, my dear," said Matthew.

"Yes, but I couldn't mistake George's car with that buckled wing, and the colour the same." Loraine was obstinate.

"Did you see the registration number?" asked Alexander.

"Of course not. I was so sure it was his car that I didn't bother to look at that. Besides, I was so surprised. I thought he was at Oxford."

"So he is at Oxford. Though I suppose he could have motored over to Maltsey if he wanted to. He's not interested in old castles, though, so I think it unlikely," said Matthew.

"Not so interested as Loraine is, anyway," said Alexander quickly. "She can even tell a Norman doorway from a Saxon one nowadays, if she reads the guide-book carefully. Why didn't Harold run after the car?"

"He didn't have a chance—oh, shut up, smarty!"

"Alexander!" Matthew pretended a paternal reprimand, and then, winking across the table at his wife, he turned towards Loraine: "There is no need, Loraine, to be so secretive about your movements. In this household we have no secrets from one another. We all know you went to Maltsey with Harold. Speaking for myself, I think he is a very sensible young man, and I have no objection to your accompanying him. Why you should somehow convey the impression that you are ashamed of the association I do not know. I was never ashamed of being seen with your mother…" He went on, delivering a gentle lecture, while Alexander, overjoyed, watched the horror and disgust that chased across Loraine's face. "Love," Matthew went on, forgetting that he was teasing Loraine, absorbed by his own eloquence, his breakfast cold upon his plate, his heart warming with wisdom, "love is a noble, generous impulse, a virtue that turns all its touches into the purest—"

Loraine could stand it no longer. With a half-stifled outburst of indignation and shame, she fled from the room, knocking over her cup of coffee as she went.

When order reigned again over the table, Alison, who had watched and heard everything with an eager face, addressed herself to Matthew. "Turns all it touches into the purest what, Daddy?"

Matthew, his speech forgotten in the pandemonium of the coffee-spilling, looked at her for a moment before he understood what she meant. What he had been going to say had gone completely from his head.

"Alison," he said severely, "little girls should be seen and not heard. Love is a subject which does not concern you at the moment."

"That's right, dear," put in Mrs. Silverman. "Eat up your shredded wheat."

"You know it would be unlike Loraine to make a mistake. I wonder if it was George at Maltsey?" mused Alexander.

"Maltsey's not very far from where Aunt Adelaide lives, is it?" asked Alison, forgetful of the parental ban on her questions.

"Not very," answered Alexander, but neither he nor his mother and father knew what Alison was thinking as she bent over her cereal.

"My opinion is," said Matthew finally, "that if George had been to Maltsey he would have surely come home. It's all a silly mistake of Loraine's."

He rose from the table, gave his waistcoat a jerk, and walked out to the terrace. The morning was fresh; from the handle of the garden roller a plump thrush was serenading the household; and the trees in the orchard were thick with young fruit. Matthew drew in the scented air, relishing its tang in his lungs. A great peace hung over the town; the chimney smoke went straight up into the air, curling as it thinned and died; loungers bathed in the warmth of the sun and gossiped slowly; the roof slates, fresh washed from a shower in the night, shone bright red and grey, and through all the streets moved the scents of the surrounding countryside, a sweet invasion. Choirboys on their way to church thought of swimming in the river, the vision of dark pools and creamy breakers in their eyes; old men sat on their allotment seats eyeing the thin rows of radishes and young carrots and mourning the death of onion seedlings eaten by beetles. It was Sunday morning, a leisurely, comfortable time of preparation for worship and pleasure; some put out their hymnals and others their fishing-rods; some lay abed reading or dreaming and others were up and doing, planting potatoes or tending their flower patches.

Matthew could feel the solid, happy spirit of the town, and he was happy, too. For this was Swanbridge, his town in a way, and he was proud of it. He wanted no other existence than this, no other joys than those he had already known, and no praise except the contentment of his family and the success of his business ... The success of his business—he had little doubt of that now. Week by week the sales marked a returning popularity; sometimes they halted, sometimes they soared, but always the general trend was upwards, until he was relying upon a weekly circulation of thirty-four thousand copies and confident in time this would be exceeded. It had not been a sudden success. People who had dropped the paper bought it from curiosity, and then, comparing it with the *Courier*, influenced by their old loyalty, became regular subscribers again; some of them lived in houses which had known a copy of the *Messenger* since John Silverman had first printed it. It had at first come to their great-grandparents, neatly wrapped in brown paper, and costing sixpence; their grandparents had seen the price reduced from fourpence to threepence, and finally, with the repeal of the paper taxes, to twopence. John Silverman himself had worked the hand-press which printed the first numbers; Jacob had used it for a while and then been proud of the press driven by a gas-engine which he had installed; James had hated the gas-engine, and when he died the *Messenger* was being printed on an electrical machine which had once done duty for a London paper and which he had bought cheaply, a machine which still served the new *Messenger*.

The new *Messenger* seemed to give a fresh enthusiasm to all who worked for it. Matthew catechised, praised, lacerated, and sympathised in his editorials; Selway exhausted himself to get titbits for his gossip column and drank more beer than ever at that clearing-house for scandal, the Three Feathers; Spencer reported meetings, inquests, police courts, and football matches during the day, and read until his eyes were sore at night; Alexander immersed himself in his reporting until he seemed to have no time left for leisure; the advertisement manager went about with a glad smile on his lips, his eyes bright with the light of battle, and Phipps became almost scurrilous with joy as he watched the lovely fresh quires pouring from his mechanical god's maw. He would stand listening to the roar, his fat body a-tremble with the stir of the rollers and his lips, moving noiselessly to a string of imprecations, happy, rotund oaths which were the offerings of his devotion. In the composing room the linotype machines clicked their glad song of falling lead, and even the dirty-faced boys carrying flongs to the foundry shared in the making of a new sensation which stirred Swanbridge and lifted the *Messenger* towards its old position of glory and authority. Even scrawny-necked Miss Leeds, who sat all day in her little cubicle proof-reading the columns, stopped sucking peppermints and actually began to take an interest in what she read.

"All this," thought Matthew, "I have done. From me has sprung this wonder." Others have helped—he could magnanimously make that acknowledgment—but he had been the well from whence this pure, undefiled spring took its source. He basked in the morning sun, revelling in a slow procession of adjectives and metaphors ... and it was all for posterity; it would be handed on to Alexander (how that boy worked these days; the fire was there, the spirit that rejoiced in news, in print, and the smell of hot lead from the foundry). One day he would die—he could contemplate eternity with content—one day the carriages would roll slowly over the gravel of St. Dunstan's drive and he would be laid to rest; but behind would be the *Messenger*, the hubbub and stir of the works, and his son, Alexander. His blood, his flesh, his work, would go on ... There was no end to his spirit, the spirit of the Silvermans.

His wife's voice within the house, and an unhappy protest from Alison, told him that the church party was waiting for him. He straightened his coat, put a hand to his cravat, and then raised it to his carefully combed hair. He was coming; Mr. Matthew Silverman, editor of the *Messenger*, was going to church with his family.

XVI

"What beauty! What grace!" he thought, "and you are mine … mine."

Swanbridge Messenger (From the Serial Story)

Alexander bought a dog. A long time afterwards, when events had revealed their proper significance in the softening perspective of time, he came to the conclusion that the dog had proved a great influence in his life—not directly, of course; but the indirect influences in life are those which often have the greatest effect.

After the Farley Horse Show, which he had been covering for the *Messenger*, he had been walking away from the paddock in which the prizes had been presented when he was stopped by a bowlegged, gaitered ferret of a man, known all over the county as Foxy Thomas. Foxy was known and disliked by a number of people from all classes. He drove a shrewd deal, and often a sharp one, with a soft tongue; in drink he was quarrelsome and capable of putting his temper into his fists; he had a way with the women which was an additional reason for many men disliking him; and he was an inveterate gambler. Alexander, unreasonably perhaps, liked Foxy, although the only things he could find in his favour were an understanding of animals and a certain bawdy wit.

"Well, Foxy, what do you think of the show?"

Foxy had told him and Alexander had said that he could not print his comments, though personally he would treasure and relate them to his friends. Then Foxy had asked him if he wanted to buy a dog, and Alexander had seen that he was holding his walking-stick by the wrong end, the crook curled round the collar of a dog. The dog, Foxy explained, he had that afternoon won in a bet from a farmer, who had backed his judgment of a hunter in the jumping contest against Foxy's.

"He wanted to make it pounds, but I saw this dog with him and I felt I'd like him. The trouble is, now I've got him I can't keep him. I've a little spaniel bitch that'll kill herself trying to keep him from the house. He's yours for five bob. I could have sold him back to the farmer for more, but that would have brought me bad luck. Never sell back to a man what you've won from him. Look at him!"

Alexander had looked at him. It was a bull-terrier dog with a chest as broad as a barrel, the hind-quarters of a bull, stocky legs, a brown patch on the right ear, and a pair of eyes as bright as sea-buttons and rimmed with pink. The animal had the look of an amiable murderer, a stout, lethal butcher, a swaggering, nautical air, and a grin over its face that seemed to indicate that it found something funny about the world and could not stop laughing.

"He looks a pretty tough customer."

"Not a bit of it, my boy. Sweet as a lamb, as gentle as a dove, and as obedient as they make 'em. Not an ounce of fight in him. These bull-terriers are all bluff. Look at the ears. If he'd ever done any fighting they wouldn't be so perfect." Foxy did not find it necessary to add that the good fighters always keep their ears well out of harm's way.

A stallion went prancing by them and squealed. The dog's ears went up at the familiar sound, and its tail thumped the ground.

"Mind you," put in Foxy quickly, seeing that Alexander was not altogether enamoured of a pacific pedigree, "if it came to the point and the dog had to fight, defend himself—then he'd make the fur fly and give anything on four legs twenty shillings in the pound. I wish I didn't have to get rid of him. What do you say—seven-and-sixpence?"

"You said five shillings."

"All right then, yours for five shillings."

And the dog became Alexander's. He took it back with him at the end of a length of stout cord. It sat quietly in the bus and, tied to the leg of a table, quietly watched him as he wrote his report of the horse show at the office. In three hours Alexander had been won by its happy grin and gentle, mournful eyes.

Outside the office he let it off the string, and the dog, as though only too ready to acknowledge his mastership, trotted sturdily at his heels. He decided to call it Hannibal, because that was a good name and somehow the dog reminded him of alps and elephants; it was the incarnation of ponderous determination. As he expected, there was some opposition in Khartum when he announced Hannibal. Loraine said that one dog was enough in the house. His mother, who agreed with Loraine, but preferred to show her versatility by thinking of another objection, declared that Hannibal and Micky were sure to fight and that Alison would not like it.

Alexander had a ready answer to their objections. He argued; they replied; and Hannibal sat solidly on the rush mat by the french window, looking now at one face and now at another, his eyebrows creased into what might have been a disapproving frown at the bickering.

Alison came in as they argued and, seeing Hannibal, lost her heart at once to his ugly simplicity, and so disposed of one objection. Matthew, who liked animals, came in a few minutes afterwards, walked slowly round Hannibal, pronounced that its hind legs were too long and its neck too short for it to be a thoroughbred (an opinion which Alexander and Alison at once disputed), and said that he saw no reason why it should not remain—so long as it did not fight with Micky.

"He won't fight, I tell you," insisted Alexander. "They only fight when they're attacked. Foxy said so."

"Foxy Thomas—did he sell it to you?" Loraine asked the question incredulously. "Fancy letting that sharper diddle you."

"He's not a sharper. At least, not with me. Foxy Thomas has some very good points about him. You may not believe—"

"Who is this Mr. Thomas?" asked Mrs. Silverman.

"I'm afraid, my dear," explained Matthew, "he's not a gentleman you would approve of altogether. But from my knowledge of him, I must say there's little he does not know about animals."

"And he said Hannibal was as gentle as a lamb, and so he is!"

At this moment Micky trotted along the terrace and appeared at the open french window. He stopped, every hair on his back rising, his tubby little body stiffening at the sight of Hannibal. Then, reasoning perhaps from a comparison of bulks, Micky gave a half-hearted, friendly wag of his tail and made to enter the room and establish cordial relations with Hannibal. Micky never got inside the room. Hannibal had decided that this was his territory. He was being invaded. His hackles rose, the soft skin of his muzzle stretched back to show a row of fanged teeth, and with a sharp bark he launched his fifty pounds at Micky. Micky fled.

201

Loraine shrieked; her mother cried, "It's murder "; Matthew ran to the fireplace for the poker, and Alexander and Alison, their eyes shining with excitement, followed the dogs.

Micky took no heed of flower-beds or paths. He went straight through the screen of irises that bordered the terrace, across the lawn, over the rockery, and through the currant-bushes to the orchard. And behind him, showing a surprising turn of speed, came Hannibal. He flattened the irises, sent pieces of the lawn scudding into the air, traversed the rockery with a dexterity that would have made the real Hannibal look like a day tripper on Snowdon, and yelped ecstatically as he saw Micky leave the currant-bushes.

"Hannibal! Hannibal!" Alexander roared.

"Micky! Micky!" Alison cried, feeling that she should show some loyalty and hoping that nothing would deprive her now of a private dog fight in her own garden. Together they raced down the path, the dogs already lost to sight in the orchard.

At the bottom of the orchard they stopped short. Micky, realising he could go no further, had jumped from the edge of the pond on to the little island in its centre on which the ducks preened and sunned themselves. For a small dog it was a long jump. Hannibal was dancing and barking round the pool, his tail waving, a happy grin over his face.

"Hannibal!" Alexander made a rush for him. Hannibal dodged him, backed a few feet, gathering himself, and then jumped. He landed square and heavy on the island.

Alexander shut his eyes from the bloodshed. Alison opened hers wide to miss nothing. And the dogs disappointed them both, for Hannibal's growl died away in his throat like summer thunder over the downs, his tail wagged more violently, and Micky, losing his fear, made little snuffling noises of friendship.

When the rest of the family arrived, the two dogs were, unembarrassed by their audience, completing their friendship, so oddly begun, by an olfactory exchange of credentials which appeared to give them every satisfaction.

"You see," said Alexander proudly. "I said he wasn't fierce. They were just playing. There's no doubt of their being friends."

No one disputed him, and Hannibal became a member of the Silverman family.

* * *

Alexander was proud of Hannibal, and resented any criticism of his breeding. Hannibal slept in his room at night, curled on a rug at the side of the bed. He made an admirable watch-dog, and seemed, as though by some uncanny sense, to feel the presence of a stranger in the house. More than once, when Alexander was working in his room at night and the family were downstairs, Hannibal had suddenly raised his head and growled softly, and Alexander had known that someone had called to see his father or mother, some stranger. A word to Hannibal would stop the growling.

Only once did Hannibal disgrace the peaceful reputation which Foxy had given him. That was when Alexander took him to see Uncle Abner. Uncle Abner liked big dogs; Pelang was the latest of a long line of companions; Great Danes, collies, mastiffs, St. Bernards.

Alexander wanted Uncle Abner's opinion on Hannibal. He got it. Without announcing himself, he walked into Abner's sitting-room on a hot Saturday afternoon, proudly leading Hannibal and smiling to himself at the surprise his uncle would have when he saw the magnificent dog.

Abner, from cursing the noise of an aeroplane, had dropped into a doze in the sunshine by the window. He was awakened by a thump against his chair as Pelang rose and turned quickly.

Some men can never be friends; there is that in their composition which forbids it. Some dogs share this ineluctable quality, and Hannibal and Pelang had it for each other. They wasted no time in preliminaries; they halted for no formal growling declarations. Hannibal snapped free of the lead and flung himself towards Pelang, who rose quickly and avoided the rush and then, taking a natural advantage, closed in on Hannibal from behind.

Hackles high, muzzles bared to their fangs, paws scraping Abner's Hamadan for a hold, they squealed, snapped, twisted, and rolled in the middle of the room.

"What the devil is this?" roared Abner, rising and brandishing his stick. The melée of dog swirled towards him and he took one vicious cut at it and hopped to cover behind his chair.

"Hannibal! Hannibal!" Alexander danced in agony around the pair, making insincere gestures towards Hannibal, wanting to catch hold of the dog and not daring to risk his hand in the midst of the chopping teeth. A small table was knocked over, a loose rug tumbled across the room, and the firepieces pealed in a jangling disarray about the hearth as the dogs swept against the high fender.

"Curse the savages! Do something!" howled Abner at Alexander. "Do something! Stop them!" Then, seeing Alexander's indecision, he stepped in bravely, raising his stick aloft and using it like a broadsword. The blows rose and fell indiscriminately—and the dogs clung to one another's throats and appeared to be unaware of the blows. A wild swing from Abner hit the electric light globe and brought a tinkling shower of glass upon himself and the combatants.

Mrs. Cartwright appeared, pale and frightened, at the doorway, and fled, crying hopefully, "Snuff ... snuff."

"Snuff!" Abner had time to be critical. "There's not a pinch of snuff in the house. And who could put it under their noses?"

"They say if you bite their tails hard ..." Alexander felt he ought to do something to stay the bloodshed.

"Fool! Take that, you devils!" The stick rose again. Alexander, awed by the primitive influences that were loose in the room, watching Abner slashing like a gaunt savage, and the dogs, all wolf, all hate, tearing at each other, found time to make the trite philosophical observation to himself that civilisation is only a thin cover for natural instincts. "Nature red in tooth and claw," he thought.

And then, laughing, competent, and calm, Reginald appeared in the doorway with a bucket of water. He lifted it and hit the struggling dogs with a cold douche. They stopped fighting at once and sat back with a hurt, uncomprehending expression on their faces, and in the momentary lull Alexander grabbed Hannibal by the collar and Reginald secured Pelang, and Uncle Abner looked ruefully at the wet mess spreading over his lovely Hamadan.

"Reggie, you're a damned fool!"

"I had to stop them, sir."

"And now perhaps you will tell me, Alexander, why you brought that villainous, bandy-legged runt into my house? In another moment Pelang would have killed it."

"Oh, no, Uncle Abner. I think Hannibal was getting the better of it. Hannibal's my dog. I wanted you to see him and give me your opinion of him."

"My opinion of that—that—" Abner opened and shut his mouth like a goldfish, and then, catching sight of Mrs. Cartwright in the doorway, he decided to withhold his opinion. "Take him away, take him away! And don't bring him here again. Do you hear? Next time I may not be in such a hurry to have the fight stopped, and then you'll be taking a dead dog back with you. Hannibal, indeed!"

"Well, I don't suppose it was entirely Hannibal's fault," said Reginald, who had already met Hannibal and liked him for his grin. "Pelang is as much to blame."

"Silence!" snorted Abner. "You'd better start clearing up the mess. There seems to be no peace these days; no sooner do I get to sleep and forget the confounded aeroplanes that fly overhead all day with their infernal buzzing than irresponsible ruffians come into my house throwing water about and starting dog-fights. Now then, get out before I put Pelang on to you both." He shook his stick fiercely at Alexander and Hannibal, and they went, both grinning.

Outside, Alexander examined Hannibal for wounds and found that, except for a few patches of hair torn away and a cut on the neck, the dog was sound. He slipped in the back way at Khartum and smuggling Hannibal to his room, dressed the wound, and left him there sleeping happily on the rug.

As he went downstairs he heard a familiar voice coming from the dining-room. When he entered, the first thing he saw was George's broad face, partially eclipsed by a cup.

"Strike me pink!" he said vulgarly. "It's the prodigal son himself. What have they sent you down for?"

George lowered his cup and beamed at Alexander, who found the radiance almost too brotherly and affectionate; George was exuding good-will and happiness and Alexander was naturally curious.

"Hullo, Alex. Bit of a surprise, eh?"

"I should say so."

"George"—it was Loraine speaking, her voice bubbling over like a fountain—"George has come home for the weekend, and he's got the most wonderful news. He's engaged, Alex!"

"What!" There was surprise, humour, and some indignation in the tone.

"It's true," said George. "I want you—"

"You poor fish," commiserated Alexander, interrupting him. "What on earth did you do that for? Don't you know that marriage is a snare, the pit into which all ambitions fall? What grasping female lured you into her clutches?"

"Alexander!" The exclamation came simultaneously from his mother, Loraine, and Matthew, who was standing near the window. Then a pleasant female voice, a voice that was near laughter, said, "I'm the grasping female, Alexander."

Alexander felt himself going red, and saw that Miss Peters, his Aunt Adelaide's secretary, was seated in a small chair by the fireplace. He had been so taken up with seeing George that he had not noticed her.

At once he was all apologies. "I say, I'm terribly sorry. I didn't mean that, Miss Peters. Joking, you know. George and I … we … well, you know how it is with brothers."

"I've never had any brothers; but I think I can guess," she said.

"Well, Alexander," boomed Matthew, covering the slight awkwardness which had settled on the room, "now you've earned the undying enmity of your future sister-in-law, aren't you going to congratulate the lucky pair?" When engagements and weddings were in the air, Matthew found his mind falling back on the time-honoured cliches of "lucky pair," "happy couple," and "future bliss."

"Oh, rather. Here's wishing you all the best"; and he drank their health from the cup which his mother had diplomatically pushed into his hand. He went on, "Won't Aunt Adelaide be mad at losing a good secretary!"

"She won't lose her for a while," said Miss Peters. "Will she, George?" She looked up at George, and he shook his head gently, and Alexander thought to himself, as he saw George's eyes, "Save us, the poor fellow's got it bad. Talk about a hen with one chicken."

Matthew, although George had surprised him, thoroughly approved of his choice. He had heard a great deal about Miss Peters from Aunt Adelaide, and from his own acquaintance with the young lady he had formed a good opinion of her steadiness, sound judgment, and good sense; qualities which were essential in any wife and lacking in a great many.

"And it was you I saw at Maltsey Castle?" Loraine saw an opportunity to establish her story without doubt.

Hildegarde Peters nodded. "Yes. I was staying near by for the weekend with a friend, and George ran down from Oxford on the Saturday to see me. We never dreamt that our conspiracy had been observed."

"You were quite safe. No one would believe my story."

"Hum!" Matthew coughed disapprovingly.

"But I believed it, Loraine?" Alison cried. "I knew it must be George and Miss Peters. I knew they were in love."

"Alison!"

But Alison went on unperturbed. What was wrong? If they were in love—and they must be if they were going to get married—why should she not mention it? " 'Cause Miss Peters used to get letters from George when I was staying with Aunt Adelaide. I could tell the writing on the envelope, only—"

"Only I made you swear to keep the secret!" Hildegarde laughed. "You kept it very well."

"Yes, didn't I?" Alison was delighted by the compliment. "It was hard sometimes. I wanted to tell."

"Alison, dear, don't try to eat as well as talk," came Mrs. Silverman's soothing voice.

That evening they had, to use Alexander's phrase, "a thoroughly hearty time." Matthew, in honour of the occasion, produced bottles of Sauternes and of port for dinner, and the last vestige of awkwardness disappeared. Hildegarde was accepted into the family, and introduced them to demon grab, and found that she need not overlook cheating but could add her vigorous denunciation to those of Matthew and Alexander when Loraine and her mother occasionally weakened. They played paper games and argued fiercely; Alexander contesting with his father the legitimacy of hatchet ranking as a kitchen utensil; Loraine insisting, against all opposition, that, for a vegetable beginning with p, pickled cabbage was admissible; Mrs. Silverman protesting that, for one word beginning with s and ending with e, sewing-machine was entitled to be correct, and overjoyed when reference to a dictionary proved her right; and Alison, allowed up long after her bedtime as a treat, falling off to sleep on the rug jealously watched by Micky and Hannibal.

Tired of games, George played the piano, and they sang songs—the old-fashioned songs—and Hildegarde, looking so lovely that George frequently hit the wrong note, sang a comic song about an Indian merchant who came from the East to sell carpets in London.

Thoroughly hearty and sentimental Alexander found the evening, conscious that his modernity should make him despise it, and yet glad that he was, for all his opinions, enjoying it as much as anyone.

Such evenings were rare in Swanbridge, and, for that matter, anywhere. The wireless was mute on its pedestal, the urgency of the nine o'clock news forgotten; the gramophone stood silently in its corner, the records in their dog-eared folders a decrepit column. The family made their own amusement, finding company in themselves. Matthew shepherded them affectionately. This reminded him of the days when he had been a young man and found nothing strange in standing at a piano, singing *Admirals All* and *Glorious Devon* (last verse in dialect), while a young girl, her dress glorified by a blue sash, played. In those days everyone contributed; every man could sing and every girl recite and play.

He was glad George was engaged, and glad that the woman was not a stranger. Surprised though he had been by George's announcement, the shock was tempered by the fact of Miss Peters being known to him; she was almost one of the family whether she married George or not. He watched the two; George, usually reserved in his emotions before the family, filling the room with his exuberant happiness and conscious only of Hildegarde; and Hildegarde feeling her right place, taking all they were so ready to give and yet doing nothing to embarrass them in their generosity. She would be good for George; she was mature, wise, and would add vision to George's steadiness.

And Mrs. Silverman, standing blushing before them, reciting *The Armada*, the words so firmly a part of her past childhood that age could never steal them from her, blushing not from the intimate publicity, but for pride and happiness that George had delighted Matthew by getting himself engaged to such a nice girl … *the richest spoils of Mexico, the stoutest hearts of Spain* …

Some day, thought Loraine, I shall be as Hildegarde, welcomed by a family not my own, sliding into a new world, standing, a little afraid, at the gateway of a new experience, an experience already dimly acknowledged and guessed, like a distant view of the grey and golden towers of a cathedral lying away in a valley, holding promise of new joys, fresh beauties. She shared Hildegarde's happiness vicariously, and thought how pretty even now her mother looked when she blushed.

They finished the evening by sitting round the fire with the biscuit-barrel on the hearthrug before them, dipping into it as though they were Arabs at a communal feast, Loraine picking only the chocolate creams and Alexander taking three Garibaldis at a time, unchided, for this night all was permitted. Gibby brought lemonade and lime-juice, and grumbled about the crumbs and the wet ring marks, and was met by laughter from Matthew, who dismissed her disapproval of informal meals and justified his right as master to light the fire on a summer evening.

"Man needs fire not only for warmth, Gibby. It is a companion, too, and should be allowed to share his happiness. And this is a very happy night for us."

"He's going to get sentimental now," thought Alexander.

But George, insisting that Hildegarde must be tired, anxious for her health already, brought the evening to an end, while Alexander, disappointed of his father's speech, found another pleasure in George's solicitousness for his beloved, telling himself that he could never come to this.

Matthew and his wife stood by the open window when the rest were gone to their rooms, letting the cool night air bathe their faces free of the warmth of the room. His arm held her shoulders and they said nothing, both of them too happy for words, contented and drawn into a mysterious, joyful communion as they watched the moon push the clouds aside and with its light turn the orchard to a fairy forest, the white, lime-coated trunks spectre shapes immobilised for ever in the moment of a dance ... They stayed for a while, conscious of the night's beauty and their own happiness.

XVII

There are several ways of dealing with boiled bacon.

Swanbridge Messenger (From "You and your Kitchen.")

Mr. Clewton liked rivers, and he had seen enough of them in his lifetime to have acquired a severity of judgment which refused to be impressed by size or commercial importance. He liked the River Troon. It was shallow with summer drought, and choked in some stretches by rank growths of water-buttercups, wild irises, and flannel-weed. Spits of sand which, in winter, lay five feet below the water, were laid bare, and covered with a flotsam of dead branches and quickly grown spikes of sorrel and meadowsweet that would be swept away in the first autumn flood-rise. In the cool places of the overhanging banks, grilled by trailing tree-roots and the damp fronds of meadow plants that yearned for the water, big fish—barbel, pike, and an occasional trout—lay, moving seldom, lazy with the heat from the tepid water. Above Mr. Clewton's head was a twisted crabapple whose blossoms had drifted in a pink fall to the river in May, and whose small apples, set only to fall before their time, now dropped with rich splashes into the stream and were carried away, bobbing like buoys in each cross-current, to a variety of fates.

The Troon curved and looped itself through the wide valley plain, now running close under the shelter of thick beech and fir woods, now through an orchard where ducks worked its banks and a farmer's sons bathed. In his imagination Mr. Clewton followed the river from its birth at the foot of distant hills, along its tortuous valley, past hop-fields trellised with green, and orchards heavy with swelling fruit, towards that moment when its water would be muddied by tide banks, its surface ruffled by salt wind, and the young current, feeling the lift and fall of the mother sea, would set its shoulder against her domination and find itself overpowered, its strength lapped into the matrix of the oceans. Mr. Clewton liked doing this, because the life of a river made an analogy to his own life. He was, and he was ready to tell anyone who cared to listen, very much like a river. It was his habit of babbling like a brook which had brought him so low in the world; low, that is, if you reckon worldly wealth the real measure of exaltation. Mr. Clewton for fifty-five years had been talking himself into jobs and almost as quickly talking himself out of them. He was generous with his own goods, and thought to find that generosity returned to him by others so illimitably that he could take and waive the formality of an invitation. He had often appeared before county magistrates for petty thefts of food and money. He tramped the country during the summer and sponged upon a married sister in Birmingham during the winter.

A man and a girl came through the meadow towards him. Their passage shook the seeds from the grasses in a fine dust. The girl was striking at the heads of the knapweeds with a hazel switch. As they came abreast of Mr. Clewton, he coughed to warn them of his presence, for where he sat the tall grass almost hid him. The man looked at him and frowned. Mr. Clewton was unconcerned by the frown, for almost everyone frowned when they saw him; the shock of his unshaven face and unkempt appearance had that effect.

"I wonder if you would be kind enough," he said in a voice that was not unmusical, and he lifted his unlit pipe to indicate that he wanted a light. "I find myself without a match."

"Certainly." The man brought out his matches and tossed them down to him.

As he lit his pipe, Mr. Clewton eyed the girl over the flame and decided that she was as pretty as anyone he had seen that summer. A light cotton dress, a green floral pattern over a white ground, showed the young lines of her body. Her bare arms and legs were touched a faint tan with the sun, and the light breeze fingered her fair hair gently as though it were striving to order its pleasant untidiness. Mr. Clewton saw, too, that she was annoyed by the interruption. Because of this, as he threw the matches back with a thank you, he went on: "Would you mind telling me the name of the town up there?" He jerked his head across the meadows.

"Swanbridge," the girl answered sharply.

Mr. Clewton understood the intolerance in her voice. He almost liked her for it. It proved how little she knew of real values. She could see only his body, but he thought of his soul. She had a beautiful body, but probably no soul. That was not, Mr. Clewton decided, an insuperable handicap for a woman. If she knew about his soul ... He rolled back, sucking at his pipe, and began to day-dream about his soul, enjoying the taste of borrowed tobacco through a filched pipe and relishing the comfort in the heat of the sun. Yes, she probably had no soul ...

"He could do with a shave and a good scrubbing!" Loraine said when they were away from the man. "Dirty loafer!"

"Loraine!" Harold was hurt by her brusqueness. "Haven't you got any soul? Talking like that about the poor fellow."

"Poor fellow!" Loraine scoffed. The sight of the filthy man squatting in the lovely meadow had filled her with repulsion, and the words had come unbidden to her lips. " He's just a dirty old man. There's no excuse for people like that these days. There's always the dole."

"Not everyone gets that."

"Well, there are other things. Public assistance institutions and charities." It was silly of Harold to defend the man. She had known Harold for a long time, and there were occasions when she found herself utterly out of harmony with him, when she felt like screaming at the sight of a poetry book and became impatient with him when he defended and tried to excuse tramps and people with impossible grievances. She liked him best when he danced with her and when he kissed her.

"Not every man," answered Harold gently, "feels able to give up his freedom to such organisations—and some people, you know, don't care for charity in any form. Remember the words of Borrow: *There's the wind on the heath, brother;* perhaps that is all that poor fellow back there asks from life."

"Even so," said Loraine, who had not remembered the words of George Borrow, for she had never heard them before, "there's no reason why he shouldn't keep himself clean. Water is free and shaves are cheap enough."

"When a man leads his kind of life I suppose he is entitled to make his own resolutions about personal hygiene. I've always found you so sympathetic of other people's troubles. Last night, for instance, when I was telling you about the persecution of the German Jews, you were most indignant. For a moment, just now, it was almost as though I had a stranger by my side. It didn't sound like your voice."

"Oh, Harold, don't talk such nonsense!" Loraine felt herself growing impatient. "Hitler pouring castor oil into a Jew is one thing. Anyone would feel angry about it. But you surely can't expect me to go all sentimental over a nasty tramp."

"The system under which we live unfortunately produces such people; it is almost a sacred duty for us to accept them and treat them as human beings, not the waste of a pernicious system."

"Sacred!" Loraine's laughter echoed across the river, startling a water-rat from the bank with a *plomp* that was marked by out-reaching ripples. "Harold, don't be so solemn!"

"I'm not solemn in the way you mean. Didn't you read that book by Bernard Shaw I lent you? You know—*The Intelligent Woman's Guide to Socialism?*"

"Of course I did!" The book had lain in her drawer since Harold had given it to her. Its bulk had frightened her, and she had put it to keep companion with Burton's *Anatomy of Melancholy*, and Darwin's *Origin of Species*. When she had finished them Harold had promised— for he intended that her revelations should be liberal— that she should be lent his Everyman edition of *Gargantua and Pantagruel*.

"Then how can you take that attitude? I should have thought that Shaw's book would have convinced you about the present economic system. Didn't you agree with what he said?"

"Of course." Loraine was annoyed because he had driven her into a definite opinion. "But, after all, it's only a book."

"Only a book!" Harold was appalled by this desecration of his gods. "It was Shaw!" He was almost sure that Loraine had not read the book. She could not feel as she did otherwise. And he suspected that perhaps she had not read any of the others he had pressed upon her. Only that morning, when he had begun to talk about Browning's

Sordello, which he had given to her as a present, she had turned the conversation by making some childish joke about the title sounding like the name of one of those patent unburstable balls. An unpleasant suspicion that she was not interested in culture, that her fondness for his company was merely to escape for a while from that auctioneer fellow, made him anxious to put her to the test. He felt she was all he desired when they kissed; but passion was only a small part of his life; his woman had to be intelligent and rational as well, schooling her senses. Beauty of the body was not everything; the mind had to be considered.

They wandered on beside the river, silent with their thoughts. From a clump of tall grasses a skylark sprang, disturbed by their passing, and flighted into the sky, its edged wings beating the air in short sweeps, its song pouring down upon them. Harold, stirred by the song, remembered the poet who had heard another bird sing and wrote of it. As they watched it dive into the blue and lose itself against the defiant disc of the sun, he began:

Thou wast not born for death, immortal bird!

Loraine listened to him, savouring the music of his voice as he spoke the lovely lines, and she was sorry that she had spoken rudely about the tramp; she was sorry that she had spoiled the afternoon by a quarrel, and she was suddenly anxious to please him.

... that oft-times hath
Charm'd magic casements, opening on the foam
Of perilous seas, in faery lands forlorn.

"Isn't it lovely, Harold?" she said.

"It's god-like," he said; and then, acting with a guile that he had not known he possessed, he went on "It comes from Wordsworth. I marked it in the volume I lent you last week. Did you read it?"

And Loraine, eager to bring back peace between them, took his arm and answered, "Yes, it was beautiful." She did not mind saying that, because he was so sincere about these things that she could not hurt him by telling the truth.

Harold patted the hand on his arm affectionately, and in his heart groaned for her who could not tell Keats from Wordsworth, who could not recognise the famous ode, drummed into the ears of every schoolchild; and he saw in her dissembling not noble purpose, only a base desire to achieve her own ends. From that moment Loraine lost her magic.

* * *

Alexander spent his Wednesday half-day at Mr. Hancock's cheese factory. The building was almost finished, and it was planned to start production within the next few weeks. The *Messenger* intended to run a long article about the factory, brightened by photographs, and Alexander had been assigned to inspect this "new acquisition to Swanbridge's already considerable industries." Mr. Hancock was not there, and Alexander was conducted round the building by the company secretary, who, Alexander was glad to find, was as ignorant as himself about technical matters. Alexander decided that the machinery could conveniently be dismissed from readers' minds by the useful phrase "must be seen to be believed"; "the ingenuity of these modern devices for pressing, cutting, and packing would need an engineer to describe them and a class of technicians to understand them." Everything that could possibly be so was automatic, and the secretary stressed, with a repetition that soon had Alexander and the staff photographer making faces at one another, the absolute hygienic conditions of the factory. Cleanliness; the cheese that is never touched by hand; virgin from cow to table … the wonder of this miracle seemed to have hypnotised the secretary, and Alexander's remark that the factory itself was built on what had once been a corporation dump left him untouched.

Alexander wrote his article in the comfort and silence of his own room at Khartum. His mother and father were dining out, to return a formal call from a new bank manager. Alison was in bed, and Loraine had gone to the cinema. George had gone back to Oxford to finish the Trinity Term, dropping Hildegarde at Aunt Adelaide's on his way. At the end of the term—Alexander smiled as he thought of it—George was going to do mission work at one of the

215

University East End settlements. Somehow, although George was so deadly serious about it, Alexander had never become reconciled to the vision of his brother as a clergyman. It was like the thought of having an operation. The doctors said it was to happen, yet you looked forward to it with incredulity. It was something that had no part in your existence; it was unreality obtruding from some fairy tale into your life. And then, when it was all over, it still seemed unreal; it was almost possible to convince yourself that the minutes of blankness, when white-coated figures had cut and handled your inert body, had never passed; that the stuff under their hands, plasmic flesh, unliving in the mind and insensible to pain because it was without personality, was not your own; that it was all a creation of a momentary dream. That your body and mind which you knew so well could at any surgeon's will pass into an alien, featureless state was unreal; and that George, steady, plodding, and resolute George, with his little ponderous habits, his solid, human, sensible principles and weaknesses, could ever step from the circle that owned him on to that higher stage was impossible. It might be happening under your very eyes, but still it could not be believed ... Alexander, although he professed, according to his mood, agnosticism, atheism, and pantheism, was at heart medieval to the point of relegating the mission of religion to those who were not passion's slaves; to those who, being born of this earth, hardly realised that they were on it. George, he decided finally, played football too well ever to become a good preacher.

He finished his article and then sat reading in his armchair until it was time for bed. He took Hannibal down for a run around the orchard and said good night to his mother and father, who came in as he was going up the stairs. He lay in bed sleepless for a long time, listening with a deep pleasure to the dying sounds of the house; the scrunch of Loraine's feet over the gravel as she came up the drive, the click of bolts as Matthew made his locking-up round, and then the noises about the bedrooms—the closing of doors and the singing of fresh water coming into the roof cistern not far from his room as the bathroom taps were turned on, and then the swift swoop of silence measured by the creaking of his cane chair as it moved back to burdenless comfort after the strain of his body. Hannibal snored gently at the side of the bed, whining once in his sleep. Soon Alexander was sleeping.

He dreamed about cheeses, a dream of quick, cinematographic flashes joined only by the cognation of cheese. He walked through an enormous cheese, a mountain tunnelled and scored like the face of a quarry, and in the darkness and mould of the tunnels, where his feet were muffled by soft dust, movements of strange things swept by him in the gloom and he was glad of Hannibal walking before him, glad of the swift rise of the dog's hackles and the soft growl at each new terror. He passed from dream to wakefulness with a soft, unsudden transition, and lay in the dark for a moment before he realised that Hannibal was still growling gently and that he no longer dreamed.

He dropped his hand over the side of the bed and touched the cold nose of the dog, bidding it be silent. Hannibal was still while his hand was there, but as he withdrew it the dog began to growl again.

"Silent!"

Hannibal stopped at his command and Alexander heard the thump of its tail against the floor. Then the growl came again as the dog's instincts fought its training.

Alexander knew what the growling meant now. His senses, clogged from sleep, cleared. He slipped from the bed and reached for his dressing-gown. At his movements Hannibal stopped growling. Alexander pulled on his socks and moved to the door. Hannibal followed quietly and obediently.

They went silently down the curving stairway on to the landing. A window at the far end let in the thin light of the night and showed the top of the stairway like the black maw of a dungeon. There were no lights showing under any of the bedroom doors, so Alexander passed them and went silently into the hall. He felt no fear. He knew the house so well that even in the darkness it was never inimical, it could never harbour any danger. Quickly he examined the rooms and, finding them all empty, he opened the door to the passage which communicated with the kitchen, pantry, and the small living-room of Gibby and the servants. The kitchen door was ajar, and from it fell a hard beam of light cutting the passage into half diagonally. Alexander dropped his hand to Hannibal's collar and they advanced towards the door. Standing at the apex of the shadow that held half the passage he could look into the kitchen far enough to see the long table and the wall dresser which filled its length at one side.

Standing at the end of the table was a man. In his hands he had a carving-knife and fork, which he was using on a large piece of boiled bacon. To one side of the bacon was a plate, with a few ragged pieces of thickly cut meat, four pickled onions, and some cold potatoes. A bottle of pale ale stood opened by the plate, and, in readiness when the other was done, a large rice pudding and a pot of strawberry jam waited beyond the ham.

Alexander looked at the man curiously, then he stepped quietly into the kitchen and closed the door gently behind him.

"The great thing to remember in carving," he said quickly to cover the man's surprise, "is to use the wrists. Force won't help you much. It's like tennis or cricket or fencing—the wristwork is the essential thing. Let me do it for you."

He stepped forward and took the carvers from the man and, to hide the agitation of his heart which threatened to unman his calmness, he bent over the meat and began to carve, skilfully and easily. The exercise restored his self-control, and when he had filled the plate he laid the carvers down and smiled at the man.

"There, I think that will be as much as you can manage. You can take the rest with you when you go. I don't like boiled bacon, so you will be doing me a favour."

"Perhaps I'd better go now?" The man made a movement towards the open kitchen window.

"Oh, no! Please don't do that. You must stop and finish your supper. You see"—Alexander was almost apologetic—"I've never had this happen to me before, and I shouldn't want it to end so quickly. I expect you know that it is a favourite mental exercise of most people, imagining what they would do if they met a burglar in their house. Thinking about it one can always be heroic and calm. When it actually happens, somehow all that is upset. You see, even now, although I appear calm, I'm tremendously excited and nervous. But I have often told myself what I should do, and you must help me to do that. Do begin your supper."

Mr. Clewton—for he was the intruder—was astute enough to recognise Alexander's mood and clever enough to realise that it was to his interest to indulge it. He drew himself a chair and sat down, saying "I'm not really a burglar, of course. I'm just hungry, and when a man is hungry it is only natural that he should look for food. Is the dog safe?" He waved his fork to where Hannibal sat by the door.

"He won't hurt you," said Alexander. He went on, " Tell me, why do you do this sort of thing? It's rather dangerous, isn't it?"

Mr. Clewton looked up from his food at this question, and then he shook his head. "You'd be surprised how soundly most people sleep." He cut into a pickle, and.the kitchen was silent for a while save for the heavy crunching of his teeth on the onion. "I'll bet," he said when his mouth was clear, "that it was the dog that heard me first?"

"It was," admitted Alexander.

"Must be a good dog. They usually sleep as soundly as their owners, or else they come creeping down to you to make friends and get titbits. I don't think most dogs have any social conscience. As for why I do this kind of thing, well"—he shrugged his shoulders—"I suppose it just is that I'm a misfit. There don't seem to be any respectable place, at least what most people would call respectable, for me, so I've formed my own philosophy."

"And what's that?"

"Chiefly to please myself. You've got to be what the authorities call a vagrant to do that, and, of course, you can't always please yourself. Nothing holds good all the time. I don't suppose there's a single philosophy in the world which hasn't got to make a compromise somewhere. But mine works most of the time."

"It seems to me that your happiness depends very largely upon the generosity of those people who have a less careless, less selfish policy. For instance, you would have been in an awkward position tonight if I'd been some crusty old householder who would have turned you over to the police."

Mr. Clewton laughed and poured himself a glass of ale.

"Bad-tempered householders generally make enough noise coming downstairs to give me warning, and I'm gone before they have a chance to hand me to the police. The timid ones are noisy too, only from a different reason. They want to give me a chance to go so they won't have to deal with me. And the curious, quiet people, like yourself, are always reasonable. For absolute peace of mind there is no life like mine, because I never have to bother about myself. I only wish I'd discovered this life earlier."

"It sounds very convincing," said Alexander, pushing the rice pudding towards the man; "but I'm sure there's a flaw in it somewhere. It might be all right for a few individuals to live your kind of life, but the fact that you can do so is entirely dependent upon the millions of other people who live a normal life. You depend entirely upon other people not deciding to live as you do. In fact, you're rather like ..." He stopped, realising that the simile which had come to his mind was not altogether a pleasing one.

"Go on, say it," urged Mr. Clewton amiably. "You wouldn't be the first. We're like the fleas on a dog, parasites. But we aren't really. I prefer the other description, the nobler one, that we are like the satellites flung off from some splendid sun, different, yet dependent. Anyway, the important point is that here I am sitting in your kitchen, as your guest, having a good meal, when I don't perhaps deserve your hospitality. That being so, I must drink to your humanity." Mr. Clewton raised his glass and drank a silent toast.

"You're welcome."

"Thank you, Mr.—?"

"Silverman."

"Thank you, Mr. Silverman. Clewton is my name. This," Mr. Clewton said after a lengthy pause during which he was feeding with a quick voracity that fascinated Alexander, "is an excellent pudding."

"It was made by a good cook."

"So I can tell. This, in fact, is an excellent house. Judging by the furnishings in the dining-room, Mr. Silverman, you—or your father—must be a wealthy man."

"You've been in the dining-room?" Alexander was amazed.

"Of course, and the library. I had to find a cigar to round off my meal. I don't think your father will miss one of his."

Alexander began to laugh, his body shaking, and finally his laughter passed to coughing, so that Mr. Clewton solicitously poured him a glass of ale and handed it to him. Alexander drank and was calmed.

"Thank you. In a small way, I suppose, you would call us wealthy. Wealthy, at least, for Swanbridge—that's the name of this town. My father owns the local newspaper."

"And you?"

"I work on it. Reporter and general factotum."

"Well, well." Mr. Clewton put down his glass and began to prepare his cigar. " The gods arrange strange meetings. So you're a reporter?" He eyed Alexander critically as he spoke, his eyes taking in every detail—the tousled, sleep-rumpled hair, the dark eyes bright with this small adventure, and the quick form lost in the loose folds of a green-and-black dressing-gown which had shaving-soap stains on the brocaded lapels.

"Why do you say that and stare at me so?"

"Because," said Mr. Clewton, rubbing the cigar under his nose tenderly, " I must have been about your age when I first entered newspaper life."

"You're a newspaperman?"

"I was for years. Once I believed that I should be a newspaperman all my life. I started on a provincial paper, the same as you. But it wasn't long before I was dissatisfied with that, and made for London and Fleet Street. Ha, those were the days. You'll soon be tired, too, of a provincial newspaper. You'll want to get out and work for a London paper. Fleet Street will probably disappoint you; but you'll go. It's irresistible."

"I shan't go. I'm going to stay on here and be editor of the paper. You can keep your dailies."

Mr. Clewton shook his head. "That's what they all say; but they go at sometime or other. Most of them come back to the country; some die of overwork and drink, and a few make names. And what names!" Mr. Clewton leaned back in a gesture of happy memory. Alexander never learned on what papers Mr. Clewton had worked, or for how long he had been a journalist, or for that matter whether he had ever really been a journalist. Mr. Clewton's life was so much a mixture of fantasy and fact that even he might have had difficulty in defining from his memories what he had imagined and what he had experienced. But, journalist or no journalist, Mr. Clewton knew his subject. Here, in the kitchen at Khartum, he laid bare for Alexander's and his own delight all that he knew of Fleet Street. He was a man transposed beyond his insalubrious self for a while to the position of worthiness which belongs to all men who can relish and revere the achievements of others even though they themselves are capable only of the meanest acts. He talked of the great Sir William Howard Russell, the first of the real war correspondents, whose letters to *The Times* saved a shattered Crimean army, and who earned a place in St. Paul's Cathedral; of G. W. Steevens, who went with Kitchener to Khartum and saw his colleagues die of shot and disease and himself found death in the Boer War; of Sir Philip Gibbs, Sir William Beach Thomas, and the other great war correspondents. And Alexander, who had thought narrowly that the *Messenger* was his destiny, heard the ring of names like George Augustus Sala, the thunderer of synonyms, of de Blowitz, who secured the full text of the Treaty of Berlin for *The Times* to publish it at almost the same moment as it was signed in Berlin—de Blowitz whose marvellous memory made the use of a notebook almost unnecessary; and of others whose writings had changed Parliaments and voiced public opinion since the days of Defoe.

For the first time Alexander saw the place of the *Messenger*, and realised the world that lay outside of the office at the Bear Yard, a world that was waiting for him. As he sat on the table listening to Mr. Clewton's enthusiastic talk men were gathering news—not local news, but the vital news of the world; correspondents were daring dictatorship's tyranny to send news of atrocities; every large city in the world held men ready to forsake pleasure, their beds, their wives, at the ring of a telephone bell. Politicians, famous sportsmen, dictators, film stars, and stage celebrities, fighting countries, sinking ships, burning buildings, disease-haunted cantons … they were all watched so that the world might know at its breakfast-table the tale of each day's hour. As he sat on the table his youthful enthusiasms left him and he found himself; for he had seen the one thing which the world had to offer him; the call had come to him as clearly as the whistle of a train is heard across the stillness of a frosty night, and he knew that from now onwards he would always have one ambition before him. At the moment it was far away, but time would bring it closer, experience would define its limits, and faith would finally give it to him.

"Here," said Mr. Clewton, raising his glass, "is to the Press!"

They drank the toast, and, as Alexander grounded his glass upon the table, Hannibal made a sudden movement towards the door, which swung open before the dog reached it, to reveal Matthew, a poker in his right hand.

He stood for a moment on the threshold, acquainting himself with the scene. Then he stepped into the room and, realising that it would not be needed, he dropped the poker on the table.

"What does this mean, Alexander?" he asked sternly. He could tell from the boy's flushed face that he was excited.

"This is Mr. Clewton, Dad," answered Alexander. "He's ... he's my guest. I hope you don't mind."

Matthew blew through his nostrils indignantly. "Of course I mind. I object to being wakened at this hour of night by people talking in my kitchen. You should have more consideration for others. Do your guests usually come in by the kitchen window?"

"Perhaps I should explain—" Mr. Clewton began; but Matthew stopped him with a fierce look.

"I don't want any explanation. I fancy that I can understand everything that has happened. If you're wise, sir, you'll retire from this room in the same way as you came—and quickly!"

"But, Dad, he's not—"

"Silence, Alexander!"

Mr. Clewton wisely got up and made for the window, without even a glance at the bacon which had been promised to him. With one leg over the sill he turned and grinned at Alexander. " I shall remember your kindness," he said, and was gone.

Matthew turned to Alexander and said kindly, "It's a mistake, Alex, to let your generosity get the better of your good sense. There are too many men ready to impose upon such a weakness. Now get along to bed and we'll forget all about it."

"Forget all about it!" Alexander was shocked. "Why, you can't mean that?"

"I do. Why shouldn't I?"

"But don't you see, Dad, if it's nothing else it's a glorious story for the *Messenger*. Tramp breaks into Swanbridge house and is entertained at supper. It'll make a nice half-column."

"It will make nothing of the sort. Don't you realise that it was your duty as a citizen to hand that man over to the police—my duty as well? We've let him go, and I can't possibly make a point of it in my paper, so say nothing about it to anyone. Now go on back to bed and no more of this nonsense."

Alexander recognised the tone and said no more. He went back to his room, leaving his father to lock the kitchen window and tidy the place so that Gibby should not be suspicious in the morning. Some day, thought Matthew as he washed the plate Mr. Clewton had used, Alexander would realise that quixotic behaviour helped very little; that the only virtue was in being just, even though justness implied harshness—meanwhile he was rather glad that the boy had shown enough courage to behave quixotically—it was an indication of character, and the word character had a solid, nineteenth-century appeal to Matthew, for by it he understood an innate goodness.

XVIII

We are all young enough to enjoy a day at the seaside.

Swanbridge Messenger (From an Editorial)

Each year the employees of the *Messenger* had an outing, generally on a Friday, which, being the day after publication, was more convenient than any other in the week. The first outing had been in James Silverman's time, when the work-people had gone in wagonettes to Maltsey Castle for a picnic. Since his day the wagonette had disappeared and the range of the outing increased. Year by year a large motor-coach had taken them in succession to most of the seaside resorts of the south coast.

It was Matthew's theory, and an often repeated saying of his father, that an employer should see his staff at play at least once a year in order to appreciate that they were human beings and not just workers. It had a healthy effect upon his attitude towards them. James had always accompanied the outings, and spent most of his time arranging entertainments and generally foiling any attempt of individuals to enjoy themselves in their own particular way. Matthew, however, remembering the irritation his father's fussiness had engendered in him on the outings, never arranged anything. The only fixed thing was the tea, which was held in a restaurant; the people were free to do as they chose for the rest of the time so long as they did not keep the coach waiting when it was time to go. The result was that the outing was looked forward to and enjoyed, even when it rained, and it was surprising how often rain came to mark the day.

But this year the weather promised to be fine. The day was in early August, after a July which had been full of warm days with opaline skies and still evenings when the brume over the Troon hung almost motionless, disturbed only by the shrieking passage of low-flying swifts and the arcs made by swallows.

Alexander went with the staff in the coach while Matthew and the others of the family followed in a chauffeur-driven hired car. With Matthew was his wife, Loraine, Alison, and Uncle Abner.

At first, because he had a slight cold, Mrs. Cartwright had wanted to keep Abner at home. He had persisted.

"A cold is nothing! The fresh air and sea will do it good. To hear you talk, anyone would think I'm an invalid."

And so they went, though he left Pelang behind with Mrs. Cartwright, who did not care for outings.

Abner, who cared for cars as little as Aunt Adelaide, sat beside the chauffeur to order his driving. Matthew, his wife, and Loraine had the wide back seat, and Alison was happy alternating from Matthew's lap to the small tip-up seat underneath the speaking-tube which communicated with the chauffeur.

The coach started before them, and they saw nothing of it until they reached Herne Bay, which was their destination. At one point in the journey a long red sports car rushed past them and disappeared over a hill with a disturbing rattle of exhaust gases. Abner cursed the car, and Loraine, sitting in the back, wished she were in it, for it belonged to Philip and was being driven by Reginald, with the owner as a passenger. Riding in Philip's car with Reginald driving was her idea of real travelling. Beyond Canterbury they passed George's baby car. Hildegarde waved a hand to them as they passed. George's term had finished, and he had broken away from the settlement for a day to join in the outing.

* * *

"I see Uncle Abner has taken the place by the chauffeur to keep him in order," chuckled George. "It would only need Aunt Adelaide sitting behind with the speaking-tube to send the man crazy."

"Aunt Adelaide would never ride in the same car with Uncle Abner. I honestly believe that she hates him—really hates him."

"She doesn't really," said George, anxious not to think ill of anyone; "she just tries to give that impression. She may have disliked him at one time, but all that finished years ago. She just goes on playing her part out of habit now. If anything happened to Abner she'd be as upset as anyone."

"Perhaps she would. I wonder why she never married?"

George was silent for a while before replying. Then he said solemnly, "You know, I think she would have, only her sister married the man she wanted to marry. I think she fell in love with Abner, too. She turned it into something else when she saw how hopeless it was."

"Why, George!" Hildegarde turned towards him, her dark eyes under their sheltering lashes lively with a sudden appreciation. "Do you know, I thought I was the only one who had realised that. I think it is true, too. When you love something, and your love is never seen or appreciated, it may make your love turn to hate."

"Yes, I know that. I've even felt a bit like that lately." George did not look at her as he spoke; he kept his eyes for the road.

Hildegarde glanced up at him, puzzled by the remark and his tone. They passed a field of fleshy green sweet corn, and the car bumped over a bridge, giving her a glimpse of a water-meadow. She felt that George had offered the observation as an invitation to make her persuade him to some revelation. She was lost for a while, groping for some contact with his thought. When he spoke of such love, she knew that he could not refer to her. Their love was one of those unquestionable realities which existed solidly, evenly, and seemed to carry a mark of undestroyable vigour. Then she thought she understood. "What is it, George dear?"

George could have made an evasion. Then he admitted that he had been longing for this opportunity, and must take it. He said, "As a matter of fact, it's this mission work. I'm not getting along very well, and I'm afraid I've made a mistake."

"You mean you don't like it?"

"Not that exactly. I like it, but I don't seem to fit. I don't seem to be able to communicate with people somehow. You see, in the quietness of my room, when I'm by myself, I can see things so clearly, and know what I must do and say. When I'm alone I can feel what is needed. Yet when I try to do anything it seems to me that I become just a plain bungler, not even second-rate."

"Can't you make that more explicit?" Hildegarde felt his pain within her, and her whole being ached in sympathy for him; yet she knew that to any man in the moment of his depression, sympathy could sometimes be of harm.

"In a way, though perhaps I shan't make myself much clearer. I don't seem to be able to make the contacts, although I can see quite clearly in my own mind what I want to do. The other night, for instance, we had a crowd of young fellows in for a talk. I mean the young chaps you see kicking around the streets in London slums, an odd mixture, some of them vicious, some good-natured, and all very good listeners. You know we help them in many ways; arrange sports and outings and give them clubs to keep them off the streets; but that isn't enough. I spoke to them. It was awful ..." He broke off and stared ahead, recalling that night.

"Go on," said Hildegarde softly.

"Before I stood up I knew how to talk to them. It was all inside me—not a sermon; you can't preach to them. I wanted to wake them up, to get them aware of themselves. When I started to speak I knew at once that I wasn't going to do it. It was just as though the moment I opened my mouth to speak someone else took control of my mind and began to churn out a lot of stupid, priggish sentiments while I stood by—horrified. Why is it that I can feel what is proper, yet can't say it to others? I could feel that I hadn't even touched my audience, and I could guess what they were thinking about me—just another busybody trying to do good. That's all wrong."

"Of course it's all wrong, George, if it is always to be like that. But you mustn't mistake your trouble for something more serious than it is. You're only just beginning, and to anyone trying something new there must come those moments of depression when they feel that everything is hopeless, that they aren't doing any good. Every man and woman feels like that at some time or other."

"This isn't just depression from lack of results. It's more like a conviction of inability. It seems that these last few weeks, while I've been away from the University and immersing myself in a different world, I've begun to understand myself more. You know"—there was an anguish in his voice now—"Hildegarde, I don't want to be a lackadaisical parson. That wouldn't suit me. I've got to know that

I'm doing something with my life more than just making a living for myself. I think that must be because the Silvermans have always had a strong idea of service before them."

"I think you're letting this impression get too much of a hold on you. You had the courage to leave the *Messenger* for religion; surely you're not going to be defeated by the first little upset, George? I know you too well to believe you will do that, my dear. Look, this is what we'll do. We'll have a jolly time today and clear your blues away, and then you go back to the settlement and prove that all this is passing depression. Don't plan things out so much beforehand. Wait until your turn comes, and then stand up and speak what really is in your heart, and I'm sure you won't be disappointed then. I believe in you, George."

George gave her a grateful look. "Perhaps I'm being rather foolish," he said.

* * *

Alison and Mr. Phipps sat with their backs to a groyne, drinking lemonade. To one side of them shingle ran down to the sea, which stretched away until it was lost in the dance of silver haze about the horizon.

" 'Ot!" Mr. Phipps commented as he lowered his half-empty bottle and rested its butt on his protruding belly. He and Alison were good friends, and managed always to have an hour together on the outings.

"I should undo your coat," said Alison, and was gratified to see Mr. Phipps unbutton his jacket and let the sea-breeze strike at the wide expanse of blue shirt which he exposed. Mr. Phipps's girth fascinated her. His shape was so different from other men that she decided that he must himself be different, and regarded him as a form of oddity whose chief function was to interest her. "Why don't you bathe?" she asked.

"Not me! Don't expect I could get a costume to fit."

"Don't you ever swim?" Alison asked.

"Not me. Never learned in all my life. I fell into the Troon once, though."

Alison was silent, contemplating the vision of Mr. Phipps's large bulk splashing into the Troon. Holiday people strolled up and down the promenade behind them, children played along the beach, and rowing-boats moved slowly about close to shore. George and Hildegarde, with bathing-costumes in their hands, came along the promenade. Hildegarde waved to Alison.

"She's a nice young woman," observed Mr. Phipps as they passed. "Master George is a lucky young fellow." He pushed his straw hat forward over his face and composed himself more comfortably.

"If you want to go to sleep, don't mind me," said Alison politely.

"Thank you. But you needn't go away if you don't want to. You'll find that I talk in my sleep, and the things I say are very interesting. We might even talk to one another just as though I was awake."

* * *

"In my day," said Uncle Abner, deep in his deckchair, "the costumes that girls wore when bathing were decent."

"They weren't very comfortable to swim in, though," said Mrs. Silverman.

"No one wanted to swim in them, any more than most of the girls want to swim in them today. Those four down there"—he indicated the beach below—"have not the slightest intention of bathing. Young people have altered so much that I'm almost glad I shan't be here to see what they've made of the world by the time they're old men and women."

"The young people are all right," Matthew defended them. "They seem rather irresponsible at times, but underneath I think you'll find that they're sound."

"That's what I think about Loraine at times," put in Mrs. Silverman. "Sometimes she's most peculiar. Yesterday afternoon she played the whole of the gramophone records in the house right through, both sides, and when I asked her why she was doing it she said she didn't know—or at least she wouldn't say—and when she'd finished she insisted on going into the kitchen and cooking cakes. Gibby was most annoyed, but I told her that we could eat the cakes, and it was better to have her making herself useful than playing a gramophone all day."

"What they don't seem to realise," said Abner, disregarding Mrs. Silverman and going back to his original thought, "is that a figure doesn't have to be almost naked before it can be admired. The proper place for nudity is the bedroom or bath. I like women to be dressed. Any woman can attract attention by being half naked, but there're very few can do it by covering everything but their face and hands. I think I'll write a letter about it to *The Times*."

"And if they don't publish it, I suppose the *Messenger* will have to, eh?"

"Considering the trash it usually prints in its correspondence columns, it should be glad to get a decently worded letter!" snapped Abner. "Which reminds me that some incompetent got the captions under the pictures transposed in yesterday's issue, and Stratton village fair is described as a 'quiet corner on the Troon.' "

"I know, I know," Matthew said hastily. "It was a mistake."

"The paper's full of mistakes. You'll find yourself in a libel action one day."

"Here comes the man for the chair tickets," said Mrs. Silverman soothingly, and in the hunt for his ticket Matthew forgot Abner's remarks.

* * *

The heat of the day had sent most of the *Messenger* staff into the water. Some had succumbed to the concert-party, a few wandered aimlessly about the town, and one or two—mostly elderly folk like Mr. Phipps—had found a quiet spot and sat themselves down to enjoy a long sleep.

Loraine, who had been sent by her mother to find Alison, came across Harold buying himself an ice-cream.

He held up a fat cornet and said, "Have one?"

"Rather," she answered, and then, when she was served, they turned away towards the sea. "It looks lovely, doesn't it?"

"Grand. Shall we climb up the steps and go for a walk along the cliffs?" Harold indicated a long flight of wooden steps that reached up the broken cliff side.

"What! Walk in this weather?" Loraine was incredulous.

"Why not? There'll be a breeze on top."

"But I'd rather bathe. Come on, let's go in together."

"You know I can't, Loraine. Don't you remember what I told you earlier in the summer?"

"Oh, I don't believe all that. It's nonsense. You were joking."

"I wasn't, honestly. If I go into the water it makes me sick. Literally. It has that effect. I don't know why it is."

"Just because it happened once or twice you think it will always happen. Come on, don't be a coward."

"I'm not being a coward. I'm being practical. I just don't want to be sick, that's all."

"Oh, Harold, why don't you try … just this once? I'm sure you'd be all right."

"Hullo, you two. Coming for a bathe?" It was Alexander, and with him was Philip.

"Are you going in now?" asked Loraine.

"Yes. Philip's got one of those rubber horses you blow up and try to ride. We're going to have fun. Come on, Harold!"

"Sorry, Alex. I can't go in; it upsets my tummy. Loraine and I were just going for a walk along the cliffs."

"A walk!" The cry came from Philip, a cry full of healthy disdain for such uncongenial exercise. "You're mad! Come on, Loraine; the sea's just crying to be bathed in. Harold can sit on the shore and yell insults at us, if his tummy won't let him bathe." They took her arm, and she found herself being pulled along with them, and she found that she had no protest to make. She was glad.

When they came from their cubicles ready to swim, Harold had disappeared.

"Gone for his walk," said Alexander, carrying the rubber horse and determined to be the first on it. "Must have a jolly funny tummy, that's all, to keep him out of the water on a day like this."

"I shouldn't like it," said Philip. " I feel sorry for him."

Loraine was grateful to him for his compassion. Then she forgot Harold, crying, "Come on! First one in gets first ride!" And they were pelting across the shingle towards the water, Alexander handicapped by the horse.

Loraine won the race and, helped by Alexander and Philip, she was given a lesson in riding.

They were a happy trio. Splashing, shouting, and swallowing gouts of water as the horse threw first one and then another of them, they were alone and unmindful of the throng of people along the stretch of beach. Their pleasure in the water was animal-like, the caress of the waves an unconscious delight to their limbs as they played like otters around the horse. Above them, the gulls moved in narrow circles, the music of gramophones came from the beach huts, and the cry of children died in the noise of their splashings. A rowing-boat moved close to them yet never entered their world, which revolved slowly around the grotesque rubber animal, floating fat and elusive.

After a time Loraine tired of the horse and, turning from it, swam out towards the horizon, and she knew that Philip was following her. She swam slowly, in leisurely breast-strokes, and he came up beside her, settling into the comfortable rhythm of her movements. The water, broken by their hands, sprang into a thousand drops touched with aquamarine fire and gilded by flashing shades of green, and behind them swirled a tiny wake of troubled bubbles that for a second held, mirrored on their upturned bowls, the pale pearl tint of the clouds and the cobalt of the sky, before breaking and running the colour into the dark grey-green of the sea. Ahead of them a gull floated lightly on the waves, a paper boat lost by a wanton boy.

"Isn't it lovely, Philip?" Loraine called softly, and before he could reply she did a dolphin roll under water out of sheer high spirits. She dived steeply for the bottom, wondering if she would reach it and knowing that Philip would follow. Through the green mist before her eyes a dark blue shape with waving arms and legs moved, and a face looked into hers for a brief moment, as though it were looking from the darkness of a garden into a lighted room.

She came to the top, took a deep breath, and turned upon her back, floating easily and thinking about Philip. He broke water beside her, and she noticed that even now his hair was neat, smoothed into tidy sweeps by the water, and his face was well formed, cut into a deep regularity that gave him a healthy, fresh look. At least he never was sick when he bathed, even if he could not quote from Shelley and all the other poets ...

They swam back slowly and joined Alexander, who was wearied by unsuccessful attempts to ride the horse. Loraine was still thinking about Philip as they walked up to their cubicles. When she had dressed, she came out to find him waiting for her. Alexander was still leisurely making his toilet.

"Come on," said Philip, and there was a vigour in his voice which was new to her.

"Come on where?"

"With me," he said and, catching her by the wrist, he hurried her off.

"Not so fast! You'll have my arm off!" Loraine protested, but enjoyed it. Philip kept his hold on her, leading her from the sea-front across the lawns to the roadway.

"Get in there!" It was a command and, when she was slow to obey, Loraine found herself pushed into the passenger seat of his car. As she subsided, Philip stood beside her for a moment, looking at her, and Loraine found herself blushing and vaguely happy at his look. She knew she looked nice; green suited her, and the bathe had freshened her body until its vitality and youth broke through her clothes, surrounding her with an aura of loveliness. Philip could not understand why he had never seen her like this before. She was no longer a girl; she was a woman, entirely feminine; no longer a hesitant girl, but a personality of determination and strength. His impulse, the old impulse to protect and please her, was engulfed by a new desire to force her to acknowledge her new spirit.

He jumped into his seat and started the car. They swung out of the town and turned on to the wide by-pass road to London.

"You can't abduct me like this," cried Loraine.

"I can!" he shouted back. "You belong to me, and I ought to have done this a long time ago."

"But what will they say when they know we've disappeared?"

"To hell with what they'll say!" came the answer, and Loraine, opening her mouth to reply, found that she had no answer. Into her face, over the low scuttle, came a roaring wind, and her ears were suddenly filled with the fierce cry that the car offered up to the god of speed as its wheels screamed over the firm concrete sets of the wide road. She looked down and saw, with a satisfaction that filled her soul with unnamable pleasure, that the car was travelling at eighty miles an hour.

* * *

The absence of Loraine and Philip at tea disturbed no one. Despite Matthew's reiteration of the time and place, there was, each year, someone missing, and he had come to regard this not only as inevitable, but as an indication of the universal inability of human beings to observe even the simplest order with precision.

After tea, Mrs. Silverman took Alison with her to visit an old friend who had retired, in her widowhood, to the town. Matthew did not go with her. He went off by himself for a walk in the cool of the evening. Uncle Abner and Reginald sat themselves down to listen to a military band, Abner causing covert annoyance by talking in an unguarded voice during a cornet solo.

The coach left the town at eight o'clock, which, Mr. Phipps pointed out to his friends, gave those who cared to just time enough to make themselves affable without getting drunk. So Mr. Phipps and Roger Selway retired to the nearest bar to fight out a dart-throwing match which had been declared after much abuse between them about the other's prowess, and they took with them a great many spectators. Alexander and Harold were among them for a while. By the time Mr. Phipps, with a skill and grace his body belied, had vanquished Selway, and they had finished a pint of beer each, the two had tired of their company. They went out into the evening. It was still broad daylight, and the air was warm with the glow of the day's heat.

They walked, talking, along the beaches, clambering over the groynes in the direction of Reculver. When they were out of the way of the crowded foreshore they sat down with their backs to the bleached and splintered planks of a groyne and lit cigarettes.

Alexander sucked at his thoughtfully for a while, blowing the fragrant clouds into the air and watching the light breeze take it and whirl it away into shreds, like cobwebs torn by the vigorous brush of a housemaid.

"It looks to me," he said after a while, "as if Loraine had turned you down. She's gone off with Philip again." It was the first time in the whole of their acquaintance that he had ever made so direct a remark about Harold's relations with his sister.

"I know," Harold replied. "But I don't care a great deal. After all, she's her own master."

"She's certainly not anybody's mistress," said Alexander quickly.

Harold ignored the joke, and went on, "She's good company at times; but I think I made a mistake about her."

"You did," Alexander said firmly. "All that poetry and culture business never even touched her. You didn't know her. I could have told you, but you wouldn't have believed me then, that it was hopeless. You see, Loraine has a commonplace mind, and she is incapable of concerning herself with abstractions. She's interested in food, in clothes, in romantic novels, and in herself and the effect she has on other people. Still, you did some good. Quite a lot of the books you lent her I hadn't read, so I used to pinch them from her drawer. She never knew even."

"Well, she's gone now, and I'm not sorry. She and Philip seem suited to one another."

"He's a queer bird," said Alexander. " I honestly believe that he likes being an auctioneer."

Harold laughed and tossed a pebble towards the water. With half his mind he could appreciate Alexander's attitude, but with the other half he found himself condemning it as narrow and absurd.

"You make the rather popular mistake of imagining that nothing but the thing you happen to be doing can possibly be interesting. That, in a way, is almost as stupid as believing that the master is better than the maid, or that if God had intended us to fly He would have given us natural wings. You happen to like newspaper work; because of that you find yourself pitying everyone not similarly employed."

"But I don't, Harold!" Alexander forgot Philip. "I don't like newspaper work."

"You're crazy about it."

"Yes, but what I mean is, I don't like this kind of newspaper work." Alexander was still a while, remembering Mr. Clewton and his Nestorian persuasion. "I want to get out of the provinces and work in London, where there's more scope. I think about that in bed at night now. I see myself learning foreign languages properly and becoming a special correspondent. Think of it, Harold; think what it would mean to you to have been in Vienna when Dolfuss was murdered, to interview Mussolini and Kemel Attaturk …" His eyes had the soft glow of the dreamer. He was moving in a vision of the future, seeing himself dramatised in a thousand different situations, the herald of great news.

"You're going to be editor of the *Messenger*."

"I know." There was not even bitterness in his voice. "That's what I'm going to be. I've thought about that, too. You see, first of all I wanted to be an architect. That didn't last. When George left us, I realised that here was my place, that the *Messenger* was waiting for me. I saw that as fate diverting me from a wrong vocation into a true one, and so I entered the business. Dad thought that I did it because of the Silverman tradition, but I didn't. It was because I saw that it was meant for me to take over George's place. And now, when I feel I must get away to where there's more scope, I can't do it because to do so would be breaking faith with Dad. He thinks I came into the business to please him, and I respect him too much to hurt him by leaving it now."

"Do you mean all that?"

"Of course. It may not seem very clear, yet in my mind I can see my way perfectly. Sometimes it is wiser to make a sacrifice of ambition to keep pain from others, especially from ones you love. I'm going to make that sacrifice. Don't think I'm revelling in my martyrdom: I'm no neurotic mystic. This is common sense. Not since the world began has any man ever been free to do just as he wanted. I met a man the other night who tried to be ... He was an awful failure. The old man once gave me a lecture about rights, and for once he talked sense. Strictly speaking, I suppose I should be within my rights to go up to him and say, 'I'm tired of the *Messenger*. I want permission to go to London and get a job on a daily.' He couldn't stop me; logically I should be within my rights. And yet, if I did it, I should be doing an awful wrong."

"Why?" Harold was conscious that there was being revealed to him a new Alexander, a deeper, steadier personality.

"Because I should be disregarding what I call vital responsibilities to my parents. Oh, I know there's a lot of wind talked today about the relationship of parent to child. Nevertheless, no child has the right to disregard a parent's feelings. I was brought into this world because of my parents; they inconvenienced themselves to give me a chance to live. They gave me happiness, and it seems to me that I have no right to repay them by causing them sorrow, however logically you may pick holes in my argument. If there is any sacrifice to be made—then the child should make it. Actually, I suppose, it's rather emotional, but I'm coming to see that emotion is often a far surer guide to right conduct than intellect. Man is master of the mind, and man is often wrong; but the conscience is controlled by something outside of knowledge—call it God, if you like—and it seems to be that to ignore it is to ignore life. Golly, that was a pretty good speech, eh?"

"Very good, and I think I agree with most of it."

"You flatter me." Alexander was flippant now, as a shield to this past earnestness. " If you had disagreed with me I should have known I was right. But when you agree with me, I doubt myself. I suppose we should be cutting back now. Nearly time. I'll bet there'll be some fun in that coach going home; Selway and Phipps are sure to be merry, and Phipps has a lovely voice when he sings."

They got up and started back towards the town.

* * *

Matthew was surprised to see Hildegarde sitting alone on the cliff top.

"Hullo," he said, dropping beside her and crushing a patch of brown sea-thrift. "What are you doing all alone?"

Hildergarde smiled and shook her head. " No, we haven't quarrelled or anything like that. I was incautious enough to say that I could eat an ice, and nothing would stop George from going off to get me one. He's probably scouring the cliffs for an ice-cream cart."

"Your lightest wish his law, eh?"

"Yes. It makes one realise how carefully one should speak. I have enjoyed today, haven't you?" Matthew did not reply at once. A low bank of purple cloud had arisen from the horizon, spreading around the periphery of water like heavy smoke rolling onwards from a heath fire, tormented streamers of grey wreathing into the sky as it advanced. Through this pall the dipping sun shone with a dull red sullenness, and quick cats-paws raced across the water, chasing one another.

"Yes, I have. Hullo"—he looked down towards the beach—"is that Alexander down there? You look; your eyes are younger than mine."

Hildegarde followed the line of his arm. " Yes, Alexander and Harold Spencer talking."

"Talking." Matthew shook his head softly. " How the young talk, especially Alexander. He's a funny young man in some ways."

"I like him," said Hildegarde. He's so alive. When you're near him you can almost hear the blood bubbling inside him. George, too, has a great respect for him."

"I know. George fancies that Alexander has some genius, eh?"

"How did you know?"

"You forget that George is my son, my dear, and there aren't many things a father doesn't know about his children. Perhaps George is right. Some day I hope to see Alexander filling my place, unless—" Matthew paused as a thought occurred to him.

"Unless what?" prompted Hildegarde, respecting his mood.

"Unless he decides to leave Swanbridge."

"Alexander leave Swanbridge? But why? I thought …"

"I know. But what we all think will happen the future has an uncanny knack of upsetting. Alexander is young—a young hawk, Abner once called him; and he said that you can feed the young hawk on sops, but when its wings grow strong nothing will stop it from marking prey. And Alexander is growing. Perhaps one day he will want to venture his wings elsewhere in search of more important prey than local news."

"I thought you wanted him to become editor of the *Messenger*?"

"So I do, my dear. Yet I couldn't stop him if he wanted to go away, and I have a feeling that the day will come when he will want to go. Alexander doesn't belong in a provincial town. He lives in a different world. George now—sometimes I wonder whether George fully realises the great power for good an editor can exercise, especially if he loves and understands his town—as George loves and understands Swanbridge. Alexander is intolerant of it in many ways. Do you understand the difference between them?"

Hildegarde was still for a moment, pondering Matthew's words. A gull fell across the face of the cliff, its shrewd head turning left and right as it swooped, the wings stiff like carved wood.

"Yes, I think I do. Alexander is only a Silverman by birth— some wild creature that suddenly finds itself in a cage, longing for freedom—but George is your son; that is he is another Matthew, and should be another editor." She spoke almost to herself, her mind following another train of thought, half wondering if Matthew had not deliberately inspired it.

"Time is a great healer," Matthew observed pontifically, "and things have a way of righting themselves. Well, we'd better be getting back. I believe I felt a drop of rain then."

"Yes, let's. And there's George coming back now." As Hildegarde rose, a drop of rain, heavy and cold, fell upon her hand and, looking up, she saw that the sky was burdened with rain-clouds, and that the sea had gone a metallic grey.

XIX

And those who are always so ready to accuse should remember that it is often a sign of grace when a man changes his mind.

Swanbridge Messenger (From a report of a speech by Captain H. C. Lowthern, M.P.)

The air was still under its load of scents, pressed into immobility by the sweetness that weighed upon it. The grass, dark blue in the last light of the day, was rich with a coating of dew.

Sitting at the window, Aunt Adelaide could see the thick line of the yew hedge fired at its foot by the marigolds that grew in profusion along the border. A trailer of clematis threw purple stains along the garden wall. The great crest of a sweet chestnut hid the sky, filtering its wan light through the thick leaves, sprinkling shadows over the lawn. Soon the chestnuts would be falling, and she would spend the fresh mornings of autumn gathering them for the winter, and the gardener would brush the yellow and ochre leaves into a pile and burn them, the smoke going straight into the air like the incense from a sacrificial pyre.

"You know, Hildegarde, my dear"—she turned to her companion and spoke gently—"nothing seems quite the same when one grows old; nothing seems quite so good as it was."

Hildegarde did not answer more than a smile, that meant that Aunt Adelaide could go on talking and she would listen with her ears, though her heart, her reason, could take no part in her attention. Her hands were crossed in her lap, one of them holding a letter which had come by the last post.

"When I was young, the summers seemed longer and hotter, and I'm sure that roses never suffered so much from the greenfly, and I was much more successful with anchusas than I am now, though I must say that I never did consider them an elegant flower. I suppose it is because we forget what the past was like and imagine it to be as we would have wanted it to be." She stopped talking for a moment and studied Hildegarde's face. The girl was staring across the garden, her profile delicate and clear against the light stuff of the curtains, a soft pastel of quiet colours. The sweep of her hair and the poise of her head reminded Aunt Adelaide of a Rossetti she had seen in the Ashmolean when she was young, only Hildegarde, she decided, was lovelier than the drawing. How easy it would be to envy the girl, only her heart was too old for envy, her heart was too tired to reach for the impossible. In youth one could do that— dream dreams and strive towards peaks that were cold and clear and beautifully remote.

"I presume from your inattention," she said suddenly, "that the letter in your hand comes from George. Ha, I thought the sound of that name would recall you from your dreams."

"I'm sorry."

"Don't apologise, my dear."

A knock on the door interrupted her, and the maid came in to say that Mr. Matthew Silverman was on the telephone.

Hildegarde went, and came back after a while, her face showing how disturbed she was.

"It's Mr. Cartwright. He's worse, and they want you to go in. They're sending a car out for you right away."

"Abner, eh? That man is the embodiment of incompetence. He had no right to go on an outing at his age and get himself caught in a storm without a coat."

"Shall I come with you?"

"No, certainly not. It's half past ten now, and if Abner's going to die he'll be sure to make it as inconvenient as possible for everyone by hanging on until the morning. You get to bed. I shall be all right."

But, as Hildegarde helped her from her chair, she could sense the tension in the old lady's body, the unsteadiness of her arm in her young grasp. All this fierceness was only a covering.

When Aunt Adelaide had gone, Hildegarde went back to the window, the garden a swamp of black shadows through which the pale patches of flower-clumps showed dimly. She held the letter from George in her hands still, and she was thinking of him. She sat so still and for so long that her body merged with the indeterminate contours of the night and her soul was lost in a wonder of the love that possessed her. She recalled how George had first seen her in this fragile, china-filled room, and she remembered the contrast of his sturdiness with the delicacy of the Dresden figures, his awkwardness against the old-fashioned dignity of the furnishings, his body uncomfortable upon the grace of the carved sofa, and his eyes upon her all the time as though he were a small boy absorbed by the glory of a new experience. He was still that small boy ... a small, honest boy, so honest that she prayed that the day should never come when his honesty should be the means of hurting them ...

* * *

Matthew was irritated by Abner. For two weeks the old man had lain upon his bed with an influenza chill that refused to pass, and now, on a Thursday evening, when the works were busy with the weekly printing of the *Messenger*, when Matthew was wanted in a dozen places at once—or imagined he was—he was told that the crisis had arrived. Abner if he lived the night would live. Only Abner had his own battle to fight with life. No one could help him.

He left the office at eleven. Alexander remained, for on press night there must be always a Silverman to see the last paper slip from the machine, to hear the roar cease and watch the wet rollers still themselves at Phipps's command.

And yet he was anxious, his being vibrant with definite sorrow. He had known Abner so long, and liked him in spite of his mannerisms. The *Messenger* without Abner ... He did not care to watch anything that touched him and his life go from him, rebelling against the slow inevitability of every passing.

He walked sadly to Abner's house, and only when he was in the sick-room did he realise that he had in his hand a copy of the *Messenger*. Somehow the sight of the paper, fresh smelling of ink and

243

its leaves unopened, upset him, and he put it hastily down on the small table by the bed.

There was only a low light in the room. Abner lay very still on the bed, his iron-grey hair neatly brushed, his old face pale with the days of bed-lying and grizzled by a growth of stiff white hairs.

"He's been like that for the last two hours," said the nurse softly. "Miss Silverman is downstairs. Perhaps you'd better go, too. I'll be here, and will call you …"

Matthew went.

In the sitting-room below were Mrs. Cartwright and Reginald and Aunt Adelaide. They sat there, even Aunt Adelaide awed by the feeling which hung so closely around them. Reginald read, forcing his mind to the book to keep it away from what he feared, and the others made a desultory conversation, chastened by the rigid indecency of talking, of having to talk. Upstairs a man lay fighting for life, and down here they sat talking of anything but the thoughts which kept place in their minds. Pelang lay along the hearthrug, wakeful because of the unusual presences, yet calm. Matthew looked at the dog and wondered whether the beast knew, wondered if there was any bond between Abner and the dog that told the animal what was happening.

It seemed to them all that even time was reluctant to move on that night, fearful of what it might bring. They sat awkwardly and waiting. For how long they waited none of them knew; the checking of time was forgotten.

Then there was a sound outside the door and the nurse came in. She stood, a faint hygienic odour coming from her white starched uniform, and, although she spoke no word, they knew that the time had come. Reginald rose and, as he did so, Pelang left the rug and slipped very quietly out of the room and upstairs.

When they were all there they saw that Pelang had jumped to the bed and was lying across its foot. No one said anything to the dog, for all their attention was upon Abner.

The old man was conscious now, and fighting as only those who see death near them know how to fight. His face was flushed with the struggle, and his breath, coming more quickly, forced a tiny line of foam about his lips.

They watched fascinated, for suddenly this struggle became impersonal. It was not Abner there; it was some alien being exhibiting its strength, a nameless, impersonal will moving against another will.

"Can't you …" Mrs. Cartwright turned to the nurse. The woman's face told her that all that could be done was in the power of the old man. Matthew saw the thin body move beneath the bedclothes, almost felt his own muscles tightening as the muscles tightened in Abner's old limbs, and he was aware suddenly of Aunt Adelaide beside him, her eyes wet with tears and her thin hand on his elbow for comfort.

For five minutes they watched Abner fight, watched this old man who had domineered, slighted, and beaten others in life, facing something which matched his own obstinacy, and then the struggle ceased, the body was still, and the colour moved from the cheeks, leaving them washed over with a pale tinge.

Matthew felt Aunt Adelaide stiffen and saw the anguish that sped across the faces of Reginald and his mother. This was the moment. Abner had finished his fight. He was poised now on the threshold … Matthew shut his eyes from the sorrow that was coming to him.

He heard the laboured breath lose its vigour and die until there was no sound. He opened his eyes, and as he did so the man on the bed turned his head sideways slowly, and the deep lids rolled back and Abner was looking at him.

For a while the old man looked at them, not understanding, seeing them all ranged about his bed.

"Father!" Mary Cartwright moved forward and knelt at his bedside. The movement broke Abner's dullness. He moved his lips, and said in a thin voice, "What's all this?"

The nurse hovered above him, making signs for him to be still. The solicitude in her gestures, the sight of the staring women and his daughter-in-law near to tears at his side, filled him with a sudden petulant vigour.

"What the devil are you all doing here? Waiting for me to die? Reginald"—his head moved to take in Reginald at the foot of the bed—"who let Pelang up here? He's not allowed in the bedrooms. Take him down."

"Abner, Abner …" Matthew moved towards him.

The sound of Matthew's voice seemed to reassure the old man. "It's all right, Matt. I'm all right. Only get these people away. They confuse me ..." His eyes caught sight of the new *Messenger* on the table. "Is that this week's paper? Give it to me ... there's sure to be something wrong with ... something wrong with it." He tried to move his hands from under the coverlet to take the paper, but even as he did so the fatigue from his struggle beat him and his eyes closed, and he was asleep, breathing gently, at peace with himself and safe.

Matthew took Aunt Adelaide back to Khartum for the rest of the night. She was indignant.

"That's just like Abner, just like him! He's the most exasperating man I know. Well, the next time he's ill don't expect me to come running in as I did this time. I shall be warned."

"He's not out of danger yet."

"Nonsense. In three weeks he'll be as right as ever. You see. I know Abner."

When Adelaide had gone to her room, Matthew went into the library. Even now, coming back so late, with the anxiety of Abner's illness filling his mind, his old habits persisted. He would go into the library and see if the last post had brought him any letters, and then he would make his round of the house, locking up, emptying his pockets on to the dressing-table and brushing his teeth. This mechanical side of man went on as though it were a thing apart from the rest of his being, some part that was never touched by the distresses of emotion and fear.

There was only one letter, addressed from London in George's handwriting. He opened it and began to read, standing under the light to see more clearly. It ran:

> "DEAR DAD,—I have had an awful time with myself before I could write this letter. You see, I have found that I have been mistaken and I want you to know that if you still want me I would come back to the Messenger ..."

There was much more; but it was some time before Matthew read beyond the first two sentences.

XX

"The days that make us happy make us wise."

MASEFIELD

Swanbridge Messenger (Thought for the Week)

There was an air of important merriment about the Three Feathers Hotel. Mr. Jordan, the proprietor, stood at the doorway, swaying on his feet jauntily, breathing in the coolness of the September evening air and smiling at the world. In the hotel, waiters were hurrying to and from the kitchen and the large dining-room at the head of the main stairs, and in the bar the usual crowd watched the passage of these black-and-white messengers and made wise comment.

"I seed old Phipps going up," said one. "Regular toff he looked in his dinner-packet. Bet he had to have it let out at the back before he could get it on."

"Aye, and he borrowed the cuff links. I know that. Got them from our Alf's boy that plays in the Maniacs' Dance Band."

"And did you see his highness, old man Silverman? Hardly recognised him at first he was that spruced up. He's a rum un; kind-hearted, though he doesn't like you to think so, and a bit long-winded, though you daren't mention it. His old father was just the same."

In the large private dining-room the tables had been joined to form a huge T, across the top of which sat the members of the Silverman family and down the leg sat the employees of the *Messenger*. As many as had dinner-jackets wore them, and those who had not wore their best suits. Brilliantine shone on heads which were strangers to it most of the year, and even Phipps had plastered his few hairs into order.

"I suppose, Mr. Phipps, you wouldn't care to change your beer for my lemonade?" asked Alison, who had insisted upon sitting beside him. "I've never tasted beer."

"Never tasted beer?" Mr. Phipps rumbled. "That's a pity. But if you never tasted beer, you shouldn't go straight to it from lemonade—does funny things with your insides. All them as knows goes to shandy-gaff first, and then to beer."

"Shandy-gaff?"

"Yes; you shut your eyes for a moment."

Alison put her hands over her eyes and Phipps tipped some of his beer into her half-filled glass of lemonade.

"Now—open!"

Alison found her glass full of a strange amber drink which carried a delicate foam on its head. She sipped it, and then turned to Phipps. "I shall always drink shandy-gaff now."

Waiters brought lemonade, beer, lager, red and white wine, and cider; others brought in the trays of food: soups smelling of winter and cold days, fish lonely in their crisp brown jackets, cold meats, game, entrees, jellies, trifles, and other glorious dishes that the hotel chef delighted Swanbridge diners with on such occasions. The odour of food, warm and satisfying, filled the air, and put good humour into everyone; drink, even innocuous lemonade, loosened tongues, and the long room rang with voices.

"Looks as though this party isn't going to end without some folks being under the weather," observed Selway to Harold, who sat by him, and he nodded to where Alexander was lifting a large tankard to his mouth at the family table.

"As long as he doesn't start singing bawdy songs, Matthew will stand anything tonight," was the answer.

Alexander put down his tankard and caught Harold's eye. He winked profoundly. This was going to be a night; already he felt like a king. Anyhow, it was a fit time to celebrate, for not only was this the centenary of the *Messenger*, it was the celebration of his freedom. George had come back, George was going into the *Messenger*, and that left him free to leave when he wanted to.

"Enjoying yourself, Hildegarde?" he asked. She was sitting next to him where he was at the end of the table. Beyond her was George, then

Aunt Adelaide, and then Matthew in the middle. On the other side of Matthew were Mrs. Silverman, Uncle Abner, Mrs. Cartwright, then Philip, and Loraine and, making the far end of the table, Reginald.

"Rather—and I can see that you are. I suppose you know exactly how much of that stuff you can drink with safety?"

"Oh, no: that's the joy of it. But I mean to find out tonight. Would you like to keep count for me?"

"George is better at mathematics than I am, aren't you, George?"

"I'm not going to attempt the impossible," was George's reply. The words betrayed him into a thought which he would have wished to avoid. Once with him, it persisted for a while. He had attempted the impossible—and failed. Or had he failed? He was coming back to the *Messenger*, yet he would, at those times when his faith was weakened, always wonder whether it would not have been better for him to have become a second-rate preacher rather than a capable editor, whether the good a fine editor can do is comparable with the good a humdrum preacher can do … A remark from Aunt Adelaide at his side turned him from his thoughts, and he was lost again in the stir of the dinner.

"I expect your father is glad George is coming back, isn't he?" Philip said to Loraine. "I never did see George as a preacher."

"Should you have red or white wine with fish? I never know and, anyway, they both taste the same to me. Yes, he's glad all right. So we all are. Alex and I teased them both this afternoon. Called it the return of the prodigal, and said that this feast wasn't for the paper so much as for George. It was fun—we all ended up by fighting on the floor of the library, and after that we made Daddy rehearse his speech for tonight and threw in helpful suggestions." She raised her glass to Harold at the end of the other table; that, she thought, might make Philip a little jealous and it did Harold good. She did not want him to feel outcast.

Matthew, dignified in his dress clothes, was rehearsing in his mind, as he ate, the speech he was to make. It was to be simple and direct. "My friends, on this day one hundred years ago John Silverman published the first number of the *Messenger* …"

The words trickled through his brain as he ate, the flow swelling and halting as he looked around him. It was good to have them all together like this. Aunt Adelaide, dignified in her black velvet;

249

his wife, as lovely to him now as she had been when he first saw her entering her father's church; Abner, pale still from his illness, an upright figure in an old-fashioned dress suit, with a glass of Vichy water by his side … they were essential parts of his life. He smiled across at Mrs. Cartwright and for a moment wished that her husband, Peter, could have seen this moment. From her his eye went to Philip and Loraine. They were going to be married one day, and another mooring-rope would have been thrown out to fasten the Silvermans to the great bulk of Swanbridge life. Yet he was going to lose Alexander—Alexander, who was grinning at him and pretending to write on his cuff to indicate that he had better get his speech ready. He knew now that Abner had been right about Alexander; in his own heart he had known it as well, from the day he had persuaded the boy to work for the *Messenger*. He had been selfish then, letting his pride and his desire to see his life move as he had planned it usurp the wisdom which his years had brought him. Now he acknowledged again the truth that a man must take what comes, be honest with himself, and leave what is beyond his powers to work out its own salvation. Things had worked out well. George was coming back. He wondered if anyone, even Hildegarde, would know the full anguish which had lived in George's mind before he resolved to come back.

"I do hope you won't forget your speech, dear." His wife leaned across to him, and she added softly, "Put your tie straight; it's slipped to one side a little. That's better."

Everyone had finished eating, and Matthew knew that his moment had come—this moment which had been fated to him from the day John Silverman had decided to print a newspaper in Swanbridge. He looked around the table, every face a familiar one to him; his family, his workpeople, printers, reporters, typists, errand-boys … all units in the machinery of the *Messenger*.

He took his glass and rose, and as he began to speak his eyes were blurred by tears which he held to himself.

THE END

Preview

What's going on behind the doors of Fountain Inn?

When her employer suddenly disappears, young Grace Kirkstall finds herself accepting a new job at a new company in the same building – an oasis of tranquillity off the streets of London.

Ben and Helen Brown's startup company's pitch is that, for a small consideration, they will help people out of their major and minor fixes. Their first big commission initiates Ben into the gentle art of house-breaking, and Helen into the mysteries of the Society for Progressive Rehabilitation… But for Grace, it will plunge her into more danger than she could ever have imagined.

Fountain Inn, by Victor Canning

Also Available

Mr Edgar Finchley, unmarried clerk, aged 45, is told to take a holiday for the first time in his life. He decides to go to the seaside. But Fate has other plans in store…

From his abduction by a cheerful crook, to his smuggling escapade off the south coast, the timid but plucky Mr Finchley is plunged into a series of the most astonishing and extraordinary adventures.

His rural adventure takes him gradually westward through the English countryside and back, via a smuggling yacht, to London.

Mr Finchley, Book 1

OUT NOW

About the Early Works of Victor Canning

Victor Canning had a runaway success with his first book, *Mr Finchley Discovers his England*, published in 1934, and lost no time in writing more. Up to the start of the Second World War he wrote seven such life-affirming novels.

Following the war, Canning went on to write over fifty more novels along with an abundance of short stories, plays and TV and radio scripts, gaining sophistication and later a darker note – but perhaps losing the exuberance that is the hallmark of his early work.

Early novels by Victor Canning –

Mr Finchley Discovers His England

Mr Finchley Goes to Paris

Mr Finchley Takes the Road

Polycarp's Progress

Fly Away Paul

Matthew Silverman

Fountain Inn

About the Author

Victor Canning was a prolific writer throughout his career, which began young: he had sold several short stories by the age of nineteen and his first novel, *Mr Finchley Discovers His England* (1934) was published when he was twenty-three. It proved to be a runaway bestseller. Canning also wrote for children: his trilogy The Runaways was adapted for US children's television. Canning's later thrillers were darker and more complex than his earlier work and received further critical acclaim.

Note from the Publisher

To receive background material and updates on further titles by Victor Canning, sign up at farragobooks.com/canning-signup